THE LONG AND DARK

Joshua Banker

First Publication, 2019
Library of Congress Control Number: 2019914464
ISBN: 0578559358
ISBN-13: 978-0-578-55935-3

Also from Joshua Banker

The Fifth Era of Man

The Realm of Tah'afajien Series
Not Gods But Monsters
A Prison of Flesh
The Killing Kind

For my father, Rex,
who did everything he could for his children,
and who was a greater influence on me than
he would admit.

CHAPTER ONE

The Gape

"Only those beyond the caress of God can cross the Gape," Hilliard had warned as he greedily clutched at his reward, a bottle of rye whiskey. When Gareth brushed the comment aside, Hilliard opened his prize and began to gulp greedily.

To Gareth, this had seemed like the rantings of a man busy drinking himself to death. Fortunately for him, Hilliard had known how to enter Dineothan and was willing to part with the information.

Now, as he approached the first real lead of his long search, the earth itself seemed determined to impede him. Soggy peat squelched beneath Gareth Solomon's boot heels as he climbed the hillside leading away from the shore. Every step was a struggle. His gear rattled noisily each time he pulled his feet clear of the quagmire.

Behind him, tied to the rocky shoreline, was the

sailing dory he'd rented from a fisherman earlier that morning. After hearing Gareth's destination, the elderly sailor charged him a hefty fee and frowned as if he'd never see his boat again.

Gareth had met many a seaman who refused his requests. No reasonable, god-fearing ship's captain would take him anywhere near Dineothan, it seemed. Sailors claimed that no amount of money would convince them to sail anywhere in the vicinity, that the waters themselves were cursed. Even without all of the superstitions, the near-impenetrable fog which bordered the isle on all sides forced sane men of the sea to steer clear.

Whether of sound mind or not, Gareth was no fool. Over the past few weeks, he'd heard so many tales that he knew making land at Dineothan would be a daunting task, especially for someone who lacked naval experience. Sailing the dory across the Gulf of Nina had proved challenging enough. Even now, as he trudged through the mud, he felt immense relief to be back on land.

Gareth found himself thinking about how he'd come to be at this diminutive bump in the gulf's waters. Hilliard had pointed him to the tiny island, Pilsu-kimah, no more than a few hundred yards from the larger island of Dineothan. He'd spoken of crewmen who'd entered the isle's catacombs, never to return. It was here that Gareth was supposed to find the pathway into the island nation.

His recollection of the last few weeks' events was,

at best, spotty. Faces and locations swirled about in his head. His journey began with the need to find a cure; a plague running rampant through his home country had afflicted his family. Local doctors and men of science had discovered no remedy. Undaunted, he began a lengthy investigation. Each person he interviewed along the way only revealed a sliver of information. Even so, each one knew another who Gareth needed to meet, and so on. He was passed along from person to person for what felt like ages. Finally, he learned that the men who might know of a cure could be found in Dineothan.

Initially, he had brushed the suggestion aside. Dineothan was the stuff of folktales, the kind that no reasoning man took seriously. The island kingdom was allegedly surrounded by a mystical fog that separated it from the outside world.

A pagan healer from Boddenburn was the first to mention the island nation; he offered a rumor that the greatest minds of the known world could be found there. Its location, though, was unknown to him. He'd directed Gareth to an alchemist in the Golden City of Auewellian who might be better informed.

The more he dug around, though, the more convinced he became that his journey was worthwhile. The tales of Dineothan and its capital city, Upelstbohr, were the stuff of improbable folklore, but they were full of promise. Stories told of wise men, the greatest minds in all the lands, who resided within the metropolis of Upelstbohr. Concealed for decades behind the mysterious fog, they and their work were hidden from the world at large.

He'd undertaken the task not for gold, but for the sake of his loved ones, so he knew he couldn't turn it away from it. His family's needs were far more important than the doubts that haunted him. He couldn't sit around and watch them succumb to the disease.

After spending what felt like an eternity scouring the country for clues, plenty of which had been plain strange, he now scaled the sodden hillside hoping that something would stand at its crest.

The isle of Pilsu-kimah, legendary gateway to Dineothan, was a small cluster of bog-rich rocks that sat a stone's throw inside the mist. As Gareth had learned, it was not on any maps. Whether this was because of pervasive superstition or the desire to hide its location was something about which he did not care.

Gareth learned that his informant, Hilliard, once worked the gulf as a career fisherman. Rumor was that he'd sailed too close to Dineothan and found the small isle hidden on the outer edge of the mists. It was there that he and his men uncovered the underground catacombs that supposedly led to Dineothan. After some of his crew failed to escape its caverns, Hilliard returned home a haunted man. Now, he spent his time rambling incoherently while panhandling for his next drink. In the tiny slivers of sanity among his confusing words was the location of Pilsu-kimah. This revelation, though, came with a cryptic warning.

As he trudged upwards, Gareth patted at his torso and waist. There would be no turning back once he reached the summit.

He wore a boiled leather cuirass, over which draped a grey longcoat. Inside the jacket were stitched a number of pockets, stocked with items that could be used during a lengthy mission. Matches, chalk, and even a sack filled with smoked beef made up a part of his usual equipment.

Two belts wrapped across his waist. The first strap held a sextet of throwing knives. The second had loops for his limited supply of bullets. Hung from one end was the holster for his revolver. Within was tucked an oiled, black slab of steel that had a six-round chamber and cracked like thunder when fired.

Weathered cuisses, creased with wear, covered the upper thighs of his denim trousers. His steel-toed leather boots, soiled from previous journeys, were functional rather than decorative. Though occasionally something shiny and polished beckoned to him from a storefront, he resisted the lure. The soles of his practical footwear dug like canines into the rotten soil.

Slung across his back was his sword. The four-foot long blade lacked any ornamentation. It had been in his family for decades; however, except for a trio of nicks that intersected the fuller just above the hilt, it was an indistinct piece of steel. He'd not bothered to give the weapon a name. To him, it was merely a tool of his trade.

As Gareth continued his climb, he stumbled. Once again, he could feel the earth beneath him take hold of his foot. Even though the hike appeared short, the terrain tasked him with every stride.

It was only once he approached the summit that the ground solidified. The soggy peat gave way to a dust-covered crag. While Gareth cautiously placed his feet, at least he no longer struggled.

It was there, at the top of the hill, that he spotted the entrance. For some reason, he'd expected to see some ancient structure, perhaps an abandoned mausoleum or derelict chapel. Maybe he'd let the stories go to his head.

Instead, it was a simple hole lined with pavers around the lip.

He walked to the edge and saw stairs descending steeply into the darkness below. Stone-laid walls propped up the surrounding soil. Though the steps were quickly swallowed up by the subterranean darkness, he managed to spot an ancient archway marking the entrance.

Although he remained alert, Gareth felt some degree of relief. All of his inquiries had led him to the strange structure before him.

As he lingered by the cavern's opening, Gareth looked at the dense mist that separated Dineothan from the outside world. No matter how hard he squinted, he could not see through the miasma. If there was a landmass large enough to hold a city there, he failed to spot even a hint of it. Except for the whispers of the wind, and the sounds of the gulf as it lapped against the shore, he heard nothing. If the so-called Grand City of Upelstbohr existed beyond the fog, it was still as the grave.

Gareth found himself momentarily entranced. Instead of formless whiteness, he saw something in the vapors. Hints of color faded in and out as the haze slowly roiled. Small glints, like reflective pieces of metal suspended in the air, caught his eye. For a second, he swore that he spotted movement: a glimpse of someone walking alone, hunched over and with an unsteady gait, weary from their trek.

Confused by the vision, Gareth blinked his eyes. He saw only the pallid mist.

Gareth shook his head and began his descent. He paused once he reached the archway and collected a scorched piece of wood in a nearby rust-coated sconce. The tip was wrapped in cloth that unfurled as he pulled the timber down. He produced a match and, after a strike on the adjacent wall, lit the torch. The flame was slow to catch, but, within a minute, it grew into a decent orange glow that wavered back and forth.

With the light in hand, he leaned forward to examine the ingress.

On each side of the entryway was a soapstone slab, covered in ancient lettering. Perhaps if he'd been anyone else, he might have paused. To Gareth, though, they were a column of uninteresting scratches that only had meaning to those more interested in the past than the present.

Perhaps the letters warned that the path before him wasn't entirely without peril. Even if he could decipher them, Gareth would have willfully ignored these words. He was outfitted and skilled enough to survive most anything. Years of living as a sellsword made him confident in his ability to adapt to any scenario. Even so, it wasn't as if he could turn back. For his family's sake, he needed to find the cure for their malady and no possible danger was going to turn him away.

He ducked his head and proceeded. At first, he took it slowly, but the stairs proved far more stable than they appeared.

Taking the steps two and three at a time, he continued to descend. How deep did this tunnel go? For a moment, he considered the depth of the surrounding waters. Certainly, whatever catacombs that connected Pilsu-kimah and Dineothan would reach well beneath the gulf's floor. If they didn't, his trip would be short.

He listened for the anticipated sounds of water but heard nothing.

Soon, Gareth noticed the change in atmosphere. The air itself grew heavy, as if the earth and water above threatened to crush him under their weight. More than once, Gareth slowed as he took a deep breath. He looked at the ceiling and was briefly relieved that it appeared well-constructed. Even though they were aged, only a few of the palm-sized tiles were missing. A few small shards littered the stone steps.

Once he reached the bottom of the stairs, he noticed fluid in the spaces between the earthen pavers. The gray stone walls were damp with a fine layer of condensation that clung to the surface. When he reached out to steady himself, drops formed and slowly rolled away from his hand.

As he continued his march forward, with torch in hand, the pathway dried. After a hundred yards, all that remained was the ambient moisture in the air.

The subterranean path was a lone corridor, just narrow enough to feel claustrophobic. Except for the burning piece of lumber in his hand, there was no light. There were no intersecting hallways or side rooms. He knocked on the walls, only to hear a dull thud in response.

As he progressed, he raised the torch. The ceiling was so low that the flames licked the paved tiles. A clump of roots poking out from an uneven opening quickly caught fire. It only took seconds for dampness to extinguish the blaze, which left a blackened husk in Gareth's wake. A thin wisp of smoke dissipated as Gareth passed through it.

Gareth continued to move along the tunnel. He only paused from time to time to catch his breath in the dense atmosphere. He often lingered long enough for the echoes of his own footfalls to die off. Eventually, though, a faint sound told him that he was not alone. There was something else there, moving in the distance. At first, he thought it was a shifting of the earth, but then the dull thuds sounded with increasing regularity.

The noise was consistent and deep, the beating of a heavy object against the cavern's supports. When he placed a hand on the nearby wall, he could feel the shudder, even through the coarse fabric of his glove.

He removed his sword from its scabbard and held it at his side.

As Gareth covered the next hundred yards, the pounding grew in intensity. He slowed as he tried to determine the source. Large mammals in battle, like elephants, came to mind. On the fields of Rutchgale, the Gherthans had draped their pachyderms in armor, adorned them with colorful banners, and deployed them in an effort to turn the tide of the conflict. Gareth considered himself lucky that he'd not been at the vanguard of that battle.

Even as the heavy sounds continued to vibrate the tunnel, Gareth pressed on. It wasn't until he caught a whiff of something foul that he stopped completely.

Gareth groaned as he placed the back of his free hand in front of his nose. In between the odors of wild animal and feces was an aroma of rotting meat. The rank fragrance seemed to permeate the still air.

He drew a long breath through his open mouth and sighed.

Just as suddenly as it had begun, the beating ceased. Gareth straightened. He wasted a few seconds waiting for something else to happen before he continued. The source of the noise was at least a point of reference, a destination he might reach. Without it, he was now alone in the darkness with no idea how much longer his trek would take.

Soon, he noticed a faint glow in the distance. He dismissed it as a trick of the light that played on his eyes. As he drew closer, the illumination became brighter. This emboldened Gareth, who hastened.

At the other end of the lengthy corridor was an archway, formed from soapstone blocks. Beyond lay a room lit by flickering flames.

Both curious and wary, Gareth dropped his torch and snuffed it with the heel of his boot. He slowed to sneak up to the entryway. Gareth saw no reason to announce his presence.

With his back pressed against the doorframe, Gareth peeked into the chamber. The arena was dim, lit by flaming sconces along the upper rim. The circular room, which stretched at least 100 yards in diameter, was littered with piles of broken wood and stone slabs, the remains of tiered bleachers. A series of arched openings ran around the upper portion of the thirty-yard tall walls. The brick-laid floor, covered in dirt and debris, was recessed into the ground by a good four feet as it sloped downwards from the outer barricade.

Gareth looked in vain for an exit on the other side of the arena. A heap of what had once been a staircase was spread across the back side of the chamber.

Gareth ground his teeth as he let out a harsh breath through his nose. The hairs on the back of his neck stood up, and the pungent aroma in the air made his stomach churn.

Eventually, he shrugged his shoulders and continued. Just as he began to pass through the entryway, he spied the creature. He'd mistaken it for a blackened mass in the far left corner of the room, a clump of debris that had once been a part of the arena. When it shifted, Gareth recoiled. A low, guttural noise rumbled forth as it began to rise upward.

With a clumsiness borne from unwieldy weight, the beast clambered to its feet. Even hunched over as it was, the creature stood to a height of twenty feet. Beneath the coarse black hair that covered most of its torso was a dense grayish hide. The beast's arms were long and ended in meaty paws that curled into club-like fists of enormous size.

Between its hooved feet was a pile of picked-over carcasses. Gareth had no idea what the bodies once were. A few appeared fresh, which made him wonder where the beast found a consistent food source on isolated Dineothan.

He recoiled from the sight as he pressed his back against the doorway. The only stories of monsters he knew were old wives' tales, long ago dismissed. The burgeoning age of industry had proven all the ancient stories false. There were no more horrors lurking in the dark. Man was fiend enough.

Gareth had never seen anything like it before. Having spent decades in combat against soldiers and bandits, he had no clue how to deal with such an overlarge beast.

After a few seconds, Gareth returned his attention to the thing in the arena. He didn't want to die, but he couldn't retreat. His wife and daughter depended on him.

There had to be some other way through. The beast must have arrived there somehow. The hall behind Gareth was far too small for it.

Maybe I can sneak through. Use the debris as cover. If I can find an exit on the other side, make a break for it.

He nodded to himself.

The only possible way is through, he solemnly thought as he clutched the hilt of his sword in both hands. Even as the beast's overpowering stench caused his nostrils to curl, he inhaled, spun on one heel and slunk into the chamber.

Gareth moved with cautious steps, keeping one eye on the creature. He drew breath through his nose. The flickering torches threw a pale amber light that cast long shadows, making it difficult to see all but the largest piles of debris. When a sliver of wood, no wider than a finger, crunched under Gareth's boot, his heart stopped.

His full attention went to the monstrosity, whose body shifted for a moment. When it stilled, Gareth's shoulders slumped. His pace picked up ever so slightly as he scurried behind a shattered pile of wooden bleachers. Once hidden in the jagged shadows, he ducked down. Gareth ran a hand over his face as he let out a sigh.

He was now a few dozen yards from where the creature waited, guarding its food. He still failed to spot any potential exit in the low light.

Just as Gareth was about to press on, with his gaze on the nearest pile of broken lumber, he noticed the beast move. It turned sideways and reached for something on the nearby ground. When it raised the object, Gareth saw it silhouetted: a club made from a fossilized tree trunk. Roots were now merely fractured stubs jutting from the end. Only a pair of splintered limbs remained attached to the converted weapon.

Gareth started to wonder. *It uses tools. Doesn't that*

mean it has some kind of intelligence? Maybe it can be reasoned with. Maybe, no... no. I shouldn't even chance it. His gaze returned to the mass of picked-over bodies. Some appeared to be the remains of cattle. Others had more familiar shapes that gave him the shivers.

After spending a few seconds bolstering his courage, Gareth slipped out from behind his cover. He moved with measured steps as he gingerly crossed the distance. By the time he was a few yards into the open, the muscles along his shoulders had clenched tightly.

Without a sound, the beast turned towards him.

Gareth recoiled from the sight of the creature's face. Beneath the thick mane of dark fur was a visage out of nightmares. At first, he might have mistaken it for something like a lion, with an unhinged jaw that hung far lower than it should have. After a few seconds, though, Gareth realized that the facial structure was far too flat and long, as if it was some hybrid of a man and a predatory feline. Long and curved teeth, coated in gore from the recent meal, slowly moved up and down. Black eyes shimmered in the faint flickers of torchlight.

Gareth came to a sudden stop. Maybe, if he was fortunate, its vision would be like that of a toad's, based mainly on motion.

He was not lucky.

The beast hunkered down and let out a thunderous roar. The foul odor of rotten meat blew out of its mouth as a spray of spittle launched into the air. It stomped forward as it raised the cudgel.

"Shit," Gareth muttered as he launched to his right

and rushed for cover. Though the creature remained on the periphery of his vision, Gareth focused on a slab of stone only yards ahead of him. Maybe it would do just well enough to put some space between himself and the beast. He could feel the pounding footfalls as they closed on him with surprising speed.

Another roar blasted his ears. Gareth realized it would catch him before he could reach shelter. Any hopes Gareth may have had about dodging the monster were immediately dashed.

The club came down with such swiftness that Gareth couldn't avoid the blow. Even as he attempted to sidestep to his right, the blunt tip glanced off of his left shoulder and spun him.

Gareth howled as he felt the bones in his shoulder break under the impact. His arm went limp. Only by clutching his left arm with his right hand did he manage to keep a grip on his sword. The tip dragged across the stone-laid floor for a moment with a high-pitched squeal.

Gareth was steady enough to stay on his feet. Though dazed for a second, it wasn't long until he reoriented himself.

This isn't a fight I can win, Gareth realized as he reached the broken chunk of stone that angled upwards into the air. He was able to cower beneath it for a moment as he tried in vain to assess his situation. As adrenaline surged, his heart pumped fiercely. While the pain in his shoulder screamed, his thoughts were racing far too fast to pay it any mind.

Another roar sounded from only feet behind him. It was followed by a blow on his makeshift shelter. Chunks of rock rained down on him. Massive fingers reached around the far end and clutched the slab.

Gotta bail, Gareth realized as the creature peeled back the broken architecture. Even as the pain surged, he scurried out as the stone was pulled free and carelessly pitched aside.

After letting out a deep, rumbling howl that shook the air, the monster was hot on his heels. Frantic, Gareth was running for his life, hoping to locate an exit. His sword dangled impotently in his right hand.

As he dashed around another pile of broken masonry, Gareth spotted something in the distance. There it was—a darkened archway a dozen yards away, on the far side of the arena. As he struggled to increase his pace, Gareth kept his eyes on the exit that grew as he neared.

He paid no attention to the sound of something dense cutting through the air behind him.

The horizontal strike caught him across his back. Consciousness fled as Gareth flew headfirst into a nearby pile of shattered bleachers.

CHAPTER TWO

The Halls of Perpetual Arrival

Details came into focus as Gareth's eyes grew accustomed to the change in illumination. Hand still on the handle, he pulled the front door closed behind him with a satisfying click. Stained wooden planks, many of which were covered in seasonal decorations, lined the walls. Orange and red leaves were tacked to a wreath on a nearby holiday display. A crackling fire in the hearth cast a warm glow across the adjacent living room.

The entrance hall was rich with familiar scents that caused a joyous feeling to overcome Gareth. He closed his eyes and greedily drew in the aroma. Even though there were whiffs of roast meat and freshly-baked bread in the air, there was a single fragrance that he immediately picked out: a floral perfume that smelled of posies.

It was a luxury he'd purchased abroad for Nattia years ago. The crystal decanter of golden, aromatic liquid had evoked such elation that her face had immediately glowed. Since then, she'd taken to placing a dab of it on her neck every day. Every time he came home, he could easily catch hints of its aroma.

"Gareth!" Nattia called out as she raced from the kitchen to the foyer of their modest cottage. Her long black hair swayed back and forth as she rushed into his waiting arms.

Behind her trotted their daughter, Shea, whose tiny legs struggled to keep up with her mother's pace. As she joined the pair, Shea wrapped herself around Gareth's leg and buried her face into the fabric of his trousers.

After they eventually broke from their embrace, Nattia retreated a few steps as she reached out a hand and drew Shea in close. Though Shea fidgeted for a moment in her mother's grasp, she eventually settled down. Once done with the initial greetings, Gareth would remove his gear. Most of it would be returned to the wooden chest beside the fireplace. The sword would be placed in a stand in the master bedroom. Nattia would tend to any new wounds he had received while on the job. There was a pattern to his homecoming, one in which she willingly played her part.

Such a life, though, came at a cost to Gareth. He became something less than human, something hardened and violence-prone, to earn his living. He went out of the city, performed the tasks of a sellsword— fighting in foreign wars or acting as hired muscle for the rich—and ultimately returned flush with cash. Even though he knew that version of Gareth had to be abandoned at the entrance, like muddied shoes were left on the doorstep, it took time for him to return to the rational man that Nattia deemed worthy.

Once stripped of his gear, Gareth stood before them in his stained clothes. With his arms out, he remained in place as Shea skipped around him. She flitted about like a fairy as she sang a schoolyard tune. He smiled at her antics.

Nattia frowned at the state of his apparel. Sweat and grime caked his shirt and trousers. The seams along his collar were frayed. After a few seconds, she leaned in close and looked for bloodstains. Relief caused her features to soften.

"Let's get you into something cleaner," she announced in her silky-smooth way as she reached a hand out to Gareth. She led him to the bedroom, where he could disrobe in privacy.

As they moved through the house, Gareth's focus remained on Nattia and the way her locks swung back and forth. For a moment, he caught the whiff of something like burning incense. This faded only to be replaced with the smell of her perfume.

Knowing her parents wanted privacy, Shea stayed behind. Nattia stopped in the hall and motioned Gareth along. Shea's joyous singing was muffled by the door which was closed to a crack.

Their bedroom was as he recalled: paneled in dark wood, lit by the glow of lanterns, and furnished modestly. Atop the bed was a fur-lined quilt. Everything was in its place, including the stack of books on the window-side dresser. For a moment, from the way they were bunched up, it seemed as though someone was still under the sheets. Briefly, the covers moved as if something beneath breathed. Seeing this, Gareth shifted sideways and leaned over. He spotted the crown of a woman's dark head on the pillow.

Gareth knew that couldn't be right. Nattia was just outside, still speaking to their daughter. There was no one else in their home. He reached a hand towards the cover.

"Dear?" Nattia's voice came from the doorway. He stood upright and looked over at her.

His confusion mounted as Nattia closed the door and walked around in front of him. Slender fingers traced across his shoulders. A tingle ran along the skin as it ran down his back.

He glanced past her to the bed, only to find it empty. The cover was flat across the top of the mattress.

"Gareth? Are you okay?"

"Yes," Gareth muttered with a shake of his head.

He shrugged his shoulders and let her undress him. Once stripped bare, she examined him. He waited as his wife scoured every inch of his body with her eyes. She had all the scars memorized: the crescent underneath his right shoulder blade, the trio of lines above his hip, the nick on his thigh that she loved to touch. Nattia had once told him that she enjoyed the rough sensation against her fingertips.

She reached up and caressed his left arm, which

hung limply by his side. When it wiggled about impotently, she clasped it tightly and jerked upwards. A small pop sounded and Gareth began to move the limb about.

"Only a few bruises," she announced as she stood back with arms folded, signaling that her examination was complete. "Were you even in a fight?" she added dryly. "This looks like you drank too much and fell down a flight of stairs."

He offered a cockeyed smile as he stepped in close to her, hearing relief under her dismissive tone. She reached around and placed a hand on his bare buttocks. The chilliness of her touch sent a shiver up his spine. It felt like ice pressed against his flesh.

Gareth leaned in and placed a kiss on her lips. A blush caused her olive cheeks to glow.

"I was extra careful," he announced. "The less injured I am, the sooner I get to enjoy you."

"But, dinner—"

"Can wait," he cut off her objection as he wrapped himself around her. His hands slipped inside the fabric of her blouse and ran along her lower back.

As he caressed her, Gareth paid little attention to the nagging cough that shook Nattia's body. She placed a balled fist over her mouth and turned away.

He woke with every inch of his body sore. Even as his muscles and joints throbbed in protest, he raised an arm and rubbed at his eyelids. The skin around his eyes felt raw as they slowly opened to an encompassing darkness which made him wonder if he was having problems with his vision. All other senses seemed to be functioning. He recognized the texture of his glove's rough cloth as it brushed against his cheek. He could smell burning candles, incense, or possibly both. However faint, the sounds of shuffling movement and breathing could be heard.

Floating somewhere between his dreams and consciousness, Gareth's head was muddled. Where was Nattia? Clearly the sun had not risen and it was unlike her to get up during the night. Patting at his side revealed no warm, soft lump wrapped in a fur cover. He had woken on a cold, wooden floor. A lump of sadness sank in his stomach.

It took time, but eventually, his eyesight acclimated. The vertical lines of an ionic column a few yards in front of him came into focus. On his left was a circular staircase that curved up into the darkness above.

Gareth slowly shifted as he propped himself up. As the muddiness abated, he noted that his left shoulder no longer throbbed with the searing discomfort of broken bones. There was no sense of impairment or even lingering phantom pain. Except for an underlying ache that he attributed to his sleeping arrangements, he felt fine.

He began to move his left arm about, mostly to confirm that his mind was failing him. After a few seconds, he shrugged his shoulders and shook his head. His memories of the beast were so crisp that he struggled to accept his current condition. How long had he been unconscious? Had the confrontation in the tunnels even transpired? Perhaps it had only been a delusion brought on by some unknown influence.

He grunted as a sour expression settled onto his features. This was a skein of thought that made him feel uncomfortable. The more he tugged at it, the more it seemed to unravel. Simple questions begat more complex inquiries; soon, he would be wondering how much of this was real. It wasn't in him to woolgather about the nature of reality.

Gareth shook his head and chose to refocus on the strange-enough now.

Once his eyesight adjusted to the faint lighting, he began to notice familiar architectural features in the enormous chamber. He had woken in some kind of cathedral, lit mostly by clumps of candles spaced along the outer walls. Windows were covered and furnishings he would expect to see, like endless rows of wooden pews, were missing. If there had once been colorful leaded glass murals, they were now paved over with nothing but ashen-hued brick.

Instead of worshippers, the sanctuary housed a smattering of what he could only describe as refugees. A byproduct of war, he'd seen their like before: handfuls of people huddled around crates and woolen sacks of what were possibly their remaining possessions. He had seen similar haunted, fearful eyes and hungry, gaunt faces illuminated by campfire light.

Though they seemed to give him a wide berth, Gareth certainly thought to keep an eye on the others. A quick reflexive touch of his gear gave him comfort.

The interior decoration was missing any kind of religious iconography with which he was familiar. During his years, Gareth had seen many cathedrals that had been stripped of their valuables. In this case, he doubted that the building had ever contained much of value.

Eventually, Gareth stood up and dusted off his hands. As he patted himself down, he was relieved that none of his equipment was missing. At some point, his sword had been returned to its scabbard. He made a mental note to thank whoever had brought him here not only for their kindness, but for their integrity.

Once Gareth was upright, he noticed that the interior did not entirely follow the standard design of any cathedral he'd seen before. While not a devout man himself, both Gareth's and Nattia's families had been staunch parishioners; he'd seen his fair share of worship houses over the years. While the narthex and nave hinted at familiarity, everything to his left served a different purpose. Beyond the transept, where a traditional choir and apse should have been, was an atrium that served as the ground level of a massive tower. It rose what seemed like dozens of yards above him.

The floor of the atrium was a solid sheet of glass which was covered in painted symbols. Scrawled with a quicksilver ink, many were simple arcs and circles that intersected to form a strange pattern. Through the oddly-adorned flooring could be spied a greenish mist that obscured everything below the first few feet.

Encircling this was a series of six-foot-tall obelisks. On each was carved a unique bas-relief. While some of these had worn down with age, many clearly represented something: a priest, a doctor, a university professor in gown and cap, a gravedigger, and a bride holding a lantern among others. Due to damage and age, as only piles of rubble remained, the images on a few of the monuments were indecipherable.

Behind the circle of etched slabs were two sets of stairs that led upward. Both disappeared into open archways a couple of yards above Gareth. Further up, he spotted a series of staircases that ran along the outer rim. Many of these, which skirted the curved surface, were only a few yards in length. Each appeared to be bookended by darkened doorways. He had no specific reason to climb upwards.

He gazed for some time at the tower's upper levels, hoping to spot something of interest. Despite a cluster of candles that were barely visible on a balcony dozens of feet above him, Gareth had difficulty determining how tall the construct ultimately was. A murky darkness shrouded all sign of the ceiling.

Gareth now turned his gaze to the other inhabitants. Except for the shuffling of feet and a series of coughs from one corner of the room, they remained quiet. That no one attempted to approach him struck Gareth as a bit strange. Still, he kept a hand on his shoulder, ready to draw his sword at a moment's notice.

He began to look more closely at those around him.

A few yards on his left, tucked into a back corner and barely visible behind a column of rosewood, was an older gentleman who reclined on a stack of wooden crates. With a piece of cloth, he diligently polished a strip of leather. When their eyes met, he only grimaced and returned to his work.

Seated across from Gareth was an elderly man who seemed absorbed by his presence. In fact, he was the only person that seemed interested in Gareth's awakening. Long scrawny arms were draped over his knees, which were pulled up to his chest. Thin wisps of hair had been pulled back out of his face. An uneven, ragged beard hung down to his chest. Pale blue eyes bulged in their sockets.

Gareth decided to approach him. Before he was within a few paces, the grizzled refugee shifted in place and sat upright.

"Welcome, young one. I am called Alharrad," he stated with a proud smile. He reached out a hand with long bony fingers that were curiously curled at a downward angle, as if crooked by injury or age. Gareth, not wanting to be rude, took the offered palm and shook it.

"Gareth Solomon," he announced in response. Once done, he moved his weight to his back foot and gave Alharrad an examining glance. The older man began to run his fingers through his beard. A few thin, curly strands dislodged and floated down into his lap. After a long, silent pause, he spoke up again.

"I notice you've had the pleasure of meeting the Gatekeeper of the Gape. Special you must be to survive it," he said with a grin that cut across his face from ear to ear. It took Gareth a moment to process the comment. When he realized that Alharrad meant the beast that had assaulted him in the tunnels, he leaned in.

"How? H-how did I make it out?" Almost absentmindedly, he clutched at the once-injured shoulder.

"How indeed," Alharrad replied as the exaggerated smirk remained in place. For a moment, his gaze went to the ornamented glass flooring.

"Do I have *you* to thank for dragging me from there? For making sure I had all my equipment? My sword? If so, you have my thanks."

"Oh, no. No, no, no. I'm not so brave as to chance returning to the Gape. Not even sure how one might go about such a process. Bit of a one-way passage, I might think. One such interaction with the Gatekeeper was more than enough for the likes of me. Too frail. Too frail."

Alharrad's responses immediately grated on Gareth's patience. Alharrad seemed to be taking perverse joy in giving cryptic replies.

"The Gape? Is that what they call the tunnel between Dineothan and the outside world? I assume I've somehow arrived in Dineothan. If not, perhaps you'd be kind enough to advise me otherwise." There was a sarcastic bite to his words.

"So many questions! So many queries!" Alharrad bellowed as he rocked back and forth in his seat. He laughed with a childlike glee. His cackling caused more than one of the other inhabitants to look warily in his direction. "For one so newly-arrived, you ask so much. You've not yet earned even a sliver of the answers you'll be wanting. Knowledge of that kind has value. Must be earned. But not bartered for with gold, mind you. No value here that has."

At this, Gareth scowled. His tolerance for the man was already at an end. For a moment, he considered walking away. He noticed a nearby woman who was dressed in layers of dark-hued wool with a white coif pinned to her head by a gray veil. A few strands of sandy blonde hair had fallen down across her face. Seated against a column, she was surrounded by stacks of books and a half-circle of melted candles.

"No, no, no, don't, uh, don't you scurry away with so much, uh, haste." Alharrad patted vigorously at the air between them. "You'll not find half the answers you want from them. Too a'feared to walk through Upelstbohr anymore. Not alone. Not without the certainty that they'll be returned here a little less than they were. Smaller and smaller every time."

At this point, Gareth'd had enough. "Well, I'm grateful for your time, but I must be on my way," he announced.

Alharrad paused for a second. "Do you even know where to go? Can't be traipsing outside without knowing where step one must be placed." He pointed to the vaulted wooden doors at the narthex.

"I need to…" Gareth trailed off as Alharrad's comment seemed to catch him off-guard. He'd just met the man and despite Alharrad's seemingly welcoming nature, however bizarre it was, there was something untoward about his interest. While others in the cathedral shied away from him, Alharrad had seemingly gone out of his way to watch Gareth.

Alharrad leaned in, ever so slightly, and turned his head.

"I'm looking for a doctor or someone well-versed in medicine. Even a man of science. Someone knowledgeable in either field would do for starters. I came to Dineothan in search of the kind of advice one in those professions might provide."

This caused Alharrad to scowl as he leaned back. Gareth fully expected him to reply that the island of Dineothan was filled with such men and that his request was far too nebulous. He was stunned at what came out of Alharrad's mouth.

"Ya'll be hard-pressed to find any of their like left in the city of Upelstbohr, anymore. Certainly not in the city proper. Though, *maybe* one or two are still in residence at the Grand College of Amaru-ma-mudu. Perhaps one still tending to patients at the Sanatorium of Lyceed's Asylum. Still doing the Lord's work in trying to keep men as men. In the wards of Chorazin? Naught but those of us taken to sanctuary." One of his gangly arms flung out in a sweeping motion to others in the chamber.

Briefly, Gareth's mouth opened. Just as he began to

press for clarification, he stopped himself. He doubted Alharrad's response would be any more informative. The man barely flirted with coherence.

However, Alharrad continued. "If you're damned to press on, you'd best see your way to the Lord's Chapel at Burngwent. Scurry, scurry, blocks to the east. You must move with haste if you're to make it there in one piece. You'll see the double spires stabbing up at the sky on your right as you leave. Two angry fingers pointing at God. If you aim to head upwards through the city to either the College or the Sanatorium, you'll be needing the sigil key to be found there."

Dubious, Gareth shifted his stance and looked the man in the eyes.

"A key? To what, or where? Actually, forget that. Firstly, you know this key is there, how? One would think that if access to parts of the city requires it—"

"You've not been outside these walls," Alharrad noted. "Perhaps once you see what walks the streets, you'll understand the situation proper. *Then* you can make assumptions about what is known."

When Gareth opened his mouth, Alharrad waved both hands in the air.

"Go, go! Only when you see what remains of the outside world will you understand why folks cannot walk through the wards as if they own the city." He insistently pointed at the massive doors that barred the arched exit.

This was enough for Gareth. He thanked Alharrad and left him behind. Gareth could feel the old man's eyes on him as he charged down the center aisle.

As Gareth approached the doors, he noticed movement on the periphery of his vision. While Alharrad had not moved, he watched Gareth pensively. The others, though, appeared as though they were preparing for something terrible. Many shrunk away from the entrance. A few even covered their faces.

Gareth snorted derisively as he placed his hands on the dense wooden surface and pushed. The weight was as he expected, and it took him a second try to force the barrier ajar. The hinges groaned against the effort, as if they hadn't been used in some time.

A sharp stream of cold white light cut an angle across the narthex. Though he heard the gasps and whimpering of others, Gareth paid little heed.

With one shoulder, he pushed the entryway open just wide enough to pass through sideways. Once outside, he paused to take in the opulent vista that was his first view of Upelstbohr.

Someone rushed to close the door behind him.

CHAPTER THREE

Lord's Chapel at Burngwent

Gareth stepped forward and was immediately stunned by the overwhelming vista that loomed menacingly over him. No amount of prior warning could have prepared him for a city which towered skyward in precariously stacked tiers of gothic structures. Open-mouthed, he stood in place for what felt like minutes.

As he attempted to process the baroque landscape, Gareth slowly made sense of it all. Upelstbohr was clearly a metropolis that had been constructed over a lengthy span of time. Over what he could only assume were centuries, the city had been built up in levels growing more ornate as they rose. The ground floor, fashioned from stone, steel, and concrete, served as foundation for the more ornate, opulent wards. Multiple strata rose, in some places as high as a quarter-mile from the earth. There seemed to be some never-ending need to build garish domiciles on the literal backs of the poorer districts.

The skyline itself was a porcupine, thick with towers and steeples, all of which stretched to obscure the sky above.

To Gareth, it appeared as though someone had hoarded these buildings from throughout the world; they were stacked tightly as if the island of Dineothan served as warehouse for the strange collection. Though he was not some yokel from the boonies, Gareth had to admit some degree of astonishment. In his time, he'd seen many an overdeveloped metropolis. Boddenburn to the south was particularly dense and overpopulated. The Golden City of Auewellian was glaringly gauche, even as seen from the adjacent waters of the Sea of Auewel.

Still, Upelstbohr was something altogether unique and Gareth struggled to process its grandeur.

As he looked at the sky, Gareth took note of the sun's position. Examining the orange-hued haze that ringed it, he tried to estimate the time of day. *It's late in the afternoon. 4ish or maybe close to 5. What was the hour when I arrived at Pilsu-kimah? Early... before noon, I think. Is this... the same day? No, it couldn't be. To travel so far on foot alone would have taken longer. If someone dragged me here, I can't imagine it going any faster. Seems unlikely. I wonder how much time I've lost. Maybe I'll be fortunate enough to find someone who knows the date. I could have... No, I doubt Alharrad has the sense to know the year, much less the day.*

After he blinked a few times to diffuse the lingering

glare burning his retinas, Gareth shook his head and continued on. He crossed the courtyard in a few strides and began his way down a small set of curved stairs to the pathway below.

Just as he cleared the last step, Gareth looked over his shoulder to the building he'd left behind. The stone-laid edifice rose above him, sullen and gray. A series of overly-ornate columns framed the entryway. Now paved over, rows of steep archways lined the exterior. What had once been a rose window was now a featureless circle of brick and mortar. Two sets of steeply-sloped buttresses flanked either side of the main building. Only separated by a wrought iron fence, adjacent edifices were crammed tightly against the cathedral's property.

From where Gareth lingered, he spotted the cylindrical structure which loomed like a lighthouse over the sanctuary and surrounding wards. Atop it was a crown of thin, jagged, obsidian steeples. Even now, he was surprised at its towering height.

Gareth began to look for signs leading him to the Lord's Chapel at Burngwent. He had no idea what or where Burngwent was, just that it was "blocks to the east." His head bobbed back and forth as he attempted to parse Alharrad's direction. Through the forest of wood and steel, he eventually spotted a pair of black spires. Visible through a sliver of space in the skyline, the pointy structures appeared to be no more than a mile away.

With his course set, he turned to his right and trotted towards the alley's eastward exit. It wasn't long before he was swallowed up by the ornate landscape.

Precipitously-angled rooftops hung over the cramped, crooked alleys that connected one intersection to another. The streets themselves were laid out in a maze, wherein many of the walkways folded back at strange angles. He spotted the occasional square, littered with refuse and the signs of a city in decline. Staircases and metal ladders were crammed oddly into the creases between claustrophobically-organized housing blocks.

More than once, Gareth paused to examine where these might lead. Those that appeared to descend below directed him to even more dank tenements beneath the shadows of the upper tiers. Above were more affluent settlements, propped up by a massive skeleton of steel and stone.

Gareth pressed on. He had yet to spot a living soul outside of the sanctuary. While there were faint echoes of movement from elsewhere, they were barely audible over the whistling breeze. Missing was the usual muffled din of people moving within their homes. Though there was some damage and dilapidation, Upelstbohr did not strike him as a city ruined by some all-encompassing catastrophe. He'd seen cities under siege and near their ends before. There were no neighborhoods razed to the ground, no piles of plague-riddled bodies left in the streets. The sky was not choked with the black smoke of the pillager's fire.

Gareth picked up on the first signs of life as he put some distance between himself and the cathedral. What was usually lost in the buzz of bustling civilization now stood out starkly among the murmurs of creaking abodes. From somewhere far off came a dull bass rumble, like that of distant thunder, which pounded at regular intervals.

His pace slowed as he tried to make sense of it. He vacillated between two separate notions: that it was either a large drum being beaten or that something of great size marched with a deliberate gait. Before he could mull it over for too long, the sound ceased. Disappointedly, he shook his head and resumed his trek.

As Gareth approached the intersection of two walking paths, a feeling caused him to slow down. Uncertain why he felt the sudden apprehension, Gareth chose to heed it all the same. He crept forward to the juncture where the alley crossed the side street. Gareth paused as he leaned against the building's corner. Beneath the echoes of his own footfalls, there was something else.

He peered down the narrow strait. The lane was just wide enough for foot traffic. On either side were multistory townhomes that appeared to bow inwards under their own cumbersome weight. An overhanging balcony dozens of yards overhead hinted at the existence of a courtyard far above his position.

The nearing sounds of muffled footfalls caused Gareth's gaze to drop back to street-level. Gareth leaned out and spied a silhouette through the wisps of fog that wafted through the adjacent walkway. It swayed back and forth as it moved, so at the very least, it was another living thing. Its mere presence proved that Upelstbohr's streets were not entirely abandoned.

The mists swirled as they parted and allowed the thing to amble forward. Horrified, Gareth struggled not to gasp aloud. With one hand, he reached for his sword, but stopped short of withdrawing it from the scabbard.

Swinging side to side, the beast's face was twisted in an unholy mask. Part man and part canine, with a matted white pelt, its toothy maw was askew as the lower jaw hung like a broken gate. Reddened lips peeled back to reveal a mouthful of ivory daggers.

Hunched over, the creature continued to lurch forward. It had two arms and two legs and moved in a grotesque imitation of a man's gait. The only parts that could be mistaken for human in the beast were its lanky, fur-coated appendages. Long, gnarled talons scraped along the tiled avenue as its arms dragged behind it. The torso was misshapen and top-heavy, and the legs were deformed to the point of being only partially useful. By the way it slowly loped forward, Gareth wondered how fast it would move if it spotted him and gave chase.

Just as that thought rolled about in his head, the creature came to a stop. Its head reared back as crescent-shaped nostrils sniffed the air. Cold blue eyes rolled about in their sockets as its mouth hung agape. A serpent-like tongue hung pendulously from one side.

While he waited and watched, Gareth's grip on his sword's hilt tightened. When his glove creaked against the leather bindings, the beast's ears twitched. Gareth clenched his jaw in anticipation as the rest of his body went rigid.

For what felt like forever, Gareth waited and
observed. The beast stayed in place as its eyes stared
at the other end of the passage. The creature's posture
shifted. With the same lurching speed as before, it
turned away and began to drag itself back through
the fog.

After a full minute, the thing disappeared into the
mists. Gareth let out a sigh. He lowered his weapon and
slumped against the wall.

What in the hell have I gotten myself into? Gareth
thought alarmingly as he ran a hand along his jawline.
He brushed a dotting of sweat from his brow. *What was
that? Something that… No, don't think too long on it.
First, the Gatekeeper and now… Is-is this Hell? What have
they done here? How did I…*

Panic began to settle into his chest, causing his heart
rate to accelerate. He fought to keep his breathing in
check. Before he let his imagination run wild, he shook
his head vigorously. Eventually, somehow, he would find
answers.

He stood upright and resumed his march down
the darkened passageway. Rather than follow the more
direct route to the Lord's Chapel, he stuck to the back
alleys.

He arrived at the Lord's Chapel before the hour
was out. As the noise of other living things in distant
neighborhoods became more and more evident, Gareth
considered himself fortunate to reach his destination

unscathed. Gareth anxiously wondered what else he would run across.

A trio of passageways and a long, sloping set of stairs eventually led him to the open square that surrounded the ancient house of worship.

An image of the building had already formed in the back of his head, even from Alharrad's strange blathering. Much like the sanctuary, the Lord's Chapel had outsized proportions. Grand arched doors on the western face were ajar. Thin window-frames, many of which no longer contained glass panes, lined the upper floors. Twin coal-colored steeples rose to the sky above the main structure. The courtyard was bordered on all sides by tiers of the surrounding ward.

He kicked at the dusty path beneath him and continued. With each step, he grew increasingly nervous. He could feel something in the air.

Slowly, Gareth withdrew his sword and held it out in front of him. For only a second, he reached towards his revolver. He thought better of it since gunfire might draw the attention of creatures in the adjacent wards. Because of the city's morgue-like silence, the crack of a gunshot might carry for miles.

Hunched over, he stalked towards the entrance. He could feel something there—an aura that extended beyond the confines of the building.

There were no recent tracks in the pathway that led to the entrance. No birds were perched on the withered trees at the back. He didn't spot so much as a lone insect crawling along the ashen soil. While there were certainly things that roamed the streets around him, the immediate vicinity was hauntingly abandoned.

That was not to say that everything was silent. There were tiny, skittering noises, like the scrabbling of vermin seeking the safety of darkened hiding places. Having visited many a rat-infested slum, he paid them no heed. To him, it was the first sign of normalcy he'd encountered.

As he reached the entrance, he placed a free hand on one of the doors. The dense slab of wood refused to budge as he pressed his weight against it. The current opening would have to suffice. Fortunately, there was enough room for him to pass through with only the slightest shift of his shoulders.

Once inside the foyer, he came to a sudden halt. His nose curled at the aroma of something like soggy fur. It was pungent enough that Gareth was immediately on edge. A low-grade nausea caused his stomach to turn over. He placed the back of his fist against his mouth.

Seconds passed before he composed himself and marched forward. It took only a few strides across a soiled carpet, past the broken remnants of wooden furniture, to get to the worship hall.

While he was reminded of the earlier sanctuary, the Lord's Chapel felt smaller, more claustrophobic. Except for an altar at the far end, the main chamber was largely empty. Though a few broken candle holders and slivers of shattered planks had been dashed to the far corners, there was nothing to indicate that anyone had visited recently. Even though slivers of light cut across the nave from the empty windows, much of the illumination originated from an oblong hole in the roof.

After looking at the gaping tear in the ceiling, Gareth turned his gaze to the parquet floor. He found it odd that there was no sign of a recent structural collapse. The flooring itself was worn and scuffed, but if part of the roof had fallen in, it left no perceivable damage or debris.

He paused within the shadows as he gazed across the empty chamber. On the far end was a long altar, adorned with silk and bronze and layered with melted candle wax. An exhibition of five oil paintings, each of which featured old men in regal clothing, was lined up along the back wall. A stack of rosewood curio boxes stood at the center. On either side of this display was a scattering of gold coins and gemstones. Even from a distance, Gareth could tell that the treasure trove was of significant value.

Despite temptation, he held his ground. The hairs on the back of his neck rose. There was a clear prize arranged atop the altar and nothing was set before him to halt his advance.

And still, he couldn't compel himself to cross just yet. He'd heard tales of traps set by a band of rogues. Victims were often robbed and left for dead, and their belongings divvied up and sold for a tidy profit. The guide who provided directions often received a cut of the proceeds. To Gareth, Alharrad didn't exactly seem trustworthy. He could have arranged just such a scenario.

Gareth bolstered his courage and began his slow

march to the far side. He was relieved when the floor thumped dully beneath his boots. Despite the wear and tear on the interior, the chapel's foundation felt solid and unyielding.

No more than a few yards across the nave, Gareth came to a sudden stop. He felt a sour, musty gust of air blow across the back of his head. This caused strands of brown hair to fall across his brow and over his eyes. He brushed these aside as he went into a defensive posture. For a moment, he looked at the opening in the roof.

The direction was all wrong. It had come from—

He could hear the scraping of something sharp on wood. From the sound, Gareth knew it wasn't metal. Perhaps bone or claws dug into the timber. On some level, he expected something inhuman.

Like a rank amateur, he'd stumbled into a trap, just not the one he expected.

He spun around just in time as the creature let out an air-rending roar. Spittle fanned out in a balmy spray that reeked of decay. Behind him, clutching the upper walls with long, curled talons, was a beast that was hunched over, much like a catlike predator. Long bristling fur that was mottled shades of gray and tan fanned out as its brass-colored eyes locked with Gareth's. Circular pupils expanded as its head bobbed forward. While its snout protruded, more humanoid nostrils flared as it sniffed at its prey.

Once again, he was face-to-face with something he'd never seen before in all his years. Decades of killing his fellow man proved inadequate preparation for the fight before him. Something that might have been fear curdled in his stomach.

Gareth held out his blade and shifted his stance. He began to take careful steps to the side. Though the beast remained attached to the upper levels, it was to the right of the still-open entrance. Gareth began to consider his chances; if he made a break to flee the chapel, he might be able to skirt along the left-hand side before it could close the distance.

As Gareth took a pair of strides towards his exit, the creature dropped from its perch. It screeched again as it landed with all the grace of a lion. The impact caused a dull vibration to rattle the floor. Gareth felt it in the heels of his feet.

Gareth was now able to get a sense of the creature's scale. Though it remained hunched over with its hindquarters raised, Gareth could see that it was approximately twelve feet in length and weighed somewhere in the neighborhood of five hundred pounds. It had no tail and each of its limbs, despite their fur-covered bulk, held anthropoidal shapes. The front paws had thumbs that curled inwards as the hawk-like claws scraped against their palms.

The beast began to tighten its muscles; it was about to lunge. Gareth's eyes glanced at the exit for a second. He was nowhere near close enough. When the creature attacked, he needed to move quickly, if only to dodge the blow. Years of combat caused his battle instincts to take over. For Gareth to survive the encounter, he would need to fight back. Perhaps, if he was fortunate enough, he might land a blow.

When it once again screeched loudly, he knew the swipe was imminent. A second later, it launched forward with an arcing pounce. Anticipating the incoming strike, Gareth lunged to the side. Thin, blade-like claws swung past him as they rent the air itself. Purely out of impulse, Gareth fanned his sword to his right. The edge bounced off of the meaty shank of its back leg. A swath of fur was trimmed from the hide as a thin gash appeared in its place.

As it landed and came to rest, the beast turned about with a violent spin of its arched back. Back claws dug into the flooring as it snapped its jaws. Despite the dripping blood that marred its pelt, it did not favor the wounded limb.

His sword was not the greatest weapon, but he knew such a blow should cause noticeable discomfort, if not impairment. In a normal opponent, the strike, however awkward, would have cut into the muscle. Instead, it had only served to enrage this beast.

Something else occurred to him. Gareth was now between his attacker and the chapel's entrance. A hasty glance over his shoulder confirmed this assessment. He had dodged the initial strike and had managed to cover a quarter of the distance. There was a possibility that he could put the dense doors between himself and the creature, if only to give him a moment of rest.

Just as its muscles coiled for the next attack, Gareth turned tail and went into a full sprint. He heard the ungodly screech as powerful legs propelled it after him.

He remained focused on the sliver of light that meant escape.

He had crossed halfway before the impact from behind toppled him.

When the talons struck him across the back, Gareth was knocked off balance. He stumbled forward and dropped to his knees. His sword bounced off the tiled surface and slid out of his reach. Gareth did not attempt to retrieve it. All he could think of as he began to crawl for the exit was survival.

Even as the wounds on his back throbbed with the kind of pain that promised permanent damage, Gareth forced his muscles to push forward. He could hear the deep rumbling breath of the beast as it neared. Each footfall thudded against the tiled surface. Even as the pain and overwhelming panic dulled his senses, Gareth knew that it was drawing in close. Nevertheless, he kept his sights on the still-open doorway. A halo of red-orange light illuminated the archway.

Hand over hand, he progressed. It never occurred to him to get back to his feet.

He saw the exit growing larger as he moved ever closer. He ignored the sanguine breath that blew against the back of his head.

The second blow lifted him off the ground and flung him out of the chapel. One arm went limp as it thudded against the right-hand door. He blacked out just as his body tumbled clear of the building.

CHAPTER FOUR

An Unexpected Revisiting

His head throbbed. For a moment, he wondered how he could possibly be hungover. He was at home, with his family and there was no reason—no excuse, really—for him to drink to excess. He didn't usually carry on in that manner unless he was with those of his ilk, usually in the midst of victorious celebration.

Early on in their marriage, Nattia made it clear he wasn't to bring that type of foolishness into the house with him. He was forbidden to be a rowdy lush around Shea.

Then, how did he end up with this headache?

His eyelids remained tightly clenched. When they opened with a flicker, the brilliant glare caused him pain. It was as if he was directly under the sun. Nausea caused his stomach to turn. He flinched at the discomfort and reclosed them.

His other senses began to pick out additional details. The aroma of a slowly-roasting hunk of beef, seasoned with garlic and wine, caused his mouth to water. He could hear the murmur of people shuffling about, sounds of daytime traffic along the side-street which abutted his home. There was a faint sound of someone coughing, heard just over the ticking of Nattia's heirloom clock.

Gareth could feel a familiar weight on his lap. It was small and wiggled about as if uncomfortable. It carried Shea's baby-powder smell that he knew well. She was trying in vain to get comfy on a seat made of muscle and bone. As she did, she let out a chirpy giggle that filled the air.

This triggered so many good memories that, for that moment, Gareth was overcome with joy. Even as those feelings grew, the throbbing in his head persisted.

Despite his dread of the sunlight, Gareth opened his eyes again. This time, the light wasn't nearly so powerful. A sliver of white fell diagonally through the living room and cut across the right side of his face. He sneered as he shifted in place. Once the beam no longer struck him, he turned his focus downward.

Gareth reclined in a padded chair with his daughter seated atop him. She appeared to finally settle as her backside pressed against the left side of his hip. Even as Shea sunk into his lap with a book open on her own, Gareth felt strange. A twinge of sadness sat like a dull weight in his stomach. He couldn't shake off a lingering dread.

He looked down at the pages. He fully expected to see a colorful illustration along with a string of short sentences. Instead, he found an amorphous blob that continued to undulate no matter how long he watched. The strange lettering shifted from one unrecognizable image to another.

Shea continued to read aloud as if there was no problem. At the end of each sentence, Gareth praised her. He had to assume she was reciting correctly.

From the other room came a violent bout of coughing. Only now did he recall that Nattia was ill. In fact, she'd been sick for some time, and despite Gareth's efforts to locate someone who could help her, she seemed no closer to recovery. He found himself spending more and more time with Shea to keep her from fretting too much about her mother's worsening illness.

Before he could linger, Shea began to squirm. She wanted him to notice something.

"Daddy, what does this say?" Shea beckoned as she pointed to the open book. Her tiny finger tapped at the paper.

Gareth leaned forward and attempted to reread the page. The letters were blurry squiggles that morphed in shape just as he came close to deciphering them. After a few seconds, he grew frustrated. This was a child's book. Why was he struggling with what should be the simplest phrases and words?

"Maybe we should put this up," he suggested. This caused Shea to frown. "We should check on dinner," he added.

"Okay," Shea agreed as she slammed the thin hardback closed and jumped from his lap. As she touched down on the floor, she stopped.

Though Gareth didn't notice it at first, Shea began to wheeze. She released the book and placed both hands over her mouth. Within seconds, her tiny frame shuddered. He leaned forward and attempted to wrap his arms around her.

When he did so, they passed through her. Shocked, he sat upright as his eyes widened. Still struggling to breathe, Shea did not move.

As he reached out for her a second time, again he was unable to touch her. There was something primal about his growing panic. The terror at his unexpected impotence latched onto Gareth. He was unable to tend to her in this time of need. What kind of father was he?

His arms continued to pass through her as if she was smoke. The world around him began to blur.

Nattia's coughing grew louder. Eventually, Shea's matched Nattia's in volume and tempo.

Gareth was overcome by a confusing mixture of relief and disappointment when he awoke flat on his back. The warmth that he associated with home was slowly replaced with a cold, candlelit gloom. The aromas of baby powder and roasting beef faded. In their place was a mixture of melted candle wax, incense, and smoldering wicks.

He let out a long, heavy sigh as he propped himself up. Joints creaked as he sat upright. Even with the horror that bedeviled his dreams, he longingly wished he could return. There was comfort in the hazy familiarity that he craved.

Gareth eventually rose to his feet. Though there was a dull soreness in his muscles, he did not feel impaired by recent injuries. He reached a hand to his back and ran it along the unmarred cloth of his outfit. There were no tears in the coat's fabric, no claw-marks, no blood. As far as he could tell, there was no sign that he'd even been in a fight.

For a moment, he began to question his memory. Perhaps in this strange environment, his mind was playing tricks on him. Gareth shook his head, as if that would push the growing doubts from his mind.

As his senses began to adjust to his surroundings, he recognized where he was. Gareth looked down at the sanctuary's familiar glass flooring. Between his feet, he spied the slowly-swirling fog that roiled underneath the transparent surface. Candlelight caused the painted markings to come alive as they reflected the illumination.

While he watched the mist beneath him, he felt the presence of another person nearby. Someone shuffled toward him. He had a fair idea of who his visitor would be.

"I see you've returned in one piece," Alharrad cackled from his seat on the left-hand stairs just above him. Gareth's head snapped upwards to find the old man gleefully bobbing back and forth in place.

Gareth's jaw clenched tightly as a short snort blew out through his nose. A deep scowl marred his features. The old man appeared to be having a laugh at his expense. Gareth had no time to waste on what was, at best, petty foolishness, if not outright malice.

Without a word, Gareth went for his sword. When his hand closed, only to clasp empty air, he realized that he no longer possessed the weapon. He swore under his breath when he recalled the attack in the Lord's Chapel, where his blade now rested. To his good fortune, though, he still possessed his revolver and knives. They would have to do.

"Oh, ho, ho, hoooo," Alharrad chortled as he clapped his hands and kicked his feet in the air.

That was the last straw for Gareth. He reached out and swiftly grabbed the old man by the ankle. Alharrad's eyes grew wide as Gareth dragged him from his perch. With a scream, Alharrad dropped to the ground with a painful clatter. That none of his limbs broke in the impact was a small miracle. Gareth moved in and seized him by his ragged, tan garments.

Gareth yanked Alharrad off of his feet and slammed him against the side of the stairs. As his lanky limbs flailed about, Alharrad screeched like a distraught animal. As he babbled loudly, Alharrad begged for his life. Gareth was too furious to care. Instead, he scanned the cathedral to see if any of the other inhabitants would intervene. When none of them moved from their places, he turned his attention back to the old man.

"Don't hurt me, I beseech you. You'll gain naught from taking Alharrad's life!" he bellowed as his hands clawed fruitlessly at Gareth's arm. "I am hollow, with nothing left not already taken by those what patrol the city streets. I've been returned here far too many times to be any more than a taste. Certainly nothing worth replacing what you've lost."

"What are you on about, madman?" Gareth snarled as he shook his prisoner. He reared back a balled fist as a threat. Despite his seething anger, Gareth wouldn't strike Alharrad. The old man was frail enough that the blow might kill him outright.

"I-I-I, uh, I knew you wouldn't die. Knew it, I did."

"And yet you didn't think to warn me about what I was walking into?"

"How else might the young child learn not to touch the flame?" Alharrad retorted cryptically. At first, Gareth struggled against his anger. Once Alharrad's comment began to sink in, though, Gareth's posture slackened.

Though he didn't want to admit it, Gareth *had* learned something about Dineothan. Many things, if he was being honest. Even now, he was acquiring the island's strange brand of wisdom. Whether his sane mind still fought the abnormal was irrelevant. Things happened differently on the island than they did in the outside world. Until Gareth began to grasp this concept, he would continue to fail. He needed to stop acting as if this was a regular job in a familiar destination with distinct orders to kill or protect.

As Gareth began to settle down, something emboldened Alharrad. "I remembers something of import. I forgets that you can't hurt me here, anyway. We are in sanctuary, protected from the deviltry what haunts Upelstbohr." He banged a balled fist on Gareth's arm. "Unhand me, you brute. You can't harm me here. You can't!"

Irritated, Gareth eventually released his grip. Alharrad dropped gracelessly to the floor. Once free, he scrambled backwards until his back was pressed against the stairwell. Before Alharrad could flee into the darkness, Gareth moved in close and leveled a finger within inches of the old man's face.

"What kind of trap did you send me into? What in the hell was that *thing*?" Gareth growled.

"If'n you'll recall I didn't direct you there exactly. You were damned and determined to be on your way. I only pointed you in the right direction. My answers were naught but the truth. You'll still be needing the sigil key to move on from these wards."

"A *truth* that you conveniently left out was that you sent me to a certain death. Without a single warning, I might add." He shook the accusing digit at the old man. His gloved finger brushed against the tip of Alharrad's nose. "Again I ask… What. Was. That. Thing?" Gareth was seething as the words came out one at a time. Even though he fully expected nonsense, he wanted an answer all the same.

After quivering in place for a few seconds, Alharrad mustered enough courage to reply.

"The Lord's Chapel is home to Sindex, th-the Scavenging Weasel. What was once a house of worship for the Church of Grand Ilu is now his place of rest. Many a tale says that in a fit of rage, he slew his brother. In a fit of madness, he, uh, he *consumed* him. Whole, they say."

This caused Gareth to recoil. Though he was loath to admit it, his brief experience in Dineothan made Gareth more likely to believe Alharrad's bizarre story. Previously, he might have discarded the response whole cloth. After his time on the streets and the failed battle with Sindex, he was beginning to take the ramblings with a little less skepticism. Now that he was in a strange land, he might have to heed the advice of others. He couldn't just rely on his own skill; even someone as shifty as Alharrad might prove to be useful.

Before he could continue, Alharrad made the most of the brief pause.

"Y-you, uh, you're a fortunate one. Born with a bit more luck than others, I think. Wear it on your skin, I see."

"How so?"

"That Sindex, either him or his vermin-kin, didn't consume you whole, make you not be anymore, says that you weren't deemed precious enough. You didn't have any more than what you walked out them doors with. If you'd slain some of them, devoured them complete, you would have had been a meal so desirable as to beckon all their kind for miles around you."

"Speak sense, you senile old crank!"

"I, uh, I am. I-i-it is you that are ignorant of the way of things. Y-you, uh, you don't yet ken what it is to exist in Dineothan. To strike on me would not make you a smarter man."

Gareth let out a sardonic snort of laughter. However obtuse it was, the old man had a point. Something else occurred to Gareth.

"And when I arrived here?" he inquired. "The first time, I mean. Why was I returned, then?"

It took a second for the question to sink in. When it did, Alharrad's eyes lit up.

"The Guardian of the Gape?" Alharrad said with a dry cackle. "That one… he has no need to consume. No need to devour, really, and it does no good as he resides within the Gape. On the cusp, he is. Can not rise higher than his current post. Had no desire, long as he properly recompensed. That's not to say he goes without. The Ikkibu, those what work behind the scenes, have given him more than his fair share. He does not go wanting. His services are paid for. Richly one might suggest." Alharrad's volume dropped as he mumbled under his breath. "Would that any man could partake of such a benevolent contract."

For a moment, Gareth wanted to press the matter. He ultimately decided against it. Even though Alharrad had willingly offered something of value, Gareth did not want to delve any deeper. Gareth decided against asking how he'd returned here. A part of him didn't want to know the answer. His situation was bizarre enough.

Before Gareth could comment further, Alharrad

spoke up with a query of his own.

"Do you still intend on throwing yourself at certain death?" Alharrad inquired.

With a snap of his arm, he reached out and grabbed Alharrad by the throat. Even before the old man could attempt to pry himself free, Gareth began to speak.

"If I discover you're behind this—that you profit from what happens at the Lord's Chapel in any fashion—I will drag you out into the streets and stake you to the nearest courtyard. Leave you for the things that roam the streets. Let them perform the deeds you so clearly fear."

The color drained from Alharrad's complexion as he began to whimper. Even though he felt like thrashing Alharrad, Gareth released his grip. The old man slumped back into the wall. Once back on his feet, he scurried away with an arm over his head for shelter. Eventually, he disappeared up the stairs to the tower's second level.

Gareth made no effort to stop him.

Once the sounds of scrambling footsteps above him ceased, Gareth turned his attention to the doors at the far end of the building. For the briefest moments, he was hesitant to depart again.

Into what madness had he stumbled? Gareth propped himself against the column and rubbed at his temples. He was clearly out of his depth here. Usually, he was so sure of himself and his skill, but he was starting to have doubts in the face of such horrors.

As he blew a breath out of his nose, he scowled.

No. You have no choice. You struggled too hard to get here. There is no turning back without some kind of cure. There is no other option.

He refocused on the reasons for his quest.

With doubts pushed aside, he charged down the main aisle. No one bothered to look in his direction. They all went out of their way to avoid meeting his gaze.

Once again, Gareth left the building only to have someone slam the door behind him.

Chapter Five

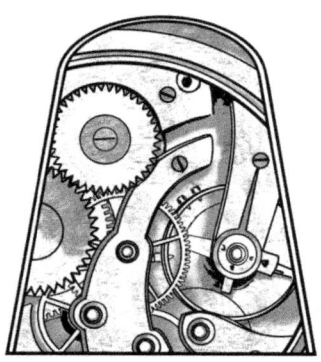

Naze

Now familiar with the streets leading to the Lord's Chapel, Gareth moved quickly along the winding lanes. With a hand on the butt of his revolver, he kept an ear out for the sounds of movement. Though certain he wasn't alone on the streets, Gareth was relieved that he'd not yet drawn unwanted attention.

Even as Gareth maintained his pace, doubts began to gnaw at the back of his brain. He was out of his mind to charge back to the cathedral without a viable plan for how to deal with Sindex. He wasn't at full strength. If he was honest with himself, even his sword wouldn't immediately swing things in his favor; it hadn't been effective against the beast during their first encounter. On top of that, he had no battle experience in dealing with such a creature. He would have to hide in the shadows and watch for a flaw that he could exploit.

That's a pretty big assumption you're making, he

thought to himself. *That it'll have a weakness.* He bit down on his lower lip and rattled his head. The sting helped him refocus.

He looked at the orange-hued sky above. From the position of the sun as it peeked through the towering city skyline, Gareth figured that it was late in the afternoon. He'd lost an entire day. Time was not on his side, and he could ill afford to squander any more. Even though the plague was a slow death to those infected, he'd been gone for far too long.

As he neared the junction where the inhuman beast had loped through the dense mists, Gareth slowed his pace. Softly, he moved up to the right-hand turn and cast a quick glance down the alley. There was no movement. The scraping of claws on pavers seemed to echo from all corners, though none sounded near enough to warrant a retreat. If the way was clear, he might cut through to reduce his time on the streets.

Just as he moved into the open, he heard a sound. Its plainness caught him off-guard.

"Hey."

For a moment, the word didn't even register. It was merely a whisper lost in the winds that whistled through the surrounding ward. His eyes focused on the crooked lane, looking for something to lurch its way out of the fog.

"Hey, yew, deaf arse."

Gareth straightened as the words sunk in. His head jerked around.

"Up *here*." The voice, which was soft and feminine, came from above.

Gareth looked up to find a lean woman dressed in black, watching him from the eaves over the street. A scowl creased the pale skin of her forehead. Fiery amber eyes met his own.

"Get off tha streets, ya dolt." She motioned off to her right. "Thar's a ladder on yur left. On tha side of tha buildin'. Get up here a'fore one a them sees ya."

It took a few seconds for him to understand, but once he did, he moved down the adjacent alley. Relieved to discover another human on the streets, he didn't think twice about joining her above. He located a column of metal rungs mounted on the brick wall. Hand over hand, Gareth pulled himself upwards.

Once atop the sloping roof, he found her crouched a few feet from the steep edge.

Choppy, shoulder-length brown hair fluttered in the breeze. When a particularly stout gust revealed most of her face, Gareth noticed her thin features. Even in her hunched-over position, Gareth could tell that she was maybe a half-foot shorter than he was.

Beneath a curtain of tattered cloth that hung from her fur-lined shoulders was a black bodysuit, composed of densely-woven fibers and reinforced with thin, molded armor plates. When the wind blew her cloak aside, he could spy her lithe form. Strapped around her waist was a belt lined with throwing knives. Hanging from one end was a curved dagger. From the other was holstered a sawed-off, double-barreled shotgun. It was a smart weapon for defensive purposes; if one of the monsters got a bit too close for comfort, she could fire the wide spray of pellets.

Slung from one shoulder was a leather rucksack, closed tightly with a cord. Though it made little sound when she moved, it swung with significant weight. Either the pack was padded to reduce noise or filled with soft items, like clothing.

After scanning the surrounding ward, she slumped backwards, sat down on the roof and turned to Gareth.

"What in tha damned hell are yew doing out here? Besides lookin' fer all manner a trouble."

She spoke with an unfamiliar brogue. In his travels, Gareth had heard many different accents. He was well-versed enough that he was usually able to place a person's region of origin. Her speech, though, caught him as something altogether new. He considered the idea that she might be a native of Dineothan.

"I, well… I, uh," he sputtered.

Noticing his reluctance, she spoke up. "Apologies, I guess introductions are in order. If I'm ta get an answer proper outta ya, maybe we should be on a first-name basis. I'm Naze." She made no effort to offer her hand.

"Gareth."

"Well, Gareth, now that I know yur name, what in the *bloody hell* are yew doing out here? Traipsing about tha streets like it ain't no thing. Do yew not even know what's out and about in these wards?"

At this, he offered a thin grimace. "I've seen them.

One of them at least."

"And yew didn't run back to the Halls lickety-split? A brave man yew must be. Or stupid. Maybe both as they ain'ts exclusive things."

This caused Gareth to snort loudly. He felt himself already beginning to dislike Naze.

"Well, I have little choice in the matter," he announced with a hint of spite. "I was told that if I'm to be gone from this place that I need to get back to the Lord's Chapel—"

"Tha hell you say," she interrupted as she shifted in place. "And who gave yew such bad advice, as it were?"

"A man who chooses to remain within the cathedral." He pointed back over his shoulder. "Goes by the name of Alharrad."

This caused Naze to chuckle lightly to herself. "That poor boy is still at it," she muttered.

At this, Gareth grunted as he moved back to the ladder.

"Whoa, there." She reached out and grabbed him by the sleeve. "Did yew not listen ta me? The Lord's Chapel is not a place yu'll want ta go. I'd rather not see yew feed Sindex any more than is possible. He's powerful enough ta be a danger fer those left in the Chorazin wards. Him and his vermin-kin."

"Well, I need to locate a doctor or a man of science. I was told that to do so, I had to reach either the Grand College of Amara… Amaru-ma-something or other or the asylum. And to do that—"

"Yew need the sigil key from tha Lord's Chapel," she finished the thought. Gareth hoped she wouldn't ask questions. He had no interest in explaining his situation. While Naze struck him as a saner source of information than Alharrad, he still knew nothing about her.

"Yes, yes I do. Unless you know of another way."

"No, no. Alharrad has the right of it. If yur wantin' ta reach tha College from here, tha sigil gate that keeps tha two separate is yur best option." Even though her physical cues were subtle, Gareth noticed the resignation in her posture.

There was a moment's pause. Naze's face contorted. Eventually, she let out a sigh and rose from her seat.

"Well, if yu'r damned an' determined, a'least let me show yew tha way." She brushed the dust from off the seat of her pants.

Uncertain, Gareth held his place. He knew how to get to the chapel from here by way of the convoluted streets. For all he knew, she might be the one to lead him into a trap. *Don't fall for a pretty face,* he reminded himself.

"What'cha waitin' fer?" She eyed him warily. "Yu're not thinkin' of goin' back down are ya? Don't be daft 'bout it. Ain't safe ta walk about on yur own. Follow me along tha rooftops and I'll get yew close as can be." She paused for a moment. "Yew think I'm gonna trick ya, right? I ain't got no time fer such nonsense. This ain't no charitable act. I just want ta keep them—" She motioned to the street below. "—from getting' all riled up. Yu'll only make it worse fer me if'n yew do."

"Okay," Gareth responded with a terse nod as he rose. When she said that any aid that she offered would be solely for her own benefit, it had the ring of the truth.

"At the very least, it's a fair bit safer up here. At least in the wards o' Chorazin, they don't have nae interest in climbin' up after ya."

With this said, she turned on one heel and scurried off at a crouched run. Before she disappeared around a nearby chimney, Gareth took off after her.

Naze had been correct in her earlier assertion: there was nothing that posed an immediate danger along the tightly-packed gables. None of the creatures noticed the pair as they raced across the rooftops. Despite the danger of leaping from one building to the next, Gareth was relieved at the fortuitous turn of events. Since so many structures lodged firmly against one another, they moved for dozens of yards without needing to alter their course.

On several occasions, he was able to spy the things that roamed the alleyways. Between the jagged eaves, he spotted more than one fur-covered mass as it trudged from door to door, as if patrolling some small territory. Much like the first creature he'd seen, these human-like monstrosities traveled in short, predictable patterns. From time to time, a beast would turn its head to the sky and sniff at the breeze, as if it had caught their scents.

Ahead of him, Naze moved with impressive agility. She climbed from one building to the next with a grace and efficiency that hinted she'd been along this route multiple times. More than once, she slowed down for Gareth to clamber clumsily after her.

As they scurried from one rooftop to another, Naze paused to make polite conversation.

"There're many a thing out there yur never gonna want ta run across."

As he struggled to keep up, Gareth only nodded quietly. His breathing had grown labored; even now, it blew out of his open mouth in gusts. When a stray thought popped into his head, he brought it up.

"Would you—do you have any idea about the pounding in the distance? Sounded like something big. Something moving about on the other side of the city."

This caused Naze's stride to drop off as she looked back over her shoulder. "Don't, uh, don't go huntin' fer its source, ya hear me? Ya'yahul tha Pale still wanders tha wards of Pyramaden. Out by tha eastern harbor. Fortunately fer us, he's found himself a place ta sleep. One where tha others leave him be. Tha last time he came too close ta tha central wards, he downed many a city block."

Gareth was about to complain that Naze's reply was cryptic when he decided against it. His head already felt overfull of information about the malformed oddities that populated the city. If he didn't need to know more, it was best that he let the topic drop.

As it was, his sides were beginning to ache. He was by no means out of shape, but chasing Naze across an uneven skyline was beginning to wear on him.

"Hold... hold up," he requested before she could take off again. He held out a hand to beg for a few seconds. As he did, he leaned over and inhaled deeply a few times.

With a dry snort that might have been a laugh, she trotted back to where he stood. She was about to comment when her head cocked to one side. Her eyes widened and she dropped to her knees.

Eventually, Gareth heard the tinny jangle on the avenue below. He spun about in an attempt to pinpoint its origin. Briefly, he wavered as he struggled to balance on the inclined surface. After scanning the winding lane, he eventually spotted a woman in a long cobalt-hued dress. Atop her head was a cloth headdress that was pulled back out of her face. Even from a distance, the frilly lace-and-silk outfit radiated with an aquamarine glow that both lit up her face and obscured her features. In one hand was a lantern that cast a blue-white beam on the cobblestone walkway.

As she casually made her way forward, Gareth began to move from his position.

"Hold," Naze said as she clutched him by the sleeve.

"She'll be killed—"

"Wait and watch."

With a sigh, he slumped down beside her. How could Naze leave this woman to certain death? Naze had offered him aid, even if it was for her own benefit. Why would she not do it for another? The woman was certain to rile up the local creatures.

After a few tense seconds, he watched the woman pass through the pack of monsters unscathed. None of them gave her a second glance and he thought one or two of them actually recoiled from the lamplight. As she disappeared beyond the distant crook in the road, he turned to Naze. She shrugged her shoulders in response.

"There are things far scarier than tha man-beasts that prowl tha streets." She paused for a moment as she looked over the neighborhood. "If you hear her wailin', I'd strongly suggest fleeing fer yur life."

"What—"

"I never stuck around long enough to find out. The inhuman racket of whatever she summoned was enough ta haunt my sleep. I can't imagine it wasn't nothin' pleasant ta behold."

With this said, Naze turned away and took off. Gareth grunted as he followed.

After scampering across rooftops for five minutes straight, Naze finally came to a stop. Gareth, who was hot on her heels, came up beside her and dropped to one knee. To his right, maybe only a few hundred yards away, were the twin spires of the Lord's Chapel. As far as he could tell, he was no more than a turn or two from the empty courtyard that bordered it.

"We're as close as we can get, I figure," she announced as she hunched down and set her pack between her legs. "Jus' down tha ladder over there and yew should have a straight shot. Doesn't sound like any of them are nearby. Should be able ta get there no problem."

"Well," he began. Gareth fleetingly wished she would offer to join him, for companionship during the impending challenge. An oppressive anxiety caused his muscles to tighten. "Thanks for your help. Hopefully, I'll see you again with tales of victory on my lips."

He shifted as he started for the nearby ladder.

"Hold up," she said with a palm raised in his direction. She reached into her rucksack and began to root around. He spotted a pair of bottles, their mouths stuffed with rags. Beside them was an object that looked suspiciously like a grappling hook, though the trio of angular claws was folded tightly against the shaft.

Eventually, she unearthed an oblong item, tightly wrapped in cloth and topped with a fuse.

"There's gonna come a moment where yew should use this. It'll do a fair bit o' damage ta him." She forced the explosive into his hands. "Yew have matches, right? It'll do ya no good without 'em."

Gareth nodded as he held the item away from himself.

"And you never thought to use this yourself? If you knew how best to deal with—"

"I have nae interest in tha petty jockeyin' of men, lookin' to climb up some proverbial ladder of power. Just 'cause I figured out how ta do some harm to tha thing, doesn't mean I wanna."

When Gareth opened his mouth, she brushed her

hand in the air.

"Look, yew seem like someone who would nae be here if yew didn't have ta. Like someone who just wants ta go back home. Not here ta plunder like so many that came before yew. That's the only reason I'm givin' yew an ounce of aid. Don't let it get to yur head."

She reached up to playfully tap him on the forehead. He recoiled just as her fingertip brushed the skin.

"Now get gone while tha streets are clear."

She retreated a few steps and sat down on the slanted roof. One of the tiles shifted under her boot. Gareth nodded appreciatively in her direction before he gingerly pocketed the bomb and made for the ladder.

Gareth hit the street at a light trot. Without the weight of his sword across his back, his steps felt unnaturally light. Sadly, this didn't make him feel in any way better. With that in mind, he knew that Naze's efforts were more than a kindness. She'd shown him a safe shortcut and handed him a tool that might even the odds.

Or at least give me a chance to get my blade back.

As he walked across the courtyard, Gareth paused to examine the ash-coated tiles. Except for a single set of footprints, which he took to be his own from earlier, there was no sign that anyone else had visited recently. Stranger still, there weren't the drag marks that a limp body might make. Without tangible evidence, he was left to wonder how he'd been returned to the sanctuary.

He shook his head and made for the open entrance. His footfalls softened as he stepped inside. Once through, he huddled in the darkened narthex. It didn't take long for him to spot his blade. From where he hid in the shadows, it rested a few yards away on his left. Though he could feel the desire in his limbs, he resisted the urge to scramble out and retrieve it.

While he had a strong recollection of being struck across the back, there was no splatter of blood on the floor. In fact, except for his abandoned weapon, there was no sign that he'd ever been there before.

No longer perched in the rafters, Sindex was now seated on the far side of the nave. From the way it reclined, it reminded Gareth of a domesticated canine. Its back legs were folded up beneath its haunches and its head rested on outstretched forelegs. Fleetingly, he felt a strange sorrow that he would have to fight it. That reminder of a more docile animal tugged at his heart.

Keep it together. Remember why you're here, he reminded himself. *Go for the sword. When it gets near, light and toss the bomb. Worst case scenario, run for the exit and regroup. Don't let it get too close.*

After a few seconds spent bolstering his courage, Gareth scurried across the floor and collected his blade. It clattered loudly as he lifted the hilt and raised it in front of him. As he did, Gareth's gaze went to Sindex, who'd clearly noticed his return. Eyelids fluttered open as its back arched.

The beast extended its front legs and slowly rose

on all four. Stretching its mouth wide, it bellowed with a howl that sprayed vile fluids into the air. The screech was layered, with deep rumbling tones under the more piercing wails. It crept forward one stride at a time until it was halfway across the nave. Only when a small chunk of the roof dropped down and bounced off of its head did the monster pause. It snorted in defiance as it gazed skyward for a second.

Gareth could feel his pulse in his ears. His breathing became shallow. Both hands gripped the hilt tight as he waited for the beast's next move. In his head, he attempted to measure the distance. How long would it take to light the fuse? Would it need extra seconds to burn before detonation?

Just as Sindex began to once again stalk forward, a pair of flaming bottles fell through the opening in the roof. It wasn't until the first struck the beast flat on its back and exploded that he realized what was happening. By the time the second incendiary hit Sindex, its entire backside was alight.

It screeched in pain with such volume that Gareth immediately recoiled. The monster collapsed to the floor and began to roll about to put out the flames. Small patches of the worn parquet caught fire, but the flames were hastily snuffed out as Sindex flailed violently. Pain sent the creature into a frenzy.

"Tha bomb!" Naze bellowed from her perch. The top of her head peeked out from the hole in the ceiling. "Use it now! This'll be yur only chance!"

Gareth paused for an instant, but then reached for

the explosive and a match from the belt pouch on his hip. With a flick, he had a flame sizzling between his fingers as he brought them against the curled fuse. Once the gunpowder-coated paper flamed to life, Gareth dropped his hand to his side.

He watched the beast's thrashings slow as the flames died to reveal large patches of blackened skin and scorched fur. Inhaling deeply, Gareth flung the explosive forward in a low arc. A strand of thin smoke trailed behind the oblong bomb as it skipped off of the floor. Eventually, it came to rest only a few feet from Sindex's front paws. The beast paid no mind as the fuse slowly disappeared.

Incapable of turning away, Gareth waited with his breath caught firmly in his throat. Time seemed to grind to a halt. The last blue-grey plumes floated upwards.

The bomb wouldn't detonate. It was a dud. It wouldn't do—

The flash that came was blinding. Gareth placed an arm over his eyes in a vain attempt to shield himself. He could feel a wave of pressure buffet his ears. The room didn't spin so much as it wavered back and forth. He was disoriented for what felt like far too long. His senses were so muddled Gareth doubted he could defend himself.

With a few vigorous shakes of his head, he finally turned to locate Sindex. As the smoke began to settle, Gareth was able to pick out the slumped form of the beast, sprawled across the floor, in the middle of an expanding pool of its own blood. Both of its front appendages were now ragged stubs. Bones, partially defleshed, protruded from the meat. The underside of its chest was torn open. Multiple ribs jutted from the flesh.

Sindex's face was a ravaged mess. Its lower jaw was gone and most of its face had been reduced to pulp. One fang dangled at a ninety-degree angle from its mouth.

Although its breathing was shallow and erratic, Sindex's chest still heaved.

As Gareth lifted his sword, he began to move forward carefully. Though Sindex remained foremost in his vision, Gareth glanced at the room around him. The explosion had carved a number of small divots out of the parquet floor. Through these, the sanguine fluid began to seep into the basement below. A soft drizzle pattered to the hard surface beneath. Gareth could hear the sounds of movement underneath him.

"Ya gotta strike 'im now," Naze stated through the open doorway behind Gareth. He glanced over his shoulder. She was coiling a length of rope in one hand. Swinging from the other end was the grappling hook. "Do it, 'fore he begins ta recover."

Gareth nodded. He clutched his blade in both hands and marched across the remaining distance. Sindex made no move as he closed in. Gareth sidestepped a few burning patches of wood as he made a beeline for the beast's head, which was now splayed to the side.

As he raised it, Gareth wasn't even certain where to plunge the blade. He tapped the tip along the ragged hide until he found a softer spot. Putting his weight behind the blade, he drove the sword in a downwards arc. It sunk almost two feet before it came to a sudden stop.

Sindex made no noise, no cry of pain. The faint movement of the monstrosity's chest ceased as its last breath expelled a soft mist over the crimson puddle.

As he withdrew the weapon and cleaned the steel on a patch of unmarred pelt, Gareth was overcome with a strange sensation. Perhaps he was suffering from a mild concussion. Gareth compared it to the warm fuzziness of drunkenness, but that didn't seem quite right. There wasn't a soggy giddiness that came with the feeling; instead, it was as if a burden was lifted from him and he was now weightless.

With every passing moment, the sensation transformed. Before too long, he felt supercharged, much like he had been given a potent stimulant. His skin felt overtight, as if his muscles and bones were expanding by the second.

"What... what was that?" he mumbled as he rubbed at his brow.

"I'd say that ya got the rest of yew back. Maybe even a touch o' Sindex as a reward. Or at least a taste of everything he's ever consumed. A buffet o' lesser things." She was now only a few steps behind him. He was briefly shocked by how quickly she'd crossed the distance.

Gareth looked at her with a mixture of irritation and confusion. "What does that even mean?"

"It can wait," she announced dismissively.

"But—"

She pointed a finger downwards. With the sounds of movement beneath, Gareth knew that the previous events had rousted something—many somethings, at that.

"Get tha sigil key and let's be gone from here, 'fore we have ta deal with tha vermin wantin' a taste of their master."

At this, Gareth marched to the altar. As he reached it, he cast a look over his shoulder. Naze remained where he left her, a few steps from the abomination's fresh corpse. Her nose curled as she reluctantly turned away from it, as if resisting some enticing lure.

Gareth glanced over the display of curios, coins, and candles. In that moment, he wasn't even certain what he intended to find. In his mind, he expected a comically-large key that stood out like a sore thumb, covered in gold and garish gemstones, intended to unlock a massive gate that kept people from leaving the damned ward. When nothing that matched such a notion turned up on first glance, he frowned.

Nothing in this damn city works the way it should.

"The circular thing there," Naze announced as she slipped up beside him. With a thin finger, she pointed to an object nestled between two wooden jewelry boxes. Gareth reached in, as he carefully navigated the forest of still-burning wicks, and plucked the item from its place.

The sigil key was a construct of brass and bronze circles, layered into an interlocking pattern that held no immediate significance to Gareth. He held it close to his face and attempted to figure out how such an item would be employed. Just as he spotted something like a series of tiny gears in the tightly-pressed layers of metal hoops, Naze spoke up.

"Let's go," she said as she headed for the exit. There was a hint of worry in her tone.

"Where? W-w-wait a moment."

"Do ya even know where ta go? Or did yew get sent here without any notion as to where yur next step was?"

"Well, I was told—"

"That yew needed the sigil key. Lord's alive, ya have no idea of what ta do or where ta go." She rolled her eyes.

Gareth frowned at the dismissive way Naze spoke to him.

"I was plannin' ta take yew ta the sigil gate that separates tha wards of Chorazin and Bethsaida. Yu'll be able to reach tha Grand College from there. Well, if'n yew can keep clear of trouble." She beckoned with a wave. "But, first thing's first: we need ta be outta here as soon as we can."

Gareth said nothing else as he pocketed the key and trotted after Naze. He stopped for a moment as he reached the exit. From the open archway, he stood with a hand against the wood as he waited. His gaze was not on the slumped carcass of Sindex. Instead, he glanced at the shadows that bordered the hall. As the seconds passed, the unnerving chittering of dozens of smaller creatures escalated. Before too long, a swarm of misshapen rodents scurried across the floor to the slumped body. With their clawed hands and curled fangs they began to dig into the cadaver. It wasn't long before a vile orgy of consumption was under way.

As they enjoyed the flesh of the fallen monster, changes in their forms became noticeable. Whereas many had scurried to the meal on all fours, some began to stand upright. Limbs began to grow thicker. The rodent-like features flattened as they took on a more human aspect. Gareth was stunned by the sight.

"Let's go before they want a bit o' dessert," Naze said as she tugged at Gareth's sleeve. Still horrified by the ongoing feast, Gareth followed as she dashed across the courtyard.

He could swear that he still heard the munching of tiny fangs on Sindex's singed hide as he began to climb the ladder.

Chapter Six

The Sigil Gate

For a short while, Gareth paid no attention to their path. Still exhilarated, he was perfectly fine to let Naze lead him wherever she may. Without a thorough understanding of the city's labyrinthine arrangement, he deferred to her judgment. Her already-invaluable aid went a long way to lessen his earlier apprehension. While he wouldn't pretend that he knew her on any level, Naze had been more practically helpful than anyone else he'd met on his entire journey.

Truth be told, the surge of energies from slaying Sindex still swirled about in his head. There was a buzz inside him that electrified his nerve-endings. Though he was no longer lightheaded, he did feel stronger, faster and more agile. His senses were sharper. From atop the maze of interconnected gables, he was certain he could see farther than before. He no longer struggled to keep up with Naze. When she paused to reorient herself, he only needed to take a few deep breaths. His heartbeat thudded with a deep resonance inside his chest.

Based on the position of the sun, it seemed that they were returning to the sanctuary. Before too long he grew increasingly concerned that they weren't headed directly to the gate. Logic dictated that they should be heading away from familiar territory.

"Hey! Uh, not to question your sense of direction, but where are we headed?" he called out as he cupped a hand at the side of his mouth. "Is this the way to the gate?"

"Don't ya fret," she replied, skipping across a gap between two townhouses. "We're makin' a single stop at mah nest—"

Gareth gave her a strange look at the word "nest."

"—ta replenish mah stores. I'd ask ya ta spot me tha stuff ta replace what I used, but I don't see anything like glass bottles and flammable liquid on yew. This is the quickest way about it, unless yew'd like ta help me go on a scavengin' raid."

When he said nothing in reply, the topic was dropped. His concern about their course waned as he continued to follow her.

At the top of what Gareth could only assume was once a legislative building—its domed rotunda reminded him of the parliamentary halls of Boddenburn—stood a belfry. Hidden in the shadows cast by the city's upper layers, the tower was invisible until they were almost upon it. Once within the smothering shade, Gareth's pupils contracted. As his eyes adjusted, he spotted the hip roof that peered out over the expansive skyline. On three sides, the exterior openings were boarded up with wooden planks.

As he slipped inside, Gareth noticed that the iron bell was missing. With that gone, the bell chamber had been converted into functional living quarters. Where an open atrium had once gazed down into the heart of the tower was now a makeshift floor, cobbled together with mismatched slabs of linoleum and oak panels. Some of these looked as if they might have once been interior doors. Stacks of crates and a single bookshelf held down a trio of worn and discolored rugs. A lone cot, covered by a pair of ragged blankets, was tucked into the back corner.

The longer Gareth examined the room, the more it became clear that there were no personal effects displayed. Though Naze had either converted or uncovered the room and made it into somewhere she could rest, there was nothing here that revealed anything about the occupant. There were no picture frames filled with happy families or sentimental knickknacks. He began to wonder if she had somewhere else to claim as home, if she'd migrated from a location elsewhere that might be in harm's way.

Naze began to rummage through her belongings. She muttered to herself as she shuffled some objects around in one of the boxes.

As Gareth waited in place, only a few feet from the entrance, a topic came to mind. "So, uh, I have a question. One that I hope you may be able to answer. Uh, what… what are *they* called?"

"Eh?" she intoned without looking back. Her hands moved quickly from one crate to the next. The occasional elated murmuring hinted that she'd uncovered something of value.

"Those… uh, those *things*. The creatures that roam the streets. I assume you have some kind of name for them. Or something." Gareth noticed that when people shared monster legends, the beasts were always named. It made it easier for the storyteller to communicate horrific threats to the listener. Once a teller described its appearance and gave it a name, each time they spoke of the creatures, the listener recalled this information to be scared or horrified.

Naze seemed to pause, as if uncomfortable with the question. One hand hovered midair. Her shoulders slumped, ever so slightly, as she eventually replied. "I've heard them referred ta as foulkin. In tha old Mericoinne, I think they were called Dalhakhu."

That short reply caused more questions to rise in Gareth's mind.

"Mericoinne?"

"Mericoinne were tha original settlers of Dineothan. Natives. Lived here well before anyone else showed up. Before Upelstbohr was a twinklin' in some rich white man's eye."

Before Gareth could press further, Naze pulled a

pair of bottles out of one crate and a silver decanter out of another. Gently, she placed them on the floor. She dropped down to her knees and produced a strip of cloth that she immediately ripped in two.

Sensing that Naze wouldn't divulge more, Gareth shifted gears. For some reason, he felt a compelling need to make conversation.

"Well, at the least, we can say that we made the neighborhood a little safer," Gareth commented as a flame of pride warmed his chest. Now that he had put some distance between the present and his earlier fight, he felt overwhelming relief that they'd been successful.

This did not last.

"Don't be foolish. Sindex was at tha bottom of tha food chain. That you felled him by yur own blade should tell yew what yew need ta know." Naze's comments snuffed out his enthusiasm. "The only thing yew did was remove his immediate presence. Without much more than a sliver of soul left, he won't be returnin'. His maker did'nae think about such a thing when birthin' 'im. But, yew left him there ta feed tha others of his kind. The vermin-kin that used to serve 'im. Now, there's a legion of his former servants roamin' tha streets about tha Lord's Chapel, more powerful and more dangerous. Yew took one problem and turned it into dozens."

Gareth snorted as his face scrunched tightly. While a part of him knew he was ignorant of how the transference of power, or anything, worked in Dineothan, he was still infuriated by Naze's comments. Could she not allow him a moment to enjoy the victory?

He almost retreated from the opening to find the sigil gate on his own.

Naze looked up at him as she finished preparing the makeshift explosives.

"Yu'r not one fer planning, are you?"

He scowled at her comment.

"I've watched ya charge from one place ta another with all the subtleness of a tornado. Ya let Alharrad tell you what ta do, where ta go. Do yew not have an idea of what ya should do of yur own?"

At this, Gareth became defensive. "Well, he wasn't exactly wrong, now was he?" When he patted his pocket, he could feel the outer curve of the key. In truth, doing something was better than the alternative. If Gareth lingered too long in contemplation, he might have to consider things that dredged up anxiety and grief.

"Yew really can't put too much faith in Alharrad." She slid the bottles into her rucksack, pulled the drawstring tight and stood up.

"How do you mean? You talk like someone who has history with the man."

"Yew could say that, but no, I won't explain myself so don't keep pesterin' me 'bout it. Let's just say that I know enough about him ta know tha foolishness of tha lad."

Gareth raised an eyebrow in her direction. His anger was quickly replaced with curiosity. Before he could open his mouth, she continued.

"Craziness runs in tha blood, Gareth. I'll say nae more than that." She slung her pack over one shoulder.

"We should be on our way."

They traveled for another hour across the interconnected rooftops before Naze came to a stop. The impression that the sun was locked in place confused him. In the slivers of space between the dense architecture that was piled above them, he had difficulty finding the burning orb. Still, the quality and color of light remained constant, which led him to believe it was still somehow midafternoon.

Naze got his attention with a wave of her hand. She came to rest beside a trio of chimneys and motioned for him to join her.

"Yes?" He knelt down beside her as she pointed to the north.

"There. Yu'll need ta get down on street level ta cover tha rest of tha distance." She then gestured to the surrounding structures. Fitted with steel beams that supported their upper levels, many of the adjacent buildings towered over the three-story block of houses. There was no easy way to reach their rooftops.

Gareth looked down to gauge the danger on the winding pathways below. As far as he could tell, there were no signs of foulkin nearby. Perhaps the enticing meal in the Lord's Chapel had drawn some of them away.

As if reading his mind, Naze spoke up. "If you're wonderin', they don't usually come out this way. The College grounds aren't exactly welcomin' to their kind.

Any kind, really."

Gareth sighed. He was tired of the vague statements. Ambiguity permeated every conversation he'd shared since his arrival. Was it too much to ask that someone tell it to him straight?

"Yew can see tha top of it *right* there," she noted as she held out her hand. "Tha gate, that is." Beyond the sharp curve in the road to the north, he spotted what looked like the outer edge of a guard tower. It was a good hundred yards from their position.

"And the College?" A part of him fully expected not to receive an answer.

"Yu'll not be able ta miss it. It's at tha center of the district. Yu'll end up there whether yew want to or not. Just keep headin' forward. As they say, 'All roads in Bethsaida lead to Amaru-ma-mudu.' "

After a silent nod, he went for the ladder at the nearby roof's edge.

As he began to climb down, Gareth noticed that Naze stayed at her perch. When his brow furrowed, he opened his mouth to inquire. Before the first word was out, she interrupted him.

"I'll not be going with yew. This is as far as I go."

Though this came as a disappointment, Gareth quickly came to accept it. He'd just met her and the journey was his alone. That she'd helped him so far was more than he could expect. It was beyond what anyone else had done for him.

"Well, thank you for your aid," he said as he

continued his descent.

"May yew find what yur lookin' fer," she replied with a flick of one hand. "And stay off tha streets as much as yew can."

By the time he set foot on the paver-lined walkway, she was out of sight. He withdrew his sword and trotted off.

Gareth wasn't certain what to expect from something called a sigil gate. The city's architecture was such a pastiche of styles, he couldn't predict what he would find. With the device in his pocket, he assumed that it was some barrier with clockwork mechanisms to keep it in place.

What he came across, though, was immediately striking in its imposing stature. Standing at a height of thirty feet was a massive bronze-plated gateway, barred by two doors. Through the bars that lined the barrier in a trio of rows, he could spy the adjacent ward, which appeared to be currently uninhabited. Lacking even the faintest noise he'd expect even in the smallest township, Gareth assumed that Bethsaida was also abandoned.

In the center, a chest-high panel overlapped the crease between the matching gates. A lone depression, lined with strange symbols, in the circular display appeared to match the sigil key.

On either side of the gate stood a trio of stone columns. Carved into these were a series of bas reliefs. The images were of proud knights with their weapons held aloft. At the top of the innermost pillars were a pair of scholars; in their hands were an open tome and a lamp. On the side of the burning lantern was a single lidless eye that stared down at the adjoining square. He was reminded of the carvings in the cathedral.

Probably built around the same time, he reasoned. *If not, one probably influenced the other.*

Littered about the adjacent courtyard were stacks of discarded luggage, many of which were standing in the middle of the passageway. Resting against one particular pile was a timeworn stuffed bear that looked as though it had been dropped carelessly. This odd collection of debris initially struck Gareth as strange, but, as he considered it, an account of possible past events began to form. He'd seen something similar during the siege of Karthune, when citizens from the neighboring lands attempted to flee to the safety of the walled city. When the Auewellian army, by which he'd been hired as a mercenary, arrived at Karthune, he witnessed waves of non-combatants flee for their lives. The abandoned personal effects suggested a similar exodus into the northern ward; it also suggested that the refugees had been coldly turned away.

Gareth lingered in front of the barrier, gazing at the luggage in the courtyard for what felt like minutes. He eventually dug into his coat pocket and removed the key. He rolled the mechanism around in his palm as he observed it in the light. Colorful glints reflected off of the polished exterior. There was an iridescent sheen on the device's surface.

Gareth stepped forward and placed the object into the circular depression. It fit snugly into the recess, and before he'd fully withdrawn his fingers, tiny gears began to spin. In response, larger mechanisms inside the doors came to life. A dense banging of metal on metal echoed from within. Stunned, Gareth stepped back into a defensive posture. He scanned his environs. As his head cocked to one side, he listened to the surrounding ward. Fear that the gate's opening would attract unwanted attention caused his heart rate to accelerate.

He clutched his weapon tightly as he shifted his stance. Nothing came out of the darkened corners. No white-furred monstrosity lurched from the adjacent lane.

When he heard only the whistle of the wind as it cut through the narrow, jagged alleys, his shoulders slumped. He dropped the tip of his blade for a moment.

From somewhere off in the distance, the deep thudding of something heavy pounding the ground began to resonate. Though he couldn't be certain, Gareth thought he felt the paved courtyard shudder beneath him. Instinctually, he brought his weapon back up.

He was reminded of his earlier discussion with Naze. *"Ya'yahul tha Pale still wanders tha wards of Pyramaden. Out by tha eastern harbor. Fortunately fer us, he's found himself a place ta sleep. One where tha others leave him be."*

If this Ya'yahul was as dangerous as Naze intimated, Gareth did not want to be around if the gate's activation drew its attention.

Once the doors had opened enough for him to pass, he scurried forward. It would take another five minutes, as the gears banged slowly one spoke at a time, for the entranceway to completely open. Gareth was well into the wards of Bethsaida when the massive metal slabs came to a halt.

CHAPTER SEVEN

The Grand College of Amaru-ma-mudu

Following Naze's advice, Gareth climbed back to the rooftops once he cleared the courtyard on the other side of the sigil gate. As he reached the sloping clay shingles that spanned for hundreds of yards to the north, Gareth paused to take in the panorama.

Unlike the wards of Chorazin, whose buildings were inspired by the ecclesiastical religious designs, Bethsaida appeared utilitarian. Instead of a confusing maze of overlapping lanes, the streets formed a wheel-and-spoke pattern with the university campus at its heart. Rows of multi-story lodgings were flanked by more opulent subdivisions that Gareth presumed were reserved for the administrative staff and tenured professors.

Though they were barely visible in the distance, Gareth could pick out the outer walls of the Grand

College. Gray monoliths were packed in tightly behind the barrier and seemed to loom menacingly over the adjacent neighborhoods.

Gareth picked up his pace. For once, he felt relieved. He had been dependent on others for information, some of whom he deemed unreliable, and he was pleased now to have a tangible point on the horizon to walk towards. Sure, it would take some time to cover the distance, but he was fine with that. Knowing exactly where he was headed suited him just fine.

On top of that, it seemed that with every step, he felt drawn to the university grounds. As he kept moving, the effect was almost imperceptible. Only in the moments when he stopped to gain his bearings did he feel it, like a magnetic pull that urged him northwards.

He noticed no movement in the nearby streets—no shuffling scramble of foulkin as they ambled along the stone-paved lanes, no cacophony of inhuman things as they wandered to and fro. When he looked over the edge of the nearby gables, he found the alleyway empty. Except for a few strange shadows, which initially looked human, Bethsaida appeared devoid of life.

Gareth did notice something off in the distance. It sounded like the rustling of leathery wings. After a quick scan of the skyline, Gareth found nothing, not even the usual dotting of birds in flight. Gareth dismissed it as an auditory illusion, something else that unnerved him about the city.

Once he felt acclimated, Gareth continued his march forward. He covered half the distance to the College before he ran out of rooftops. Here the apartment blocks were disconnected from one another. Gareth began to look for a way down. When he realized that he'd have to backtrack, he sought an alternative, even if it meant making a more hazardous descent. He eventually dropped down to a fourth-story terrace littered with terracotta pots full of long-dead flora.

As he lingered on the townhouse's balcony, Gareth realized that he was left with no safe option. Without Naze to lead the way, he had strode foolishly into the dead end. The street below was a forty-five-foot drop. He glanced back up and hastily discarded that idea. Even if he attempted the challenging climb, a return to the rooftops was pointless.

Rather than double back for an alternate path that might not exist, Gareth turned and faced the frosted glass doors separating the fourth-floor terrace from the rest of the residence. Ornately-patterned panes that were muddied made it difficult for him to peer within. A loud rap on the frame did not bring anyone to the entrance.

He turned the handle and was surprised to find it unlocked. Beyond was a master bedroom that, despite the lavish decoration and furnishings, felt cold and empty. As he moved through the abode and eventually found a stairwell that led down to the first floor, it grew clear that the home was abandoned. There were drawers left half open and piles of clothes scattered on the floor, indicating that the occupants left in a rush.

When he reached the first floor, he discovered the front door was ajar. A thin layer of dust, which had blown in over weeks, if not months, had accumulated on the wooden floor of the foyer. The woven strands of a door-side round rug were frosted with soil. There were no footprints marring the gray coating.

Just as he was about to reach for the door, something appeared at the edge of his vision. Standing by itself in the adjacent sitting room was a longcase clock. While such a device, even one as elaborately decorated as this mahogany and brass one was, would not have usually drawn his notice, there was something about it that made Gareth pause.

He hadn't seen another timepiece since his arrival to the city. He'd been in Upelstbohr for what felt like a few days now. Getting the hour might help him better track the passage of time.

He took a few excited paces towards the heirloom as his gaze focused on the ivory-and-gold face. When he noticed the stillness of the pendulum within, his relief quickly dissipated and disappointment set in. Locked in place, the delicate hands pointed at 3:58. Gareth could only learn the instant of the contraption's failure.

He threw a dismissive hand in the air, turned on one heel and strode out of the room. His boots dug short scuffs into the layer of dust as he barged from the home.

Once on street level, Gareth took in his new surroundings. It only took a quick glance to locate the roofline of the university's prominent halls. In contrast to the opulent archways which decorated many of the structures in Chorazin, the Grand College was formed from bleak, featureless slabs of marble. Thin, unlit windows ran in tight parallel rows along the upper levels. Unlike the sharply-angled gables of the southern wards, the huddled collection of buildings here was topped with flat, asphalt-coated surfaces. There was a clean, geometrical pattern in the campus' architectural motifs.

His destination grew closer with every stride, Gareth continued his northward trek. He was only a few paces forward when he sensed movement in his peripheral vision. What threats had he not anticipated? Naze made it clear that he needed to stay off the streets, if possible. What had she not told him?

When something came out of the shadows, Gareth stumbled backwards. Instinctually, he withdrew his blade and turned his focus on the unexpected presence. Because sullen silence permeated the ward, he'd become lax in his vigilance.

As he focused on it, the darkened silhouette on the adjacent townhouse appeared to stretch outwards towards him. It slithered like an amorphous tendril across the brick pavers. When it moved into the thin patches of stark daylight, Gareth began to pick out the details of its form.

Standing just a few inches shorter than Gareth, the apparition held the shape of a man dressed in a finely-tailored suit. While it had no face, it did not appear to react with menace. Gareth twisted in retreat to his left.

Just as it strode halfway across the path, the shade

disappeared, as if it was never there. Thrown for a loop, Gareth waited in place. His eyes danced back and forth in a vain effort to locate its presence. Seconds later, a similar silhouette appeared out of the shadows and traced the original's steps. It too vanished before it reached the other side of the lane. When a third followed, Gareth wasn't entirely shocked when it suffered the same fate.

He assumed that the manifestation acted without any awareness of his presence. It was locked into some form of repeating pattern, unaffected by the world around it. For the briefest of moments, he considered reaching out in an attempt to touch it. Gareth wanted to determine if the entity was as immaterial as it appeared to be.

Gareth drove this impulse away. If the man-shaped shadow did not register his presence, it was in his best interest not to engage it. After returning his blade to its scabbard, he slipped away, tossing the occasional glance over his shoulder as he went. When he felt as though he was safely away, he turned to the towering buildings of the College in the distance.

As he left the side street behind, Gareth came across more of the phantoms. Much like the first, they moved in short paths and immediately faded, only to return to their point of origin. All of them were faint outlines that hinted at human forms. Some were smaller or thinner in stature. A few seemed to be dressed in finer clothing.

Before long, he grew used to the infinitely-looping shades. He let down his guard. Even so, Gareth made certain to give them a wide berth. When he came across a particularly-dense grouping, he detoured around them by way of another alley.

He arrived at the lane by the College's campus, where he was met with a dense wall of steel and stone. A few yards to his left, he found a bronze sign next to a massive gateway of wrought iron. Stated on it in tall, thin letters was "THE GRAND COLLEGE OF AMARU-MA-MUDU, est. 1354." Etched beneath that in a smaller script was the phrase *"See and Know."*

Though he danced around a few shades street-side, Gareth headed for the open entrance. Once he was though and on the main grounds, he paused to assess the property.

Even with the cold, clinical appearance of the overbearing edifices that rose above him, the college's front acreage was as expected. Long swaths of foliage, wild and unkempt from years of neglect, swayed in the faint breeze. Two rows of trees lined the main aisle which linked the entry to the prominent hall on the other end. Sections of stone pavers were disturbed by overgrown roots which had forced their way up through the soil. In the distance, a sign that stated "ADMINISTRATION" could be plainly seen above the distant building's main entrance.

There were more shades drifting about the property, in a seemingly never-ending patrol. Many huddled in groups, as if locked in some eternal conversation. As Gareth sidestepped a particular gathering, there was an unexpected movement from two. Though he tried to dismiss it as a trick of the light, it seemed they turned to watch as he passed them by.

When Gareth approached the front of the administration building, he noticed a series of ashen-colored mounds, each with ragged black cloth that fluttered in the breeze. He assumed they were piles of discarded debris, left in place during whatever catastrophe had caused the ward's evacuation.

Once he drew in close, though, he noticed that they appeared to be human bodies on their hands and knees in some form of supplication. With the toe of his boot, he tapped at the uncovered leg of one. Unlike the shades, these were solid. Even as kick thudded dully, the inanimate human form did not react.

Gareth leaned in to take a closer look.

Draped in layers of weathered fabric, the bent figure appeared mummified. The skin, dry and ashen-colored, stretched tightly over the skeletal frame. Skeptical even in the face of the reality of the desiccated remains, Gareth dismissed the forms as strange sculptures, perhaps arranged in some eccentric display that he failed to understand.

After a shake of his head, he pressed on. Though the hinges on the double doors proved temporarily unyielding, they eventually gave way. The tarnished brass knob creaked in Gareth's grip.

Once through, he bounded into an atrium that rose multiple stories above him. Except for shafts of light that shone across the upper floors from the front windows, much of the chamber was choked by darkness.

Gareth paused long enough to let his eyes adjust.

There appeared to be no sign of the manifestations that haunted the surrounding property. Though he'd yet to have reason to fear them, Gareth didn't want to push his luck.

He crept forward as he looked for signs of life. He'd come to the College to find a man of science who could potentially speak to him about a cure for the plague. Despite his idiosyncratic manner, Alharrad indicated that he'd run across someone who would meet his needs. As he mulled over the memory of their conversation, Gareth struggled with his doubts. So far, he'd not seen a living soul since he parted with Naze. Now, as he stood on the ground floor, there seemed no evidence that any of the staff remained.

In that moment, doubt clouded his resolve. Everything about Dineothan seemed arranged to task him. He began to wonder why he didn't flee this madhouse, locate a boat at the nearest harbor and leave.

Because there's nowhere else to go.

The doctors he'd interviewed before had made it clear that there was no known cure for this strain of the plague. Anyone afflicted would slowly drown as their lungs filled with fluid. His journey to Dineothan was the last resort of a desperate man. If he abandoned his quest now, his efforts would all be for nothing.

I would have left them to die without me for no good reason. I left...

This admission caused his stomach to roil.

When anxiety began to intensify, Gareth bit at his lower lip. The sharp pain brought him back to the present.

At the center of the massive entrance hall was a marble fountain. Long ago dried out, it only contained dust and a smattering of coins. Gareth didn't recognize any of the profiles of old men imprinted on the currency. In the middle of the fountain stood a single stone column, on which was etched the now-familiar lamp-holding scholar.

Gareth felt an undeniable urge to reach across and run his fingers along the carved surface. Before he could raise a hand, he shook his head and walked away. When he was a few paces away, the compulsion disappeared.

Without a definite direction, he slowly trudged up the nearby stairs. His boots pounded loudly in the empty chamber as he reached the top.

Once on the second floor, he began to wander, only stopping to check the occasional door. A few were locked, but those that were open failed to reveal anything of value. Most led to unlit offices and an occasional storage closet.

Eventually, Gareth stumbled across a sizable auditorium, where a stage was surrounded by rows of staggered wooden benches. At the center was a podium, behind which stood a rolling chalkboard, covered with nearly-illegible writing. Flanking these were a pair of tables, topped with an assortment of books and equipment.

As Gareth slowly crossed the chamber, he wondered what was once taught here. A few blurred symbols in white chalk could have indicated anything, from advanced mathematics to a foreign language. Either way, the lines of partially-smudged formulations were incomprehensible to him.

Once he climbed the riser to the central platform, he paused. There was something about the scene that piqued his interest. He couldn't quite place what, like the feeling of a presence that lingered. He scanned the room for signs of the humanoid shadows but saw none.

Gareth was drawn to the worktables. A trail of footsteps on the dusty floor had stopped beside the area. A spot was cleared, as if a book had been removed. A stack of handwritten notes were scattered across a leather-bound tome titled *"An Examination of Biological Energy Transference in Carnivores."*

Gareth ran his hand over the haphazard collection until he eventually settled on the heap of memos. They were entries torn from a bound journal. As he scanned them, Gareth lingered on a few of the passages.

-M. 17, 33

These extracted enzymes have such peculiar properties. I made the mistake of getting a few drops on my hand and I felt muddled for countless hours. Attempted to scrub it off before the effect became worse, but I only managed to do a number on my skin. After a long night's rest, I was able to shake the worst of it. The last time I felt anything like that was during my second year when Keith and I imbibed wormwood spirits. Though, if I'm willing to admit it, these hallucinations were a bit (some words were scratched out) *more real feeling than I would have liked. The voices in my head were particularly unexpected. Will be diligent in wearing gloves going forward. That's not something I wish to repeat.*

-M. 26, 33

Garem Cullis asked me to review his proposal today. Don't know whether to consider it a compliment or not. He seems a bit nervous about it and wanted to get another set of eyes on the paper before submitting it to the review board. I read through it twice and gave him some notes on the more "procedural" aspects. The content, well, I don't think he was looking for someone (of my stature in the college, at least) to offer any opinions. To be honest, I wouldn't even know where to begin. The crux of his research was to be on some phase of temporal logistics. He wants to prove that time travel is possible, but not for a single entity. That one person or object cannot travel backwards and forwards in time alone. That we're all linked together—the world all over—and for time to move in one direction or another, it requires the lot of us to make the proverbial trip together.

I have to admit that I'm curious as to how Garem would even attempt to test such a theory. Strikes me as a proposal doomed for failure, even if only because of the grandness of his scope. I won't be surprised if he's told to scale it down, to prove some minor cornerstone element first. Nail down the ground-level science a step at a time. Prove his work with irrefutable mathematics first. The testing phase of his proposal strikes me as untenable. At least not possible without introducing some questionable morality into affecting those not a part of the experiment. That alone may get his application denied. If only he could conceive a way to produce a more limited trial, something that could be duplicated. Perhaps his theory is just too ambitious.

-Jl. 14, 33

That bastard Paimon!

He declined my proposal, YET again. Said my theories were the rankest of tripe. His EXACT words. The gall he has to say such a thing in front of my peers. Tried his best to dissuade me from this course of research, but I'll be damned if the old man is going to drive me away. I was about the barge into his office and give him a piece of my mind when Ellis pulled me aside. Bless Ellis for being a friend and bringing me to my senses. I don't know what would happen to my work if I'd been dismissed because I let my temper get the best of me.

-Jl. 15, 33

Ellis did some snooping over the past day. His report of recent events put to light the crux of mine and many others' situations. It appears that once again Lyceed and his ilk have blocked us from access to the Begeondan samples. They refuse to return to the College to answer why. Ellis feels that if Lyceed continues to be obstinate, Paimon and the senior board will be forced to take action. Perhaps even resort to censure, though I fail to see how that will result in the return of the more important materials in their possession.

Such knowledge doesn't improve my mood about Paimon, but it does give me hope that I can revisit my submission in the future.

Gareth flipped through more sheets. Near the bottom were a few pages from another journal. The paper was a different hue and the handwriting sloppier, as if done with a hurried hand.

-O. 12, 33

Things are worse than first thought. There are claims that the last of the Begeondan have already departed. If true, it won't be long before we're at each other's throats. My own research will be dead in the water before it was even started. Perhaps I should start dropping some inquiries, maybe get myself attached to someone else's project.

-O. 22, 33

While most of my inquiries have been fruitless, I did make some inroads today. I spoke with Garem Cullis about his time with the Begeondan that once resided in the chambers in lower Capernaum. Despite his blathering about the voices in his head and daily hallucinations, he assured me that he learned more in a week there than in the past eight years at the College. It was as if information seeped into his head. When I laughed at him on this, his tone grew grave and he pulled me to the side. It was as if I'd offended his family name.

"Laugh all you want," he told me. "But, there was always a constant buzzing in the back of my head,

telling me things I didn't quite yet know. At first, I merely brushed it off. Thought that I was really learning, taking to the new information like a sponge with water, but before long I recognized it wasn't my own thoughts but another's."

I would have scoffed at him had Garem not been so menacingly close. I feared he might strike me if further offended.

"That's not the worst of it, though. In the moments when I'm tired or not paying attention, it's as if the world about me is an illusion. I see it in flashes. The walls turn into blueish metallic panes, each rotating on some alien clockwork ceaselessly clicking and clacking in the background. And then I would look up and it all returns to normal."

Though I was too scared to say it to his face, I fear that Garem's studies may have worn on his mind. And still, he may be my best option to continue with the college.

-N. 15, 33

The delegation dispatched by the senior staff to Lyceed's Asylum has yet to return. There is fear that something untoward has happened to them. Would Lyceed and his staff resort to violence? I don't know the man well enough to say.

Best I focus on what I can accomplish. The mood is so tense around here that I doubt anyone is capable of focusing on their work. Despite some reservations, I'm packing up for an extended stay with Garem in Capernaum. Whether it does my nerves any good or not, I need to leave the College for a while.

Once at the bottom of the stack, Gareth returned the documents to their place. He shook his head as he mulled over their contents. He was no closer to his goal; the writings failed to give him coherent information.

He stood in silence as he listened to the shifting of the empty building around him. Though he could hear the random creaking of wood panels, he failed to pick out the footfalls of living humans. The longer he lingered, hoping for some sign of where he needed to go next, the more concerned he grew. Had he spent so much time and effort only to find the College abandoned?

Would he need to head to Capernaum to locate the author and his co-workers? Would they even be able to help him? The journal sounded like the words of a research scientist rather than a doctor. Still, they might know more than he did. He couldn't stop now; he was too far along. If so, he would have to uncover the ward's location in relation to the campus grounds.

As he struggled against the despondency that threatened, Gareth finally heard something. It was a soft, dull thud, as if something was dropped on a carpeted floor. He cocked his head to locate its direction. Gareth determined that it came from somewhere to his right, through his point of entry.

He spun sharply, charged back into the hallway and took a sharp left. He struggled to locate doorways and turns in the poorly-lit corridor. Fear that he could become lost inside the building began to take root.

Then, he noticed the muffled muttering of a man's voice.

"Hello?" Gareth hailed without thinking. Only when he heard his own voice bounce off the walls did he regret his impulsive action. He grimaced as his shoulders tightened.

As he skulked forward one step at a time, he turned the next corner. He saw a faint yellow radiance beneath the closed door on his left. He reached out cautiously and gripped the knob. With a twist, he opened it. A flood of warm light caused him to recoil until his pupils could process the sudden brightness.

Upon entering, Gareth was assaulted by the thick aroma of incense. Without thinking, he shrunk away from the dense scent between the chamber and the adjacent hall. He recalled a similar smell, that of frankincense and raw iron, from his time at the sanctuary in Chorazin. He took a deep breath and pushed on.

Once he drove past the overpowering aura, he found himself in an expansive library, with three floors connected by staircases throughout. While the upper levels were drenched in shadow, what he could see was packed with row upon row of bookcases. Choking many of the aisles were stacks of aged tomes that were unshelved. Spread across the tabletops and shelves nearest to the entrance were clusters of still-burning candles and incense. Except for a pair of lanterns, these braziers served as the room's only illumination.

Gareth's gaze turned to the right, where he found

a cluster of oak-made furnishings laden with reading materials, and a desk tucked into a corner where some of the larger bookcases met. Scrolls were left atop the few flat surfaces not littered with the college's collection. On the carpeted floor beneath him, a single leather-bound hardback, at least three inches in thickness, was facedown as if it had fallen.

On the corner of one table was a brass bowl filled with fruit. Between the fine layer of dust which coated the bowl and the way the candlelight reflected off it, Gareth quickly realized they were waxen replicas. It occurred to Gareth that he wasn't hungry, though he'd been in Upelstbohr for a few days now and had yet to feel the need to eat. He filed the thought away for later consideration.

At the nearby bureau was an older man, who only now turned away from his studies to welcome the new arrival. A tired smile crept onto his face as he locked eyes with Gareth.

"Ah, a visitor," he creaked with a voice that sounded weak. As the words left his mouth, he smacked his lips.

The man rose from his seat to a height that towered a good half-foot over Gareth. The ashy darkness of his skin stood out in stark contrast to the burgundy, purple and white of the long, flowing robes that draped across his thin frame. Silver eyes glinted brightly in the flickering flames. Thin, brittle hair hung from his scalp like withered vines.

"I heard the sigil gate open earlier and was curious as to the reason why. That it would deliver unto me a new guest is truly a blessing from the gods. I assumed that no one remaining in Chorazin had the courage left to travel, which leads me to believe that you may be one of Upelstbohr's newest citizens." With a sweep of one arm, he gathered up the excess fabric that hung like an oversized comforter on his body.

Gareth only nodded as he lingered by the doorway.

"Please, please, take a load off of your weary feet. It's been some time since I've had a visitor." He motioned to a nearby chair. "Or one in a physical state that I would want to call upon me. As you can tell, the college grounds are not so welcoming. You've seen them, have you not? The things that used to be men, trapped in the never-ending loop of their former lives?"

As Gareth slowly moved toward the offered seat, he spoke up. "And they don't trouble you?"

"The Umbral? They've been properly disincentivized." With a slim grin, he made a wave to the burning candles and incense. His smile faded into an uncomfortable grimace. "You'll have to pardon my rudeness. It's been some time since I've had the opportunity to interact with others. I fear my finer graces have atrophied. I am called Redbletter, of the Achoral Manse." With an arm over his chest, he made an exaggerated bow. When he returned to full height, there was a proud glow on his dark cheeks.

"Gareth Solomon," Gareth tersely responded. As he placed a hand on the satin-lined chair, he returned to the conversation. "You said the shades—the Umbral—were 'disincentivized.' What about the foulkin? I didn't see any of their like since passing through the sigil gate."

" 'Foulkin?' I've not... Ah, you mean the Dalhakhu. Their kind doesn't dare enter Bethsaida. There are... *anomalies* that would affect their condition, reduce them to something even less human than they already are. Beyond that is an inherent fear of the Umbral. In their current state, they are easily spooked by those that haunt the streets of Bethsaida."

At this, Gareth let out a long, exasperated breath. "Is nothing on this island sane?" he muttered as he sat down.

This drew a small, dry laugh from Redbletter. "Not for some time, I fear. I too wish for a return to the olden days. While the roads were bustling with the mundaneness of the human experience, sanity and sensibility were far more common. It was a version of madness one could learn to cope with."

Gareth continued. "It's been like this ever since I showed up at the Gape. Never-ending string of bullshit and even the people who were supposedly helping me seemed caught up in the madness."

This caused Redbletter to scowl. "The Gape? I've not heard of such a place."

"Really? Then how did you arrive? To Dineothan, I mean?"

"Arrive?" He chuckled loudly as if the question was foolish. "I was *born* in upper Upelstbohr. I *am* of the Achoral Manse, you see. Yes, yes, I know. I've heard all the japes. One of the Upper-Upers. It's how the slummers like to slag off on their betters. In reality, so few of us who are native-born are left. Many of those who still reside in Dineothan came here by choice. All of them settled into the lower wards out of necessity."

Briefly, Gareth was taken aback. He had assumed that Naze and those back in the sanctuary were citizens rather than immigrants to the island nation, but Redbletter's comments told him a different story.

"Since, you've been here, in the city, for some time—" *All his life, really.* "—I would ask if you know what happened here?" Any straight answer the man could provide would be beneficial. "I mean, I can't imagine this is how Dineothan has always been, right?"

"Within the city or the College?" He chuckled to himself before he continued. "One is a long tale that requires more time than I wish to spend. The other is dependent on the first." When Gareth scowled, Redbletter cleared his throat. "You must understand, that in the distinguished halls of the Amaru-ma-mudu, they practiced the strange sciences: reanimation, the mixing of chemical cocktails to shift a man's state of mind, the engineering of new hybrid forms of life, to name a few. They dabbled where they should not and when the madness took root in the populace, they were the first to be blamed. Rather than deal with the influx of mass insanity—to figure out why the common man so readily flouted taboos the second the idea was made public—like any sensible doctor might, they invented devices that failed in their own spectacular ways. Amaru-ma-mudu solved the problem of the Dalhakhu by turning those in Bethsaida into something just as dire. You see, you cannot become one of *them* if you are an Umbral."

When Gareth's face twisted in confusion, Redbletter stepped in close. He leaned in and took a long inhale through his nose, as if he was attempting to smell something on Gareth.

"Forgive the rudeness of my assumptions, but you strike me as a doer, rather than a learner. Might I inquire what brought you here? You came to Bethsaida by choice, I imagine. The College's irresistible draw did the rest, I think."

"Truth be told, I came looking for a scientist or a doctor. I was informed that… that some of the greatest minds in the world were in Dineothan. Tales from the outside world spoke of Upelstbohr's brilliant medical community." Gareth caught himself before he let on too much. Even then, Redbletter's eyes narrowed.

"Were you to come here before things went awry, you might have found more than your fair share. But, once they were tasked with tending to the mass hysteria that spilled into the streets, any entreating you may have attempted would have fallen on deaf ears. You would have been shown the door. I am sorry to tell you that there are none left. Well, none of whom are in a condition to hear your petition."

Considering his earlier experiences, this drew Gareth's curiosity. "What actually happened here? You speak of hysteria and madness, but that doesn't explain away the creatures in the streets."

"The amorality of rich men became public. And

instead of rebuking them, the mob chose to join in their practices, not knowing where it would eventually lead them. That enjoying their fellow man too much would turn them into something inhuman."

"That, uh, that doesn't exactly answer my question."

"With the promise of power, their hunt for akaluma'elusepsu, they thought to dine on one another. What you see outside of Bethsaida is all that remains of a populace gone truly mad. Those who survived the worst of the violence."

Gareth found himself unnerved by Redbletter's explanation. Cautiously, he asked, "And yourself?"

"I am a man of the cloth. A wholly irrelevant vocation in light of the city's condition, I must admit. Still, I chose to abstain. I thought it an unholy practice. Chose solitude and the safety of my manor until the worst of the chaos had abated. The gods have left us, I fear. Well, all but one as I've been told. I, too, eventually, came to the College for knowledge, only to find those who knew anything that mattered were no longer here."

When Gareth's shoulders slumped, Redbletter raised a hand into the air. "That is not to say that men of knowledge no longer exist. I am certain that one of Lyceed's descendants still tends to the sanatorium at the asylum which bears his name. There was a split some time in the early 1500s and Lyceed took his fair share of our smartest minds with him. A difference in perspective from what I heard. Considering the stories I'd heard that his servants had swept the nearby wards to collect some of those afflicted, I assume that someone there, at the time, thought to help."

This mitigated Gareth's frustration to a degree.

"And if I were to look for the asylum? I imagine that would require some additional, arcane task to progress forward, correct?"

Redbletter took another long sniff before he stood upright. "Not so much for a man of your stature. As skilled as you are, it should be no chore to reach Golyat's Ascent, which leads into the upper wards. Take the stairs to their apex and look for the sanatorium erected cliffside to the northeast. Perhaps you'll need to wet your blade a few times, but your course will not be barred by a sigil gate. The barrier that once separated the lower wards from Upper Upelstbohr is no longer tended."

Though he thought he should let it go, Gareth asked, "What do you mean 'a man of *my* stature?' "

"You are too new to Dineothan to pick up on such subtleties, my good man." He leveled a thin finger at Gareth as he hovered nearby. The longer he remained within arm's reach, the more agitated Gareth became.

"You have the scent of something else upon you, something that is not originally yours," Redbletter announced with a sneer. "Fresh to Upelstbohr and already partaking of the local cuisine. Not literally, I believe, but well enough. Not a surprise. Many a man turned to the enjoyment of his own kind when they realized it had pronounced benefits beyond satiating their appetite. Hence, the madness. First, it became the vogue. It was more desirable than stacks of gold. Then men discovered that it gave them something even greater. That, my good man, was when the knives truly came out."

Redbletter moved in close and drew in another breath. This caused Gareth to pull back as he eyed him warily.

"There is something else, there. Beneath the aroma of energies which do not belong to you. You smell of sadness. Loss." Redbletter's speech slowed to a drawl. "Not the kind that goes with a parent's death. Those are the inevitable. You grieve but you expect them to die before you. Yours... yours is a fresh grief borne of something unexpected. A loved one. Child? Or a wife? Maybe not even a wife, yet. A lover. Maybe never a wife, now."

This sudden intrusion caused Gareth to see red.

"That's none of your damn business!" Gareth snapped. The flash of anger caused a thin smile to appear on Redbletter's face.

"Not dead in your mind, I see." Redbletter backed away as Gareth rose to his feet. Gareth kicked the chair back out of his way. It flipped over with a clatter.

Redbletter immediately bowed to temper Gareth's rage. "Please, forgive my rudeness. Perhaps I've forgotten the politeness required of a host. Some topics, despite their allure, are better left unmentioned."

After a few seconds of silent stewing, Gareth nodded. He began to slowly make his way back to the entrance.

"Well, I thank you for your time and information," he stated through a clenched jaw. He felt relief when

Redbletter made no move from his position. He merely clasped his hands and watched as Gareth attempted to depart. "But, I have a deadline and a need to be on my way. You have my gratitude for pointing me to the sanatorium."

Redbletter raised a single finger.

"It would be impolite of me not to offer warning. If you are determined to leave, take some of the burning candles with you. That platter there—" He pointed to a silver tray on the nearby countertop. "—take it with you. Or one of the many candelabra. The incense should do well enough to keep the worst of them at bay. It may cause you some discomfort, but that will be nothing to what the wandering Umbral will feel."

Gareth's gaze bounced back and forth between Redbletter, the serving dish, and the candelabra. Redbletter spoke up.

"The shades within the city are but thin phantoms, incapable of much. Reacting to the movements of the tangible is more than they can manage. Those nearby—those within the college grounds—were close to the epicenter when the greatest minds knocked Bethsaida out of alignment. They are those who used to learn here. Even in their phantasmal forms, they can still influence the world. Smart as they are, they understand the laws that govern their new existence."

Though wary, Gareth reached out for the candelabrum. Relieved, Redbletter continued.

"If you have sense enough to fear for your physical well-being—your sanity, too—steer clear of the college's upper floors. Some of Elder Paimon's more brilliant scholars can smell the energies within you."

Gareth only nodded as he turned the doorknob. The flames flickered as held the trident candlestick in front of him.

"Please feel free to visit again if you are so inclined. You will find me here. As a man with all the time in the world, reading is the only pleasure I have left."

Gareth closed the door behind him.

Chapter Eight

Golyat's Ascent

With the candelabrum held out in front of him, Gareth began to feel foolish. He let Redbletter convince him that he needed the candles to walk the same halls he'd recently traversed without issue. Once again, he'd allowed one of Upelstbohr's eccentrics to influence him. How long would it take before he was dressed in a jester's hat as he danced for someone else's entertainment?

Even as he admonished himself, he resisted the urge to cast the candlestick aside. At the very least, it could provide illumination in the twisting set of hallways that now vexed him. Despite efforts to retrace his previous path, Gareth struggled to find his way back to the foyer. There were too many similar doorways, and every intersection appeared to draw him deeper within. After a few minutes, he unearthed a piece of white chalk from a belt pouch and scratched arrows on the walls.

Doing this quickly corrected his problem. He eventually came out to the long hallway that fed into the balcony overlooking the foyer. Faint cold light from the second-story windows served to highlight the interior's details. Gareth lowered the candelabrum. He considered snuffing out the wicks before discarding the candleholder.

As a form came out of the gloom, Gareth came to a sudden stop. Gareth stood still and watched as more of the human-shaped shades slid out of the darkness. At first, he thought they were the same kind of harmless entities he'd earlier sidestepped. When a few ambled towards him, Gareth recoiled from their presence.

He waited for what felt like the longest seconds ever for their forward march to stop, for the forms to disappear and return to their place. When the first three continued to skulk towards him, Gareth's free hand went for his sword.

These three weren't trapped in a fruitless loop of their lives just before the incident that had damned the ward. They displayed an unexpected degree of sentience by noticing Gareth's presence.

As he held the burning candles out as far as possible in front of him, the approaching Umbral finally halted their advance. When he nudged his arm forward, they withdrew as if repulsed by the strong aroma that wafted from the melting wax.

Despite his irritation with their vague answers, he'd once again received valuable advice.

Even through the growing throng of shades that

slowly choked the corridor, Gareth could see something waiting beyond them. At the far end, past the staircase that headed downwards, was another flight of steps that led deeper into the building. On the next landing was a form that lingered menacingly. While in the darkness it was impossible to see clearly, there was an air of menace that radiated from it. In the faint diffused light, Gareth noticed a denser outline, much larger than the other Umbral. Two silver-hued luminescent orbs flickered like eyes peering down on him.

Was this what Redbletter warned him against? Were these Elder Paimon's closest associates? Whomever they might be, Gareth needed to take his leave. His presence had done enough to draw unwanted attention.

As he slowly inched forward, he felt something at his back. Cold tendrils dragged themselves across the base of his neck. An almost uncontrollable shiver rattled his spine. It took great effort to keep a grasp on the objects in his hands.

Still holding the candles, Gareth spun and fanned his sword behind him. In the orange halo cast by the protective flames, he saw that a single Umbral had snuck up behind him.

When his blade passed through it, the shade drew back in apparent agony. A wisp of white smoke trailed away as the manifestation split in two. The nearby Umbral retreated with their arms raised defensively.

Gareth thought he heard the faintest strained hiss emanate from the wounded entity. He felt the smallest charge, like a rush of excitement, run through his chest.

He could feel his heartbeat pound inside his ears. The entity, somehow, was slain.

Can't stay any longer, Gareth thought as he turned to face the others. *Won't be long before they attempt to overwhelm me with their numbers. May be willing to sacrifice a few for the chance to get to me.*

He took a deep breath and began to charge forward. Even as he drove the candles into the crowd of retreating Umbral, the burning wicks flickered as they struggled to maintain their brilliance. It was as if something in the air was draining away their heat. Gareth swung his blade back and forth as he continued to press his temporary advantage. He felt a faint shudder as it struck one of the shades. Soft hissing filled the air.

Even though he could see his progress towards the exit, he felt as though he was caught in a bog. Every step forward took extra effort. More than once, he perceived cold digits as they scraped against his back and legs. It was as if the skin beneath his clothing was burned by dry ice.

Just as he reached the top of the stairwell, Gareth glanced up as the glowing silver eyes began to move towards him. The darkened form bobbed slowly as it passed through the faint slivers of outside light. Whatever this was that had stood silently was now willing to intervene on behalf of the other, lesser Umbral. A rush of anxiety gripped Gareth's chest.

He swore under his breath as he bounded over the balustrade and stumbled clumsily to the top of the stairs. For a second, he thought he might tumble forwards.

Wouldn't it be a farce to almost escape only to break his neck as he rolled head-over-heels to the foyer below? With a sharp snap, he bolted upright and continued his descent at a sprint.

He could feel them behind him. Muffled whispers grew in volume as they called out from the second floor. A pulsing coldness buffeted his back in waves.

Gareth reached the entrance and went shoulder-first into the dense oak. Surprisingly compliant this time, the doors swung aside and he charged out of the building. The warmth of the afternoon sun through the upper levels was a relief.

Though the adjacent court was crowded with shades, he cast the candlestick aside. The half-burnt candles splattered on the tiled courtyard as two of the three flames snuffed out on impact.

Now outside and free of his pursuers, Gareth picked up his pace as he gave the lingering Umbral a wide berth. Though a few hovered near the entrance, he didn't feel menaced by their presence. Even though more than one clearly turned his way, they appeared fixed in their places. Noticing this, Gareth raised his sword into the air. When none attempted to give him chase, he re-sheathed it.

Warmth crept along his bare skin. He realized that it had been far colder within the administration building than he'd originally recognized. He'd not noticed it at the time, but now, as his body began to thaw, his core temperature had gradually lowered. Blood flow eventually returned to his extremities.

Once off the college grounds, Gareth struggled to continue northward. It felt as if every step was labored. More than once, he found he had turned around, back towards the campus. When he became aware of this, Gareth spun about and redoubled his focus. With his mind set on putting distance between himself and the university, he pushed onwards.

Before long, the almost irresistible pull began to wane. By the time he'd covered a mile of the shadow-infested streets, Gareth allowed himself to relax. The muscles along his shoulders and lower back ached from the strain. When he felt safe, he paused to recover for a moment. Even though he wasn't hungry, he pulled out a piece of jerky and gnawed on it. The activity restored some semblance of normalcy.

Once done, he resumed his march.

By the time Gareth covered another half mile, he noticed fewer Umbral. Except for the occasional shade haunting one corner or another, their numbers were significantly reduced. Gareth now recognized the noise of movement from distant neighborhoods. The familiar sounds of inhuman mutterings and shuffling footsteps alerted him to inherent danger. Realizing that he was far enough away from the College that the foulkin were once again a concern, Gareth planned a return to the rooftops.

After discovering a circular staircase on the side of an apartment block, he scaled three stories to the interconnected paths of the upper gables. Here the way was not as byzantine as in Chorazin; Gareth was relieved to see that his course northward would be largely uninterrupted.

Even though the sky retained its bright orange hue, Gareth felt as though he'd been on the move for some time. At the very least, he doubted that he was even in the wards of Bethsaida anymore. Though they shared similar architectural themes as the structures of Chorazin, the neighborhoods here were far more organized.

As he continued, Gareth quickly picked out Golyat's Ascent in the distance. Beyond another colossal gateway, this one wide open and untended, was a massive set of stairs which rose hundreds of yards as it curled skyward to the city's upper strata. Even from where he was, he noticed the grandness of scale of the formation. Like some of the older structures in Chorazin, it felt as though it was intended for a much larger populace.

When he was a few dozen yards from the bottom steps, Gareth realized Golyat's Ascent had been carved into the earth itself. The steep rise was part of the island's natural formation.

After pausing to take in the view, Gareth turned his attention to the climb before him.

Flanking each side of the stairs was a series of statues, each at least ten feet in height and carved from weathered granite. Between the more regal sculptures of knights who brandished their swords and shields were monstrous gargoyles, many of which were hunched with clawed hands that reached over the lengthy pathway. Along the upper flights, the sculptures were of stranger entities, including thin, lanky humanoids whose faces were covered by segmented carapaces.

Though the climb appeared daunting, he let out a resigned sigh and approached the first riser. By the time, he'd made his fourth stride, it was clear that the climb was meant for someone with an elongated stride. He could feel it in his muscles. More than once, he stumbled as he misjudged his step.

Even as his own gear clattered in time with his march, Gareth could hear the movement of something behind him. Padded footfalls clambered after him as he continued his charge up the incline. For some reason, Gareth felt no need to look over his shoulder. He didn't fear the entity that tailed him as he continued. He could sense the presence and that it meant Gareth no immediate threat.

This realization struck him as odd. It was unlike him to become complacent, especially in a city populated with threats. And yet, something in his gut told him not to fret.

Before long, he noticed the labored wheezing of his pursuer's breathing. As he did, Gareth slowed down.

"H-h-hold up… brave warrior," a breathless voice hailed. "Don't be… in such a rush."

"I see that you've uncovered your spine," Gareth stated without looking back at Alharrad. He paused on a break in the steps that doubled as a small patio facing out on a neighborhood to the west. A stone balustrade was all that separated onlookers from a thirty-yard drop to the houses below. On his right, overlooking the terrace was another statue of the humanoid-like forms, this one dressed in a long robe with a bell in one hand.

"Not so much to… uh, to fear when someone as brave as yourself has cleared the way, I must admit." As he recovered, Alharrad stayed a few yards out of Gareth's reach. Gareth glanced over his shoulder as he watched the old man, who crouched to draw in a few long breaths. "The beasts of Chorazin are in a bit of a power struggle. Putting down Sindex—such as you did—sent the rest into a state. Too focused on the Lord's Chapel, they are. It'll be a killing field for some time until a new hierarchy's been sorted out. Still, none will replace what kinds of influence an anuphilim had over Chorazin."

Gareth cut straight to the point. "And what brings you out this way?" He struggled to not reveal his clear distrust of the man.

"With the sigil gate finally reopened, as it were— thanks to you, I might add—I felt the need to revisit some of the more interesting corners of Upelstbohr. My time in the Halls had grown long. Boredom was not an ally of mine, I must admit. Many a thing has changed since Chorazin was cut off. Not so much in Bethsaida, I gather, but in other locales you've not yet visited."

Gareth looked at him warily. "And these were places you'd been to before? Because it appears that the gate'd been barred for a fairly long time."

"Longer than you might think. But, there are other ways one might be returned to the wards of Chorazin.

Not through the sewers, mind you. An awful place no sane man should want to risk. The less savory elements retreated to those foul halls before the city fell into disrepair. Got themselves a cult, they did. Claimed they was tryin' to save the city. Turned their backs to the gods of man. Went lookin' for the Ikkibu, though I don't understand why. The Church of Grand Ilu was more than open to their kind."

Gareth held up a hand to wave off Alharrad's rambling. He was already tired of the madman's ramblings. Even if there was pertinent information to be unearthed, it was bogged down by seemingly-endless tangents. "Don't," he begged. "I honestly don't even care."

Alharrad's mouth hung open for a moment. Eventually, his jaw closed tightly as his brow furrowed.

"Well, that's a fine way to treat a good friend," Alharrad grumbled.

"And you think to follow after me—"

"Oh, ho, ho. So full of yourself now that you've supped of Sindex, aren't you?" Alharrad said with a derisive laugh. "Don't yet realize… perhaps you've not had the fortune to traverse the city so much as to know the best paths to get about. Golyat's Ascent is the best way to get to the upper levels. Or, the safest, if the truth be told. Bit of struggle for those not in such good health as yourself. Certainly, you could trek out to the Holy Man's Walk, but that takes a soul too far towards the harbor." He paused as if to listen for something. When that moment passed, he shook his head. "No, no, no. The Ascent is the best path to take."

"And you have business this way?"

"None that matters to you. Not everyone who heads to the upper levels is looking for Lyceed's Asylum. And before you ask, it makes all the sense in the world for you to be headed that way. If no one was to answer you in the Grand College, that is."

"So, then, you are headed elsewhere?"

"In truth, I have no need for a man of science or medicine. That's *your* burden, if I recall rightly." He offered a toothy grin. "Now, now, don't go tryin' to dig it outta me. Ol' Alharrad needs to have a few secrets of his own." He wagged a crooked finger in Gareth's direction.

With a wry smile that was largely forced, Gareth made a sweeping wave up the steps. "By all means, then, please feel free to continue on. Don't let me delay you any more."

This seemed to give Alharrad pause. Eventually, he spoke up.

"Do you… are you not curious as how to arrive at the Sanatorium? No inquisitive mind in need of direction? Or have you become so experienced in the ways of Upelstbohr that you no longer need the guidance of those who've gone before you?"

Gareth was certain he heard pettiness in the man's voice. He savored it, if only for a second. "In truth, I was advised that it was 'erected cliff-side to the northeast.' I think I can manage that."

"You were *advised*?" This caused Alharrad to stand as upright as his body would allow. His weathered brow wrinkled deeply. "By who? You must, uh, y-you must tell me!" His voice rose in volume and pitch as he continued. His words became frantic. "For your own safety, you *must* let me know. There are so many out there who would send you to your demise for their own gain. They would sense what you have within, already partaken in your victories, and want it for themselves. What other souls have you come across? Their names! You must tell me. You cannot trust a thing told to you by others. They've been out among the foulkin too long. Corrupted and infected, they've become—"

Gareth held out an open palm to Alharrad. His other hand fell to his holstered revolver. "Hold your tongue. Were you not the one who sent me to the Lord's Chapel without warning? Do not claim to be better than others when your own recent actions have proved foul."

"Recent? T'was but… Still, I was only—"

Gareth raised his voice as he shifted. "I don't know what delusion you labor under, but we are not of an association. Any information I receive from you will not be taken without a hearty dose of suspicion. When all is said and done, it's best we went our separate ways." He then pointed to the stairs. "Be on your way to whatever corner of this island you wish to visit."

At this, Alharrad snorted.

"Well, I'll take my leave of you, then," Alharrad snapped. Though he was furious, he kept his peace. His eyes bounced from Gareth's face to the holstered revolver at his side. "If this is the kind of brotherhood you wish to foster, then may you find what you're lookin' for with Lyceed and those under his care. Rudeness begets more of the same, I say."

Before Gareth could reply, Alharrad scurried off like a wounded animal. Though there was a burning in his stomach from the exchange, Gareth knew it was for the best. He slowly spun and gazed at the panorama before him.

Out of the corner of his eye, he watched as Alharrad struggled upward. The older man was forced to crawl over them with both hands and feet. Soon, Alharrad disappeared around the corner as the stairs curled behind the adjoining cliff face.

For a moment, Gareth was certain he saw movement in the distance. It was only a flicker as a shadow disappeared behind a stack of chimneys. He quickly wrote it off as one of the Umbral.

With a dismissive flick of his hand, he turned and continued his own climb.

CHAPTER NINE

The Sanatorium at Lyceed's Asylum

Though the air grew noticeably thinner as he climbed, Gareth continued without a break. Feeling stronger than ever, he handled the trek like it was a casual stroll. As he did, Gareth wondered how often the common citizenry utilized the pathway. It was an unwieldy byway that would dissuade anyone not determined to reach the summit. Considering that the elevation clearly separated the city's different social ranks, he speculated that it would have been patrolled by whatever security force the rich in Upelstbohr had employed.

As Gareth neared the top of Golyat's Ascent, he stopped and glanced over his shoulder at the cityscape behind him. Despite the densely-layered architecture choking the skyline around him, a part of Gareth expected to see the sprawling wards of Bethsaida and Chorazin laid out for miles. He wanted to gauge the distance he had covered during his time in Dineothan.

Curiosity gave way to dissatisfaction. Because of the northeastward curl of the lengthy route, the city's overhanging strata blocked out all but the orange-hued sky. Except for the walled-in mansions bordering the stairs, Gareth could see little of the aged metropolis.

Disappointed, Gareth sighed as he continued to scale the steps.

Once at the apex, he came across another gateway, which was open and abandoned. Unlike the previous barriers between the wards, one of the massive doors had fallen off its mountings and now rested at an angle against the nearby guardhouse. Under its weight, the northern side of the building had collapsed. Gareth took a moment to examine the damage. Something had caused the barrier to come loose, but there were no additional signs of violence.

After passing through, Gareth discovered another courtyard. The stone-paved square looked unmarred. On the far side, near the adjacent homesteads, was a semi-circle of marble statues. Unlike those erected along the stairs behind him, these effigies were of people, most likely ordinary citizens, dressed in apparel from seemingly-older eras. Many grasped objects, either held aloft before them or clasped tightly against their chests. Gareth quickly determined that most were familiar possessions: an abacus, a telescope, a mortar and pestle, and an oversized compass and caliper. One man held a winged staff that was entwined by two serpents. Some clutched at books of unknown topics. There was one figure, draped in a long robe, which held an ankh against his head.

Though he didn't physically need to, Gareth stopped to take a breath as he stretched out his legs and back. Normally, such a challenging hike would have done a number on him. Muscles would have ached with fatigue. His feet would have been sore. Now, he only performed the activity out of a sense of habit. In reality, he felt fully rested.

As he interlocked his fingers and extended his arms above his head, Gareth paused. Though he'd surmised that the upper levels housed more affluent neighborhoods, he was still stunned by the excess on display. Overly-ornate mansions, many bordered by ten-foot-high wrought iron fences, were adorned with accents of marble, ivory, and gold. There was ostentatiousness about their décor, as if the owners placed value in the garishness in their exteriors.

Long, curling pathways wrapped around the crowded estates. Along the way were more statues, many of which were variations on those at the top of Golyat's Ascent. As Gareth continued his trek, he often stopped to appreciate the intricacies of the sculptor's work. There was a surprising level of realistic detail in the carven visages and layered clothing. From the wrist of one hung a pocket watch whose hands were locked eternally at 3:58.

It wasn't long before he spotted a structure that looked promising. On a rise in the earth that overlooked most of the district was a sizeable grouping of matching buildings, cordoned off by a two-yard tall barrier wall. Unlike the surrounding homes, this campus was formed by a more restrained hand. While parts of it reminded Gareth of the hospital wards in the Golden City of Auewellian, some architectural elements called back to the Grand College in Bethsaida. The red brick facade was lit by a ring of gas-powered lamps along the rows of sash windows.

It only took a second for Gareth to decide. Since he was surrounded by vacant estates, the distant series of buildings and their lights were most likely his destination.

Unlike he had been able to in the wards of Chorazin, he couldn't travel via the rooftops. Gareth chose to stick to the streets. Before long, he recognized the familiar sounds of beasts as they roamed the pathways. He knew that he wouldn't avoid the foulkin for long.

With his blade out, he moved along the alleys until he eventually came across one.

The beast, which lingered just outside a barred set of gates, was unlike those he'd witnessed in Chorazin. It stood tall on two legs as its lanky arms swayed back and forth. It was draped in the tattered remains of clothes. A blue suit jacket, torn along a number of the seams, was wrapped tightly around its barrel-like chest. The frayed remnants of pants covered its lower abdomen. A few patches of soiled white linen hung from its wrists like manacles.

As if he wanted to force the engagement, Gareth kicked at a nearby clump of earth. The stone clattered as it skipped forward. In the silence of the ward, this sound was enough to draw the beast's attention. With sharper, more agile movements than its Chorazin kin had made, it spun and loped in Gareth's direction. Its snout sniffed at the air. After a few seconds, as its brown eyes scanned the lane, it spotted him. The foulkin's gait became an aggressive trot.

As it jogged towards him, something curious overcame Gareth. He no longer felt apprehension. He spread his legs, raised his sword, and gripped his weapon with both hands. In the back of his head, he began a countdown. He had a handful of seconds.

Three, two, one…

The creature lunged to cover the last few yards. Gareth flicked his blade, deflecting the blow. As a second clawed hand launched at him, Gareth quickly back-stepped out of reach. When inertia carried the beast to his left, Gareth shuffled his feet sideways. Reacting as quickly as its weight allowed, the foulkin tried to shift as it tracked Gareth's movement. Before it could turn fully about, Gareth struck; he kicked at its back leg, catching it with the steel toe of his boot.

The affected limb crumpled, and the beast stumbled to the ground with a screech. It appeared that the impact knocked the bone from the knee joint. It was hard to tell as many of the foulkin's limbs defied his knowledge of how bodies were assembled.

Just as the creature attempted a lurching half-crawl, Gareth drove his blade into its torso. As the honed edge plunged into the fur-coated flesh, the beast wailed. Its arms flailed in an attempt to drag itself away. Wounded, it now only wanted to flee.

Gareth raised his sword again and watched briefly as the creature pulled itself down the lane. A stream of thick blood, which trailed behind it, began to congeal on the dust-coated pavers. Before it managed to put distance between them, Gareth charged. He swung the weapon in a diagonal arc that caught it across the shoulders.

A groan spilled from the foulkin's open mouth as its body slumped forward. Gareth moved forward warily as he watched the creature's torso move up and down erratically. An arm struggled to reach forward. Clawed fingers scraped as it curled into a balled fist.

Gareth slid his blade into the beast's back, aiming for its upper ribs. Because of its inhuman physiology, he wasn't certain where its heart might be. If lucky, he might strike enough vital organs that the attack alone would be enough. When a spurt of thick, tar-like fluid followed as he unsheathed his weapon from its trunk, he felt confident he'd struck something important.

Within seconds, the foulkin ceased all movement as its body went slack. A few prodding taps of his boot confirmed that the creature was, in fact, dead. As he returned his blade to its scabbard, Gareth felt a sudden jolt. He experienced a boost, much like the one the first cup of coffee in the morning gave him.

Gareth waited a moment for this to pass. Even though it wasn't his first time, the experience was still disorienting. His gaze went to the foulkin's corpse.

He began to examine it, wanting to make sense of its existence. The human qualities of its body unnerved him the longer he observed them.

Remaining cautious, Gareth moved to the creature's head and knelt down. He withdrew a knife from his belt and slid it into the half-open mouth. He turned his wrist and rolled it over. Inside the orifice was a row of curled fangs and a meaty tongue that flopped to the ground. The acrid aroma of spoiled meat spilled out as a final gust of breath escaped its lungs. Deeper inside the oral cavity lay another set of teeth, shaped more like human's teeth, which were deeply rooted into the hard palate. Gareth shuddered.

He retreated with a nervous shake of his head. He wasn't certain what he was expecting, but what he had uncovered did not sit well with him. Exposing familiar features in its alien physiology implied something that Redbletter had earlier revealed to Gareth.

"That enjoying their fellow man too much would turn them into something inhuman."

Even as he tried to make sense of this information, Gareth felt something else. It was like a hunger gnawing at his gut, threatening to devour his organs if he failed to sate it. It was the first time he'd truly felt ravenous since his arrival. As it grew more insistent by the second, Gareth turned to the mass of slowly-cooling flesh before him. Despite his revulsion, his mouth watered. He licked his lips.

Before he could partake of the oddly-appealing slab of meat, he snapped out of the haze that had overtaken his morals.

What in the hell...

With a gloved hand, he slapped himself across the cheek. He took a few wary paces in retreat as he rubbed his temples. After a long exhale, the urge waned. This sensation was briefly replaced by nausea which likewise faded.

When the sounds of other foulkin grew more noticeable, Gareth realized that he needed to be on his way. Even if the brief battle had gone unnoticed, the fallen body would not. He had felt the irresistible lure from the prone form, and it was certain to attract the other beasts in the area.

Viscous fluids continued to spread outwards as the seconds passed. Subconsciously, he licked his lips again. His stomach churned. As the sounds of footsteps neared, Gareth pulled himself away and pressed on.

Gareth was fifty yards away when he first heard the howls of other beasts dining upon the unexpected bounty. Vicious snarls told of a struggle for dominance. Gareth was relieved. Though he felt stronger and faster, he didn't want to take his chances with more than one at a time.

Quickening his pace, he continued on to the red-brick campus to the northeast.

After what felt like an hour of weaving through foliage-dotted lanes, Gareth came out on a clearing that sloped upwards to the distant facility. Copses of gnarled oaks spread across the hillside. As he trudged up the paver-lined walkway, he hoped that he was in the right place. Now that the foulkin were roused, he didn't want to have to go back through the ward behind him.

Before long, he came to a stop just outside a partially-open gateway which separated the property from the outside acreage. Encircling the main yard was a barricade of wrought iron bars and red-brick columns. Heart-shaped flourishes lined the top of the fence. To the left of the entrance was a bronze-plated sign that stated "LYCEED'S ASYLUM & SANATORIUM."

Gareth nodded to himself. He slipped through the gap between the rusted slabs of metal. Beyond, he found a series of interconnected buildings that reminded him of many a traditional medical ward. Besides the main structure was a pair of multistory wings that ran eastwards towards the distant cliff's edge. Gareth was certain he could hear the faint crash of waves from the rocky shore below. When he cocked his head to the side and focused on it, though, the familiar sounds faded.

A once-manicured lawn was now overgrown; thickets of trees and bushes clogged the walking paths which linked the main gate and the front entrance. Whiffs of wildflowers in bloom triggered memories of better times in the outside world. For a moment, Gareth smiled.

Eventually, he reached the double doors of the main entrance and pushed his way in. The foyer led directly into an administrative area, complete with waiting room, clerical offices, and a set of visitation cubicles on the second floor. Though afternoon sunlight poured in through the clouded panes of the skylights above, gas lamps along the outer walls burned brightly. At the center was a stone obelisk, with the image of a doctor in profile carved on the front.

There was no bustle, no welcome of a receptionist at his arrival. A thick layer of dust hinted that the facility was now in a state of neglect. Some of the decorative tiles had fallen from the walls and were now collected in small piles of broken shards.

Undaunted, he crossed to the main desk and rooted about for anything that might prove useful. A floorplan or listing of staff quarters would be of some help. As he dug inside a jumbled drawer filled with assorted supplies, he heard the rattle of something metallic behind the double doors to the east.

Jingle.

Not entirely abandoned, he thought to himself. A second later, it occurred to him that the asylum might contain the same perils as the surrounding district. He repressed the urge to call out.

Eventually, he uncovered a laminated sheet that had seen better days. On the dog-eared page was a map of the facilities, which confirmed that three separate wings were anchored to the main hall. In addition, interconnected office spaces linked the entire estate in one long pathway. He could start with the northern wards and eventually work his way around the full circuit before returning to the main building.

Written with a grease pencil, though, were handwritten notes, many of which were illegible. A series of misshapen boxes and circles were added at the ends of two sections, as if to note structures not already displayed. Perhaps the additions were not a part of the original construction? Or, maybe they were not intended for public access.

Either way, Gareth rolled up the map and tucked it into his back pocket. Hoping to find someone who was still of a mind to be useful, he hung a left and went for the nearest double doors. He kept a hand on his holstered revolver and tentatively opened the entry with a nudge that made the rusty hinges creak.

Once he entered the north wing, Gareth suspected that the Sanatorium's nature was far from benevolent. The central hall was fashioned more like a prison than a hospital. The long corridor, three floors high and lined with metal walkways, was flanked on both sides by barred cells. Two rows of thick stone columns ran down the length of the main corridor.

He paused long enough to look into the cubicle on his right. Though empty, it featured a recently-made cot and a tall window slit on the back wall. No matter how long he peered within, he saw no evidence of inhabitants.

Jingle.

When he heard movement elsewhere in the building, Gareth stepped back and cocked his head to the side. A faint rustling of living things seemed to echo from all corners. Before long, he noticed incoherent mumbling.

As he listened in, Gareth wasn't certain if the sounds were a prayer or the disjointed ramblings of madness.

Just as he was about to move forward, he overheard the clear tingle of a small bell from deeper in the asylum. A spike of anxiety jolted his heartrate. He quickly convinced himself it was nothing and continued forward.

As he marched down the central aisle, Gareth's eyes bounced back and forth. He peeked into each of the cells as he passed. Most were as barren as the first. When he spotted mummified remains in the back of one, Gareth stopped and peered inside.

With one hand, he gave a tug on the door, which stuck. The rattle of rusty metal against the frame reverberated upwards into the vaulted ceiling. Almost immediately, low whispering hailed from somewhere further in. Gareth quickly placed it as coming from above him, perhaps on the second or third floors.

Gareth made a beeline for the staircase on his right.

As he climbed the stairs, Gareth cringed. With every step, the heel of his boots banged loudly. Echoes of his footfalls rang out. Any chance he might have at stealth was gone. Anyone in the wing who was in possession of their senses was now aware of his presence.

Once he reached the second-story landing, he heard something stirring in a nearby cubicle. Curious, he stalked closer until he was a few paces from the bars. With a hand still on his revolver, he leaned forward.

Inside, with his body pressed into the back corner, was a man. Though he was coated in grime and looked frail and tired, the prisoner appeared to be roughly Gareth's age. Blue eyes that were wide with terror watched intently as Gareth moved in close. His fingers clutched at the frame of a nearby cot, as if to anchor himself. His legs curled up tightly as his bare feet dug into the floor.

It took only a moment for the man to notice his visitor. When he did, the prisoner was almost immediately overcome with elation. His countenance slackened as his jaw unclenched. His eyelids fluttered as a held breath slipped through pursed lips.

"S-s-sorry," he sputtered as he tried to get to his feet. His movements exhibited the kind of weakness that Gareth had witnessed in men left in captivity for years. "Thought you were… were one of the gaolers. Been…. been some time since one of them thought to patrol. To visit. I assumed that the master of the asylum finally concocted more experiments to conduct."

Gareth offered him an apologetic half-smile. "Sorry, no such luck."

"Wh-who are you with? No, no, never mind that." He shook his head vigorously. "It really doesn't even matter, so long as you're not one of Lyceed's disciples. You're not, right? No, no. You aren't. Lyceed hasn't had need for human aides in some time." Shuffling, he walked over to the door. "You'll forgive my poor manners. It's been some time since I've had company. Geddish Pwarma, former tradesman of the Gaillee Guilds." He offered a thin hand that easily slipped through the bars.

Gareth looked down to see fingers that were raw. It

occurred to him that Geddish, if he wasn't a part of a prison work detail, might have attempted to dig himself free with his bare hands. Considering the state of the asylum, this was not unexpected.

"Gareth Solomon," he replied politely. "If you don't mind me asking, how did you end up here?"

Geddish let out a hollow chuckle. "Long story that ends with being in the wrong place at the wrong time, I think." He propped himself against the bars. "I take it that you're privy to the tales of Upelstbohr? You don't have the look of a local. Too dark for one of the blue bloods. Had to travel too far for someone from the lower wards. Maybe an immigrant."

Gareth shook his head. Until he found himself on the trail of the fog-encircled island, he'd only overheard whispered folktales, nothing he might call comprehensive. His search had uncovered hints at a long-forgotten history, as if the outside world wanted to forget its existence.

This caught Geddish by surprise. His neck craned upwards as his eyes narrowed. "Really? I'd always heard that Dineothan was the siren's song for all who labored with want. Gold and riches in excess for any man with a sword and the willingness to pillage and plunder. Knowledge in excess for those of a learned bent. If you came to Upelstbohr and spent enough time, you could learn to warp time itself. Or, so they say. The truth, I think, is less straightforward... Even the pious themselves were drawn with whispers of the opportunity to commune with their gods. 'Dineothan is on the cusp of this world and the next,' they say. Have things changed that much?"

None of this struck Gareth as familiar.

"Well, neither here nor there, I say. I heeded the call and arrived with a crew bent on turning a profit from the endeavor. We were greeted by the most unpleasant of creatures and discovered a city embroiled in a foul scourge. People killing each other in the streets. Eating one another. For a while, we thought to exploit the madness in the populace while their greatest minds failed to deal with it properly."

Short of breath, Geddish retreated from the door and returned to his cot.

"Once I was separated from my bodyguards during the worst of the riots, I eventually ended up here. To be frank, I don't quite recall how it all transpired. A part of me recalls being corralled by a squad of gaolers looking to fill the halls with what I now know to be potential specimens."

Gareth asked a question that came to mind. "How long have you been here?"

"Hard... hard to tell. It always feels like it's daytime. When I go to sleep, when I wake... the sun is always there. I don't sleep because I need to but because it's a way to pass the time."

"What about meals? They have to feed you."

Geddish paused, as if the suggestion itself was strange.

"No need for food. I haven't hungered since my

arrival. And even if I did, the gaolers have shown no interest in tending to me. That Lyceed or his attendants haven't come for me yet is a blessing unto itself. No one they take comes back. They went through most of their detainees in the first few months. By then, the din of chaos from outside was mostly gone. Then, the days grew long, and they stopped sending for men to test on. Perhaps, they already have the answers and just haven't thought to release us."

"So, you're not here for some crime?" Gareth was dubious. There was clearly a fair bit missing from his story. It was likely Geddish and his men were imprisoned for theft and were serving out some form of sentence in the asylum. On top of that was his earlier claim at being a part of the Gaillee Guilds. Gareth knew this was a falsehood, as that organization had become a part of the Rutchgale Workman's Alliance over a hundred years ago. He only knew the name because of their place in history; the Gaillee Guilds had done business for hundreds of years before the merger.

"If only it were so simple," Geddish replied. "Though, I have my doubts that a traditional form of punishment would be meted out in any case. There was a lack of clear organization when we arrived." He fell silent for a moment as his gaze fell to the ground. Eventually, he looked back up. "Might I ask, what brings you here? If Upelstbohr's natural allure did not draw you in."

Though Gareth was reluctant to give the man much information, he hoped that Geddish could offer him even the smallest sliver of knowledge.

"A… a plague has recently reached my homeland. They say that it came from the rats. Others say it's not the rats, but their fleas. I say it doesn't much matter which. As it stands, the disease is carving a lethal swath through the poorer districts. My family… my family is ill. Through a long series of investigations, I was directed to Dineothan with the hopes that I might find a man of science or medicine who might lend aid."

Geddish burst out in a fit of laughter that devolved into a dry cough. An uncontrollable shudder caused his body to shake.

Gareth scowled at him.

"My apologies," Geddish spoke weakly. "You've come at a bad time to find a cure. The streets are the way they are for a reason, my good man. But—" He held out a hand for reassurance. "—if there is someone who might have answers, it would be the master of the asylum. When the elder Lyceed and his followers split off from the Grand College, they relocated here. His lodgings and private laboratory are somewhere deeper within the halls."

This caused Gareth to perk up. Geddish returned to the cell door. "I'll even point you in the right direction, but you must do something for me."

Though Gareth knew what the request would be, he still asked. "What *exactly* can I do for you?"

Geddish let loose a thin, hollow chuckle. "If you want to be of some aid, find the switch which would open this cage. I'm not one for fighting anymore, and I don't know what other aid I could give you, but given the opportunity, I'd like to be free. Open this cage and I'll direct you to Lyceed himself."

It struck Gareth as a fair trade. Even if he didn't really know the nature of the man's imprisonment, the bargain seemed logical, given the circumstances. He craned his neck to the left and then the right, looking for some mechanism.

"Well, I—"

Jingle. Jingle.

Gareth stopped midsentence. He looked over his shoulder. When he turned back, Geddish had retreated into the back corner of his cell. The color had drained from his face, and his eyes bulged as they frantically danced back and forth.

"What is it?"

Jingle.

It took a few seconds for Geddish's terror to abate. "A gaoler. One of them is making the rounds. Must've heard us talking 'cause they don't usually come out this way. No need to with so many of the cells empty."

Gareth's hand moved to his sword. As he grasped the hilt, Geddish reached out with a warning hand.

Jingle. Jingle.

"No, don't. You can't fight them. Go. Hide. If they see you, it's already too late. Once they alert the others, you're done for. You've not got the power to fight one much less a group of them."

Gareth considered the advice before eventually relenting. As he did, Geddish rose from his cot and crossed to the door. He stretched out one arm and pointed behind Gareth. "Across the bridge, there's an empty cell. The door's still open and unlocked. Hide in there until it's passed."

Gareth glanced over his shoulder and found the open compartment, its door slightly ajar. He turned back to Geddish, whose face twitched with anxiety.

Jingle. Jingle. Jingle.

"Why should—"

"I'm not doing this for your sake, fool," Geddish interrupted him. "If I'm to get out of here, I need your aid. Hide, now! Before it reaches the doorway to the lower levels. Once it knows you're here, you're damned."

Despite his reservations, Gareth did as he was asked. He scurried across a suspended bridge and slipped into the cubicle. After a quick scan to ensure he was truly alone, he slumped against the wall and hid in the shadows, keeping an eye on his limited view of the wing.

Jingle. Jingle.

Moments later, he heard hinges creak as doors at the far end of the corridor opened. A muted shuffling swept across the ground floor, but there was no sound of footfalls. Though tempted to take a peek, Gareth stayed in place.

When dull thuds began to ring out on the metal stairs, the urge proved more than he could resist. The visitor was moving up to the second floor and would be closing in on Geddish's cell within moments. Gareth leaned to the side and turned his head.

He almost gasped when the gaoler slid into his line of sight. He wasn't entirely certain what he'd expected, but the strange thing that arrived was off-putting. He thought that he'd grown accustomed to the oddities that haunted the island, but Gareth found himself frozen in place as the gaoler move across the walkway. Taller than him by a few feet, the lanky creature, which was draped in layers of silken cloth, skated across the floor with no effort.

Jingle.

There was a fluidity about its movements that suggested a less-than-solid state of being. Two appendages swung back and forth like pendulums from its sides. One tentacle-like extremity clasped a brass bell that jangled, ever so lightly, with each swaying of its limbs.

Though he couldn't see through the robes that trailed along the ground, Gareth heard something viscous as it moved. It was as if the gaoler's garments covered a mass of undulating semi-solid that roiled endlessly to propel itself forward.

Covering its head was an iron helm, hammered into the shape of a man's head. Through the eye-slits poured two light beams that wavered back and forth. The blueish-white rays made a wide sweep of the second-floor walkways before they turned to Geddish's cell.

Jingle.

From where he hid, Gareth could see past the gaoler and into the distant cell. As the gaoler's searchlight gaze fell onto Geddish, the prisoner curled up into a ball.

Though his features were locked in a panicked sneer, there was something else. His eyes lost focus as his mouth went slack. Shoulders that had once been tightly drawn now slumped as the tension left his body.

A seemingly endless measure of time passed as the gaoler focused on the numbed state of its ward. The longer this went on, the more agitated Gareth became. In the back of his head, a voice urged him to action. Though the tempered, rational part of his mind begged for restraint, thoughts of taking on the monstrosity grew more tempting by the minute. While the gaoler was preoccupied, Gareth could sneak up behind it and strike while its attention was diverted.

As his grip tightened on the hilt of his sword, Gareth's decision was set. He rose and cautiously stepped out from his hiding place. With each stride, he held his breath, afraid that he would alert it of his approach.

Just as he strode onto the bridge linking the two sides, the gaoler backed away from Geddish's cell and spun. The robes swished with the sudden movement. The twin beacons of light swung around to locate him.

Jingle. Jingle.

Gareth's eyes widened as he suddenly halted. Any chance at catching the entity by surprise was gone. At best, he could return to his hiding place and wait out the gaoler.

It moved with such speed that Gareth struggled to retreat. His boots scuffed on the metal walkway as he backpedaled. Once hidden behind the nearby stone column, he held his breath. As he did, the cone of brilliant light spun to where he'd only just stood.

Jingle.

As his heart raced, he admonished himself. Geddish's warning to wait out the inhuman guardsman from the safety of his hiding place had been wise. If he was fortunate en—

The gaoler slid across the bridge with a swiftness that left Gareth recoiling out of pure instinct. The spotlight turned and, even as Gareth attempted to scramble backwards, it locked on him.

Gareth's grip on his weapon loosened and the sword clattered to the walkway.

In that moment, everything failed. At first, his muscles refused to comply with direct orders from his brain. Before long, even his grip on consciousness began to loosen. As the gaoler moved in on Gareth, he felt like a trapped animal.

Jingle. Jingle. Jingle. Jingle. Jingle.

His body slumped to the ground. His vision went dim and the world around him blurred. Gareth could barely hear the bell clang insistently. Something wrapped around his leg and dragged him forward. Eventually, a second set of extremities took him by the arms.

The chime ceased its shrill tolling.

CHAPTER TEN

Akaluma'elusepsu

Despite the trance-like haze that clouded his perception, Gareth was not asleep. The near-weightless feel of his body was much the same. His limbs were limp, as if his muscles lacked the ability to function. A part of him wanted to just slip under, so he could revisit his family in the dream version of his home. It was a happier place than this one.

Instead, he was locked in the barely-conscious condition, incapable of changing his situation. He wanted to scream loudly, to struggle. Even as angst caused his heart to beat violently in his chest, he lacked the motor skills to act out. Though his brain struggled, his eyes opened occasionally. In those slivers of time, he attempted to make sense of the oddly-angled view on his surroundings.

On some level, Gareth understood what was happening. Though his senses were dulled, he was still capable of taking in some of the world around him. As evidence came in, a picture of his situation began to form. One of the inhuman gaolers had immobilized him and was now dragging him through the facility. Maybe there was a second one assisting the first. He noticed an additional set of white beams wavering back and forth.

He could tell he was being escorted through a wing populated with other prisoners. A furor rose from the occupants as he was led past their cells. A few spoke in hushed tones that sounded like human language. Others, though, communicated in growls, chirps, or low rumbles of blubbering cries.

When his head lolled to the side, he spotted something in one of the compartments. Spread out across the floor was a mass of flesh that pulsed with life. On one end was something akin to a head and two arms. Thin talons clawed at the air as a screech issued from its open maw.

Before long, he was carried from the penitentiary wing and into an adjacent hall. The cacophony became muffled as the door closed behind him. He was eventually brought into a small room. Before long, his captors pulled him up off of his feet and placed him against a hard surface, where his limbs were hastily secured by leather straps.

Though he struggled to place the sound's origin, Gareth heard a man's voice.

"Leave us."

He'd never heard the gaolers utter so much as a syllable. There was someone else there, a person who could control the strange patrolmen. In the deepest recesses of his brain, where the core of his consciousness still functioned, Gareth realized that it might be the facility's namesake. A person who could not only resist their gaze but command them at least confirmed his importance.

A shuffling of cloth was joined by the clack of a door being closed. Except for the clicking of heels on the hard floor, the room was near silent.

Away from the gaolers' presence, awareness began to return. It was a rude awakening as his brain sloughed off the miasma which had incapacitated him. A nauseous feeling sank into his stomach.

While he struggled against his bindings, he started to understand his predicament. He was lashed to a table that was now inclined at a steep angle, putting him almost entirely upright. Even as leather straps restrained all four of his limbs, he was able to move his head. A shifting of his hips caused his gear to rattle. Except for his sword, it appeared that the gaolers had not taken anything from him.

Gareth scanned the room. He quickly recognized that he was in some form of research laboratory. Along the outer walls of the two-story chamber was an unbroken string of bookcases and cabinets, many of which stored strange curios, including glass canisters filled with luminous fluids. A randomly-scattered group of tables, many on the periphery of his vision, was loaded down with equipment. Gareth was left to assume the entrance was behind him, since he saw no door.

The room's strangest feature, though, was an opening, two yards in diameter, left uncovered on the other side of the chamber. The brick-laid lip stood just knee-height above the floor. At first, Gareth wondered why there would be a well inside the building. However, he noticed no scent of well-water in the air. In fact, the atmosphere was curiously dry, almost to the point of discomfort.

When his head fell backwards, he spotted an elaborate construct of track railing which hung from the ceiling. This terminated in a rectangular mechanism mounted precariously over the chasm. Gareth wondered if the slab on which he'd been tied was attached.

As Gareth continued to thrash in vain, a man strolled around from behind him and headed straight for the nearest table. Sporting a mop of fine silver locks, he was dressed in a three-piece suit that appeared to have seen better days. There were frayed seams, and both cuffs were dirty and discolored. Once-polished shoes, now scuffed to a dull luster, tapped on the uncarpeted flooring. Long, thin fingers ran along the collected equipment as he attempted to locate some object. He grunted in dissatisfaction and stood to full height as he glanced at one of the other covered surfaces.

Eventually, he turned back to Gareth and gave him an examining glance. Within the sallow, wrinkled features were cold green eyes that moved slowly as he eyed his captive. A slender arc of white beard rimmed his angular jawline. His lips were pursed joylessly as the creases in his forehead deepened. There was a manic quality about his movements, as if he could not help the persistent flutters that twitched his hands and face.

When he couldn't take the extended silence any longer, Gareth spoke up.

"Lyceed?" Gareth croaked. His mouth felt as if it was full of fluids. He coughed to clear his throat.

"An astute assumption," Lyceed eventually replied with a sardonic cock of his brow. "Considering the conditions of the city, at large, and the fractured nature of Dineothan's scientific community, one with any knowledge of history would have to assume that a Lyceed would take residence within these ancestral halls. Though, by your appearance and the outfit you wear, I would hazard a guess that you were originally not a local. You came from abroad, yes? Perhaps someone who knew of my lineage thought to send you my way."

Lyceed took a few paces forward and stopped within arm's reach of Gareth. After examining Gareth's attire, a scowl appeared on his face. His nostrils flared as he leaned in.

"You exude a particularly… delicious smell," Lyceed announced as he drew in a whiff through his nose. "Though, I don't notice the usual sanguine notes. You've benefited from one of the city's more peculiar aspects but not yet allowed yourself to take that final step. Shown restraint where so many others didn't. Upelstbohr is as you see it because so many others lost control. Maybe you've salivated over a recent kill. You would not be the first I've met to struggle against the desire. By the look of disgust in your eyes, I would wager that you have."

At this, Gareth lashed out. "What do you know about that? What I've been told so far sounds… it sounds ridiculous, at best. Horrifying, at worst."

Lyceed wagged a finger in response.

"Well, then, at least tell me what you're doing here," he implored as his expression softened.

"Why, continuing my research is all. Now that I have all the time in the world, I can finally make the breakthroughs my father, and his before him, failed to accomplish." Lyceed turned back to his table. "Usually, I would have had you gagged. I'm not one to converse with subjects as if we are equals, but it's been some time since I've had proper company. And you can certainly attest, the gaolers are not suitable conversationalists."

"So, are you the twisted mind who created them? Those… gaolers?" Even though he knew his tone was contentious, Gareth continued. He hoped to keep Lyceed occupied as he wiggled free of the bindings. Even though the leather dug into his wrists with every tug, he persisted.

Lyceed tapped a finger on the tip of his chin. "The gaolers? Oh, no, no. Far beyond the skills of one with only a single lifetime to learn. Even with the unexpected extension as it is, I've developed no such expertise. They predate even my time on this earth. Possibly even those who originally founded Upelstbohr. From best as I understand, their creation was a gift of the Ikkibu to my ancestors. If anything, I and those of my line have been trying to divine the method of their creation."

Gareth sneered at Lyceed's rambling. It was clear he had a breadth of knowledge, but perhaps his time here in the asylum had given him a strange bent.

"Could I understand how they were assembled, by what reason their existence is propelled, I might understand the means of their generation. Most curious is their disinterest with mankind's pursuit of cannibalistic consumption as a means to further one's status in the hierarchy. You see, they have no interest in flesh. I tried feeding them once only to have them ignore the offering. Perhaps they already know their place and have no desire to advance above it. Truly a sign of the perfect servitor race. Not like the Ikkibu, who rose against their makers when it best suited them."

As Lyceed continued, Gareth tugged on the straps. Their mountings protested against the struggle. At one point, when Lyceed shifted in place, Gareth was certain that the noise had drawn his captor's notice.

"And back to the earlier topic… You must understand that I am deeply focused on my life's work. Much like my father and his father before him. Ancestral in nature, though I feel that the days in which a modicum of success would have brought forth glory for the Lyceed name have passed. What with the city being mostly deserted and all. Now, the discovery—the knowledge gained—will have to be reward in and of itself. But I digress…"

He turned about to face Gareth, who slumped against the table.

"In the old Mericoinne, it is known as

akalumaʾelusepsu. The process of transferring one's energies from a single lifeform to another. While there have always been tomes postulating about willingly passing such power back and forth, the practical application has always been a bit more… *consumptive* in nature. Destroying the source—eating their flesh, as it were—in such a fashion proved *difficult* to repeat. True, it provided good data and you could gather up more specimens, but they were never exactly the same. Their energies varied from person to person. Based on a number of factors, including what they, themselves have consumed. And the hallmark of good science is being able to reproduce your experiment, is it not? That was until Elgretamon of the Aurul Halls and his kind allied with those from the College and set forth in motion events which solidified Upelstbohr's current status—being caught up in a temporal anomaly they could not correct."

"I'm afraid I don't exactly understand," Gareth stated. Maybe, in a fit of recounting, Lyceed would turn his attention to the bookcases for reference material.

"Ah, forgive me for not simplifying it for the layman. As your attire so clearly announces, you're a man of combat rather than of learning. Hmm…" He tapped on his chin as he looked over his shoulder for a moment. "How best to proceed?" he muttered.

When Lyceed turned back to Gareth, it took everything he had not to groan.

"The first signs of such interests turned up in perverse soirées held by secret societies hundreds of years ago. The rich wishing to feel above the rabble partook of forbidden meats. It wasn't long before some realized that the rush they received was not from flouting publicly-accepted morality alone, but from the consumption itself. They discovered that there were added benefits in such practices. They became stronger, more agile, heartier in constitution. A few, who of course wished to remain nameless, were benefactors of those early minds who founded the Grand College. Of course, those in the know did not wish to let this get out. As you can imagine, they did not want the kind of unending violence in the streets that this would facilitate. That such secrets could be kept for long…"

Lyceed scoffed as he strode off towards a bookcase on the far end of the room. Shocked by the sudden movement, Gareth forgot to resume his work against the bindings for a few seconds. When he saw that his captor was distracted, he began to pull hard with his left arm.

Lyceed ran a finger along the spines of his collection. As he did, he spoke over his shoulder.

"You must understand that it was not well-known, amongst the scientific community, of the source of such influences. It would be decades before they came across the last of the Mericoinne, Dineothan's original residents, and even longer before they were introduced to the alien Ikkibu and their masters, the Begeondan. I've not read an account of any man who went to entreat with the Begeondan who then returned. If the scribes that once resided at the Aurul Halls to the north can be believed, such men merely ceased to exist."

After pulling a leather-bound tome pulled from one shelf, Lyceed slowly returned to his detainee. He opened the book and began to flip through the pages.

"Discovery of akaluma'elusepsu, and the Ikkibu in particular, opened up all manner of new avenues for the scientific community. What knowledge they deigned to bequeath to us was so beyond our own comprehension that we willingly accepted each scrap as if it was the last meal we were to enjoy. So wrapped up in the halcyon days of discovery they were that some of us were careless with the secrets of their science.

"One might suggest that it was far too late when we eventually realized our folly. That knowledge of such practices became public. Instead of being repulsed, some chose to join in. There was still hope in many that they could address the course of the calamity. In months, the streets were awash with blood. Any efforts by those in charge to corral the madness were soon abandoned. True, I was allowed to collect a number of the affected under the auspices of research. When the master of Upelstbohr's Sanitorium convinces legislators and lawmen that it's madness, they become receptive to the idea that your work will possibly lead to a cure.

"Those who remained at the College—Elder Paimon and his ilk—focused on more temporal solutions to the riots. They thought to turn back time itself, as if that would keep knowledge of the practices hidden. I and my own looked forward to embracing the new way. That the presence of akaluma'elusepsu itself, as acquired by the populace during their feeding frenzy, was catalyst for the next step in mankind's evolution."

After scanning a few lines, he closed the book and set it on the table behind him.

"The richest of ironies was that those who came to the Sanitorium and the College hoped we might tend to the madness. It caught on like a plague and even those soldiers who were sent in to police the wards eventually failed to resist its allure. Little did they know their malady was caused by those who might help. The rich lords, who'd already partaken of flesh in their secret societies. The scientists and doctors of the College, who'd toyed with unearned leaps in understanding. That, at its core, the practice of akaluma'elusepsu was not of this world. That it would eventually turn them into Dalhakhu—the foulkin as I'm sure you've heard them called. Some of the afflicted, when they saw what they were becoming, scurried to the College, with the hopes that the greatest minds in all of Upelstbohr could cure them, but when Elder Paimon toyed with the fabric of time itself, many were damned right where they lay bent in supplication."

At this revelation, Gareth's attention focused fully on Lyceed. Had the scientist revealed something that Gareth had only recently considered? Plainly, he'd admitted that the foulkin were once men.

Unfazed by Gareth's suddenly-increased interest, Lyceed droned on.

"Those of the College failed to understand the complex foundation upon which their work was built. To them, it was similar to the practices of applying leeches and bloodletting. They were on to learning things beyond their ability to grasp. My ancestor, Carl Lyceed, knew it was best to recommend caution about the gifts handed to man by the Ikkibu and those that came before them. He quickly grasped that not everything learned could be reproduced by mankind without taking the time to study the proper scientific fundamentals to employ them. Carl was fond of saying that there are no shortcuts to knowledge."

By now, Gareth's patience had worn thin. Rather than let Lyceed continue, he chose to speak up. "Are there no doctors left? No one who might be of aid?" There was a pang of distress in his words. "I was told to come to Dineothan. That I might find someone here. The plague. It's sweeping through my homeland and I need the help of someone…"

The inquiry itself seemed curious to Lyceed. "Are you… oh, my! You're… you're newly-arrived, are you not? I hadn't even considered the notion. I'd merely assumed you'd been in the city for some time now—after the worst of the violence had settled—and only just found your way to the upper wards. So many survivors still hidden away, fearing the Dalhakhu that wander the streets. Oooohhh… So fresh, so new. You've yet to understand the permanence of your situation. Little do you understand that one does not enter Dineothan through normal means. As such, the Gatekeeper is a capable ferryman, one who is richly rewarded by those Ikkibu who act as his attendants. Your passing across the Gape made you a part of the island's cycle."

The muddled reply raised Gareth's ire. For the first time since his arrival, he openly struggled against his restraints.

"Are you not capable of a straight answer?" he barked. This caused Lyceed to recoil. "Is NO ONE on this God-forsaken rock capable of that? Tell me that someone in this fucking city is capable of helping me! That I didn't waste the last days of my family's life when I should have been with them!"

After a moment, Lyceed smirked. "You've seen the Dalhakhu which infest the streets, have you not? Any *man* capable of curing a plague for you has either become one of them or fallen prey to them. The College is in no state to help and I assure you there is no one *here*."

At this, Gareth screamed in an almost-feral rage. His limbs thrashed. Spittle flew from his mouth as he howled. His grasp on his senses fled as he writhed violently. An incoherent string of invectives spilled forth, all directed at the scientist who patiently waited for him to run out of steam.

It took some time but, once Gareth was done, he slumped against his restraints. The skin around his wrists was raw and he felt no closer to freedom. Despondency swelled in the core of his chest.

"Not all is lost," Lyceed noted with the faintest hint of sympathy as his brows curled upwards. "But I fear that you've wasted your time with those who remain. The lesser minds that have come to accept their condition as it is. You're better off to inquire with those who may still have a solution, even if it is on a grander scale. Perhaps the last of the Ikkibu still reside at the Aurul Halls, the Mericoinne temple erected on the edge of the Black Basalt Fields. I've not had the pleasure of reacquainting the Lyceed name with those who best understand their Begeondan masters. Those who once served before many of their creators began a pilgrimage to their own realms."

Gareth was too spent for Lyceed's peculiar explanation to make sense. He barely understood what the man was saying. Lyceed's replies were structured like normal conversation, but the jargon and the vague revelations only served to jumble Gareth's thoughts. Gareth felt just as far from his goals as when he'd arrived by sailing dory to the island of Pilsu-kimah.

Lyceed strode up beside him and leaned in. He drew in a deep breath through his nose.

"You must understand how rare it is to come across someone as fresh as you. Your every fiber seems primed to absorb the energies still running rampant within the city. Throughout the perpetual cycle, the energy is passed between those who only grow more resistant to it—the process of akaluma'elusepsu—as time progresses, in so much as it can. Yourself, though, you're like a virgin piece of cloth, only soiled at the edges. One could still wring you clean if they were so inclined."

Contemplatively, he again tapped at his chin.

"There is something *special* about you. Once, I would have jumped at such a quality specimen as yourself, but I've spent much time in contemplation.

Practical testing on live subjects is something I'm generally disinclined to continue. Or for any length of time. And yet, I was curious as to why the gaolers brought you to me. They aren't exactly talkative about their motivations. I'm left to assume you were an unwelcome visitor, which only begged further questions. Now that I know why you came here—in search of a cure for a plague—I can only assume someone in the lower wards passed you onto me. No one left in the Grand College to think for themselves, eh?"

With tears in his eyes, Gareth nodded softly.

"Victims of their own folly, I say." Lyceed grinned. After a long pause during which he peered into Gareth's face, he continued. "You might wonder—or perhaps you don't since you've been far too focused on your own freedom—why I felt the need to regale you with such a comprehensive explanation about the situation as it is. Truth be told, I've lacked quality companionship and speaking on a matter of which I'm familiar is a rare comfort. Beyond that, though, is a recent curiosity that I felt the need to indulge. In all the experiments to test my theories on akaluma'elusepsu, I have always focused on the more visceral nature of the condition. The consumption of flesh, as it were. True, in akaluma'elusepsu's current state, there is transference found in physical conquest without the need of ingestion—you gain merely by defeating your opponents as the energy is siphoned from them—but I found myself wondering if a noticeable uptick in power could be measured when someone is provided knowledge, via literary or verbal communication. That the passing of information might have as much of a reward on someone as striking down one of the Dalhakhu. Had I the foresight—"

Jingle. Jingle.

When he heard a bell ring out from somewhere else in the facility, Lyceed stopped midsentence. He turned his head to the side and listened intently. He grunted disappointedly.

"It appears as though the Sanatorium is a rather popular location. Perhaps a friend of yours decided to join you. No?" He looked at Gareth, who only shook his head. "A sad admission. Well then, it's merely a matter for the gaolers. I'm certain I will be receiving a new subject all too soon. Perhaps I will be more careful with the new visitor this time."

Lyceed bit at his lower lip as deep creases marred his pale forehead.

"In truth, I feel I may have ruined you as a viable specimen. Too hasty was I to ramble on as if you were a welcome visitor that I didn't even think to take a measure of you beforehand. Tainted you. It was the rankest of amateur mistakes, I'm afraid. One I won't make again." He chuckled as his eyes widened. "Interacting with you ruined the experiment, and now that you're aware of it, I have to no choice but to discard of you."

Once Lyceed disappeared behind him, Gareth felt the device which held him slowly roll forward. His head jerked back and forth for a few seconds. He was being moved towards the open pit. The persistent rattle of multiple bells sounded.

Jingle. Jingle. Jingle. Jingle. Jingle. Jingle.

"At the very least, you should be thankful the gaolers have no interest in akaluma'elusepsu. You would have made a fine meal for them," Lyceed continued. "Likewise, I have no stomach for it myself. I prefer to think of myself as a control group, only taking in knowledge." The strain in his voice hinted that the constant ringing was getting to him. Perhaps the gaolers had not yet captured their prey.

Once he was against the cavity's lip, Gareth felt his forward movement halt. The heels of his boots dangled just above the brick-laid edge.

"Not to worry, my good man," Lyceed commented from somewhere behind Gareth. "The fall will not kill you. In fact, in your current state, I would say that the worst you'll suffer is a bump on the head. Or a few abrasions which will fade within moments. That is not to say that you'll get away without issue."

Lyceed came up beside him as he lowered his voice. In one hand was a cube-shaped device which connected to his restraints via a pneumatic tube. On the top was a toggle switch. His thumb rested at the side.

"I've been dumping my failed experiments for some time. Of those who were not already dead, a few *might* have survived. But, that isn't the worst of it. You might wish to keep an eye out for the one known as Madame Victross. I heard she was, at one point, referred to as the Governess in Blue. For some time as I understand it. If fortune is with you, she's still wandering the lower wards.

Never quite understood the reason for her patrols. If she's not abroad, she'll've returned to the catacombs that she calls home. I only tell you on the odd chance that we meet again. If so, I might ask you to convey your experiences with her to me."

He flicked the switch and released the contraption as a small gust of air rushed through the tubing. The straps across Gareth's wrists and ankles went slack. The leather bindings flipped aside and Gareth felt gravity take over. His weak limbs were unable to grasp the table as he slid downwards.

One of his heels hit the outer edge of the pit's lip and he tumbled forward. His vision went dark as he dropped like a rock. For a moment, he was certain he heard the insistent tolling of bells from above.

Jingle. Jingle. Jingle. Jingle. Jingle. Jingle.

The impact knocked him unconscious.

CHAPTER ELEVEN

The Governess in Blue

Gareth did not dream.

In his unconscious state, there were no phantoms of Nattia and Shea. There were no hazy remembrances of familiar places. Instead, there was nothing but unending darkness as he lay comatose.

Eventually, he came to, groggy and sore. He was face-down on a mound of something that yielded under his shifting weight. He could feel that it was mushy in places and hard in others. There were brittle sticks and clumps of ragged fabric on what had to be a long-untended trash heap. He quickly pushed thoughts of the pile's contents aside, if only for the sake of his sanity.

As his head began to clear, he noticed a pain along the side of his skull. In the fall, he'd taken a blow to the scalp that now ached like a bad tooth. His wrists were still sore and as he moved about, Gareth could feel multiple contusions on his arms and legs. That he had no broken bones was fortuitous.

When his eyes fluttered open, he was momentarily relieved that he wasn't smothered in darkness. White flames flickered faintly in wall-mounted sconces along the main gallery. On either side of the great hall was a pair of aisles, separated from the central space by a series of low-hanging archways. Some of the support columns had given way over time and were now mounds of broken brick and mortar.

On either side of him, a number of alcoves were filled with the dried-out remains of the dead. The bones, some of which were still wrapped in decaying cloth, were packed tightly into the recesses. The aging brickwork and the number interred in this underground ossuary made Gareth wonder how long the Lyceed family had been dumping bodies. There was some evidence that at one time someone worked at the site. Though coated in dust, an assortment of tools was left to one side. Maybe city officials had used this vault for Upelstbohr's burial needs; it couldn't serve just to hide Lyceed's failures. Gareth reasoned there was no way he and his entire family line could have gone through so many thousands without drawing attention to themselves.

Gareth slowly attempted to prop himself up. After shaking his head, which caused more discomfort than he liked, he glanced downwards. Though he expected it, he was still horrified to discover that he'd landed on a pile of bodies in varying states of decay. While some had once been human, others looked like foulkin. A layer of scattered bones crunched as he moved. Before he could utter a shocked moan, a gloved palm reached across and clasped his mouth.

As he recoiled, Gareth attempted to turn and face the hand's owner. In the chamber's low light, it took a moment to recognize that it was Naze who'd crept up beside him. Once their eyes met, she withdrew her arm.

"Where did you come from?" he muttered as he sat upright. His voice carried further than he'd expected as it bounced off of the brick walls.

"Shh." She tapped a finger on her lips and pointed upwards.

After a few deep breaths, which were sour with the scent of decay, Gareth glanced to the opening above him. Backlit by a pinhole of light from Lyceed's laboratory, a length of rope swayed back and forth. The end was a full two yards out of reach. No sound emanated from above. Somehow, she'd managed to elude Lyceed's gaolers. Curiosity almost convinced him to inquire how.

"We have ta go," she whispered in his ear. A hint of incense wafted from her clothes and caused his eyes to burn.

Though he wanted to protest, he bit his tongue. With an offered hand, Naze helped him to his feet and motioned with a wave for him to follow.

It took a few seconds for his gait to become stable. The impact had rung his bell. Gareth was a little relieved that he wasn't in the middle of a battle. Or, at least, he thought he wasn't. The fear in Naze's face and her insistence on quiet caused him some apprehension.

The throbbing caused him to wince as his right eye watered.

The pair scurried beneath one of the archways and paused as Naze dug into her pack. Still a little rattled, Gareth waited for her to continue.

"Use this only if yew have ta," Naze said as she pressed a bottle into his grasp. For a brief moment, he glanced down. Once he noticed the frayed rag tucked into the mouth, he quickly understood. It was a weapon of last resort; employing it would alert anyone nearby of their presence.

Gareth passed it from one palm to the other until he realized he had nowhere to store it. There were no free loops on his belt and all of his pouches were meant for smaller objects. None of the pockets in his jacket were big enough. He shrugged his shoulders and kept it in hand as he followed Naze.

Crouched over, she scurried from the shelter of one shadow to the next. Her head jerked back and forth scanning for some unseen assailant. When a stone clattered to the ground a few yards to their left, she flattened herself against the nearest structure. Only after it was clear there was no immediate danger did she continue.

Just as they moved behind another dilapidated pillar, an ominous halo of aquamarine light pulsed on the far end of the chamber. Gareth knew that they were no longer alone. Naze's apprehension was justified. He'd already assembled the bits and pieces of evidence. He knew what was coming their way and that they should give it a wide berth. Still, he admitted, even if only to himself, that he was far more curious than scared.

A clicking of heels on the cobblestone floor was joined by the sound of fabric dragging behind the approaching entity. There was a faint wheeze, like wind through hollow reeds. A jangling of metal rang hollowly against the stone walls.

Entranced, Gareth craned his neck to the side. If it was the Governess in Blue, as Lyceed had earlier suggested, he wanted to witness the horrific abomination that haunted these catacombs. Before he could see anything, Naze tugged on his arm. He scowled at her but acquiesced as she dropped to a crouch and slowly moved between the shadows.

Following her lead, Gareth kept an eye on the nearing figure. Just as he slipped behind a mound that had once been a stone column, it came into stark view.

Gareth almost muttered aloud when he recognized the frilly, cobalt-hued dress. Hastily, he covered his mouth and stopped. Gone was his earlier bravado, now replaced with alarm. His sense of self-preservation took charge.

It was the same woman who he'd wanted to rescue in Chorazin; the one whose presence served to repel the foulkin.

With his breath held, Gareth watched as the female form continued down the center of the chamber. Aloft in one hand was the familiar lantern; its blue-white beam lit up the surrounding area. Gareth now could see her features through the gossamer fabric of her headdress. There was soft, porcelain skin and a few blonde strands swayed back and forth like doll's hair. Her mouth hung limply and her eyes were not unlike glazed marble. The lamp's light reflected hauntingly off their polished surfaces.

Gareth retreated to follow Naze. The Governess showed no indication that she'd become aware of the pair.

As they continued to creep along, Gareth noticed something familiar at the end of the main chamber. A stone obelisk was carved with the image of a bride holding a lantern in one hand. Much like those in the Grand College and within Lyceed's Asylum, this sculpture matched the ones inside the Chorazin sanctuary. The woman's countenance also bore an uncanny resemblance to the Governess.

Beyond this was a wide archway connected to a staircase that led away, perhaps to the outside world. By the angle of Naze's course, Gareth knew that was where they were headed.

Not wanting to be left behind, he picked up his own pace. As he did, he stumbled over a clump of broken bricks in his path. An oblong chunk bounded off the toe of his boot and skipped twice.

Shit.

He grimaced as his body tensed. After a moment of unnerving silence that felt interminable, he heard the Governess let out a bone-chilling shriek. Gareth flinched at its punishing volume. He glanced over his shoulder to catch sight of her as she spun around. With the lamp held aloft, its beam scanned the room. Beneath the high-pitched feminine screech was another sound, a deep low-pitched roar that rattled the floor with its bass notes. Her mouth remained in its locked position.

As the layered howl cut through the air, a chill ran down Gareth's spine. Even though he felt compelled to look at the Governess, he resisted. By the time he turned back around, Naze was in a full sprint ahead of him. Not wanting to lose sight of her, he chased after Naze. He hadn't moved two full strides before he heard the rumbling of movement from all corners of the room.

From the spaces between the stacked corpses poured forth an inky blackness. In the brief glimpses taken as he glanced backwards, Gareth watched as the obsidian gel began to coalesce. Limbs tore their way out of the darkened goo as their membranes hardened into a leathery skin. Clawed hands clutched at the nearby architecture, as if they were attempting to drag themselves into this world.

Gareth had seen enough. He turned back to Naze, who was already clear of the chamber, and picked up his speed. He'd never been the fastest runner in the world, but fear proved enough incentive.

Even as he charged up the steps, he could feel them giving chase. The raucous clatter of nails on the ground rang out as a horde of creatures clambered after the pair.

He eventually realized that he still clutched the bomb in hand. Gareth dug out a match and attempted to strike it.

He struggled to light the explosive. His hands

bounced back and forth as he fought to keep pace with Naze. Despite the clear danger, he knew he had to stop for a moment. He could feel the howling flock on his heels, compelled by the Governess to give chase. What they would do if they caught him was something about which Gareth did not want to think.

Gareth's heart was racing as he skidded to a halt and finally got the match burning. He ran it under the fluid-soaked fabric. It was aflame almost instantly.

He twisted just enough to pitch the burning bottle behind him. The world went into slow-motion as the bomb arced towards the approaching mass. In that moment when liquid flared into a conflagration, Gareth finally saw the Governess's creatures.

There were dozens of them, attempting to retreat from the flames in vain. Bunched so closely together, it was difficult to determine their unique dimensions. Hunched over, none appeared to stand taller than waist-height. Strangely-angled limbs, some with three or four joints, flailed as they recoiled from the fire. Masses that approximated heads were covered in curling horns that stuck out in all directions. While there was an unnerving hiss that issued from the creatures, Gareth could not see any orifices from which the noise issued.

The blaze had done its work. A quartet, close on his heels, dropped to the ground as their bodies became burnt husks. As they did, Gareth could feel the rush as their energies transferred into him. By now, it wasn't unexpected. Still, the feeling emboldened him. If he'd had his sword, he might have considered standing his ground.

Unlike the foulkin, these were uninterested in their fallen brethren. Within seconds, the lifeless forms had decomposed into tar-like lumps. Those that remained were preoccupied with the wall of fire that barred them.

"Keep moving!" Naze called out from up ahead. As the flames began to wane, he took off. It was only seconds later that he heard the clamor of their renewed pursuit.

On the run again, Gareth attempted to locate Naze. She was far enough ahead of him that he struggled to keep an eye on her in the catacomb's faint lighting.

He lost sight of Naze as she swung a hard right around a nearby corner. As Gareth followed suit, he spotted amber light from an exit in the distance. Naze's silhouette was framed in the promising halo as the pair rushed towards freedom. Though anticipation lifted his spirits, he was still keenly aware of the Governess's minions on his tail.

Though he ran as fast as possible, he felt no further from his pursuers. Even worse, he was certain they were closing the distance with each stride. Their limbs flailed furiously as they scrambled after him. A chorus of inhuman screeches and wailing buffeted the back of his head. He could hear their claws dig into the stone-laid path.

As the image of their horrifying forms in the bomb's flare popped into his head, Gareth focused on his escape. With each stride, the archway engulfed more of his vision. The exterior light became brighter.

He'd never had to run for his life before. This wasn't like a tactical retreat, where he needed to keep his guard up as he backed away. He was without his sword with a legion of shadows that would kill him, or worse, if they captured him. Before him was potential freedom, or at least an opportunity to regroup in a more favorable location.

He didn't even notice that the scuttling of his attackers had abated.

Once through the opening, Gareth was certain he'd find himself back in Upelstbohr's lower wards. Instead, they charged out into a barren valley, devoid of anything except gray, wind-blasted soil. Flanking them on both sides was a series of earthen ridges, rising to a height of a hundred yards from the basin floor. Behind them was a cliff-face that towered high above their position. Though he could not see the facility, Gareth was certain that Lyceed's Asylum would be located at the top.

A quick glance at the gorge revealed only two sets of tracks. The first followed Naze as she pressed on ahead. The other, which appeared to weave southwards, looked as though someone had dragged a length of heavy cloth behind them to obscure any footsteps. He took this to be the Governess's trail as she'd returned to the ossuary only minutes ago.

Naze came to rest a few dozen yards from the cavern's entrance. She leaned over and placed hands on her knees as she drew in long breaths. Wheezing slowly but eventually tapered off. Beads of sweat dripped from the tip of her nose to the gray soil below.

Gareth, on the other hand, wasn't even remotely winded. There was a little ache in his thighs, but this was dwarfed by the persistent pain in his head. He reached up and felt the lump above his ear.

"Have they given up?" Gareth inquired as he glanced over his shoulder. In the stark afternoon glow, the barren valley appeared empty. The horde, which had been hot on his heels, was nowhere to be seen. There was no evidence of life: no birds crossing the sky, no lizards or bugs scurrying across the dirt, and not even the smallest of green foliage. It was as if the valley had been blasted clean.

Naze finally stood upright as she wiped at her brow. "Best I can tell, it seems like it. Got too far away from their master, I'd say. Still, we should put a little more distance between us and them, fer good measure."

Gareth nodded at the suggestion. As he turned back and continued to follow Naze, another question came to mind. "What are they? Those... *things* that chased us."

"D'know. Don't care, ta be frank about it. Just that I don't want them ta lay a hand on me. You saw that place... her *lair*, fer lack of a better word. Can't imagine that anything good'll come of being there fer longer than we were. Not all the bodies there were interred by the proper authorities, if yew catch my meaning."

Gareth grunted with dissatisfaction.

They pressed on and eventually arrived at a slope that led out of the valley. As they ascended, patches of verdant life became more frequent. While the trees and bushes appeared scrawny and malnourished, Gareth was relieved to see something approximating a normal landscape. He'd endured enough of the Dineothan's strange scenery for one lifetime.

Naze suggested that they stop to rest. It did not take long for Gareth to agree. Despite his energized condition, which had been recently bolstered to new heights, the aching of his head persisted. For the first time in this place, he felt a lingering pain that failed to quickly fade. On top of this, a cold wind came in from the west and cut him to the bone. Without Upelstbohr's dense architecture for a buffer, they were naked against the stiff breeze.

The pair collected handfuls of dried timber, most of which came from downed trees, and assembled a small fire. Hidden behind an overhanging slab of earth, they reclined beside the diminutive blaze. A few powerful gusts threatened to snuff out the adolescent flames. Gareth took off his gloves and held out his hands to absorb the heat into his palms.

"Maybe it's too late to ask, but are we safe here?" Gareth inquired. Memories of the Governess's horde and their horrid cacophony haunted him. They had all been so similar in color and shape that, even now, he struggled to discern where one ended and the next began. It was as if they were all part of a singular organism. Only when set ablaze did they separate, shed like dead skin cells.

"As safe as can be expected," Naze replied as she

stretched out. "If'n yu'r frettin' over her givin' us tha chase, fear not. We're well far enough away from Governess normal rounds."

"And how can you be so sure?"

"I've been about enough ta know where she goes. A long time ago, I was far more curious than I am now," Naze announced. "Far more cavalier. I can'nae say I know her mind—and by the lords above, I'm grateful—but I've nae ever seen her stray too far off'n her path. A creature of habit, maybe. More'n likely she's treading an old and familiar trail from a previous life. Maybe a teeniest bit of what she used ta be is still in there, keeping her on her patrol."

"A previous life?"

"Before she became what she is. I don't know exactly what. Like a ghost, trapped ta somewhere familiar. Somethin' unnatural. Supernatural."

Gareth did not press the matter. Whatever the reason, her monstrous minions had given up. For that, he was grateful.

"So, why did you leave Chorazin? You had no interest in leaving, much less following after me. When last we spoke, you were pretty clear on the matter. Something change your mind?"

This query caused her some discomfort. After a few seconds of dour silence, in which she stared at the fire, she spoke up. "Truth be told, I saw Alharrad slipping in ta Bethsaida. Headin' fer tha College. Thought he might be trailing yew and I wanted ta make sure he wasn't up ta nothing ill."

Gareth eyed her warily. "And again, you talk as if you're well familiar with him."

"We are blood kin," she announced matter-of-factly. "Seems like fate that tha Collette family line is always drawn ta Dineothan. Unlike many others who came before—and after—I did'nae come ta pillage, ta rob tha citizenry. Me? I came in search o' my ancestry. My father told a story that his parents volunteered ta go into Upelstbohr and aid in tha early riots. Ta help with bringin' peace back ta tha city streets. D'know tha finer details, but their lords knew something of tha unrest, feared it ta be some kind of revolt, and sent troops ta curb it afore it made its way ta tha mainland. None expected that no one would return."

"So, you came here to find your family?" he said with a nod. "Or to uncover what happened to them? I can... I can understand that. And your plans to return once you were done here?"

This caused Naze to look down wistfully. She appeared to struggle with sorrow. "Had not considered that matter at tha time. When I left, I told my children I'd not be gone fer long. Now here, I realize that tha way back is... not safe fer someone like me. Too, uh... time... too much time has passed."

Gareth opened his mouth, but before he could comment, she continued. It was a clear diversion from a painful subject.

"Things are strange here. Time itself doesn't work exactly right. Have yew not noticed it yet? Surely, you've seen the signs of it everywhere. How time stands still?"

She motioned to the sun, which was seemingly locked in place.

He gave her a curious glance, as if the notion itself was madness. Eventually, his features softened. All the evidence had been there since he first left the sanctuary in Chorazin. No matter how long he walked, it always felt like afternoon. His head grew fuzzy and his body slumped. Gareth let out a long breath and attempted to shake the haziness from his mind. Even if he had no idea how long he'd been on the island or what the true time of day was, he couldn't ruminate on it for too long. His brain couldn't handle the implications of that concept.

I have to… to be able to get back in time. Find a cure and get back. Doesn't matter if "time stands still," whatever that means… I can't linger for too long. Been away for too many days as it is.

After giving him a few moments to pull himself together, Naze continued. "Look ta tha sun. Even through tha worst of tha island's haze, you can tell it hasn't moved since y'ur arrival. We're stuck here, in perpetual daytime."

"I, uh, I guess I knew that something was off, but…"

"It's something those at tha Grand College did. D'know what it was but its derailed things mighty good. I long ago lost track of how much time I've spent here. I canna go back. There's no tellin' how long ago it was when I left. Considering what I've been witness ta, I think it's more days than a body can be permitted. Maybe I step off tha island and Father Time catches up with me all at once. Dead and turned ta dust afore I'm two steps towards home."

There were implications there Gareth didn't quite grasp. All the same, what he did comprehend made it clear that he needed to be gone from Dineothan sooner rather than later. A part of him wanted to wholly dismiss the matter, as if Naze was merely another person with a tenuous grasp on sanity. He'd experienced his fair share of these people since leaving home.

The pair fell silent for a while. Gareth produced another strip of jerky from a pouch and gnawed at it. Naze prodded the fire with a tree branch, which caused a few embers to float in the updraft.

Eventually, Gareth thought to make idle chatter.

"So, what do you do to kill the time? I mean, you must do more than run across rooftops and watch the foulkin go on about their business. I can't think that it's the most entertaining of time wasters."

This elicited polite laughter from Naze. "No, no, I try not ta spend any more time outside if'n I can avoid it. 'Tis fer tha best, as yew can imagine. In truth, I invest as much o' tha day in readin'. Chorazin's got a couple o' libraries. In their heyday, I imagine they were tha best in this hemisphere. Along the western acreage is tha Grand Ilu's Archives and tha Library o' Mettengauss, both of which have a pretty extensive collection. Of different focuses, mind yew, but between tha two o' them, I can consider myself well-read."

"So, you… read?" Though he didn't mean it that way, it came across as condescending.

"Beats tha alternative. Too much danger in

Upelstbohr fer much else. I've become what yew might call an unofficial savant in terms of Dineothan's long history. Sure, there may be others out there with a better understandin', but I do alright fer myself."

"So, then, you'd be the one to explain what happened here."

Naze chuckled. "Not as much as yew'd like, I think. Both collections were more 'bout tha past rather than more recent events. There gets ta a point where they stopped writin' 'bout it, like they were a bit more concerned o'er what was going on in tha streets."

Gareth swallowed a well-masticated chunk of beef. It sat like a lump in his stomach.

"I'll tell you this much, there were already tales of things like Sindex livin' in tha darker corners o' Dineothan. Other creatures that existed well before tha riots began. Predated it by a fair stretch o' time. At first, people just treated them like old wives' tales ta keep people from diggin' 'bout in places they should nae visit. Then, some of tha scientific community began ta grow interested. Couldn't help themselves from a bit o' professional curiosity. Started writing about entities they called 'anuphilim.' Sent men to peek into tha darkness and report back tha things they saw."

Gareth leaned forward. Though he'd heard the term 'anuphilim' before, he failed to recall where. He'd taken in so much new information that it blurred together.

"The earliest recorded entry I found was some time around 1223. Sir Alles Goodsmith, lord of tha Goodsmith Manse, took a retinue of men with him inta

Abheth Hollow ta track down such a beast. They failed ta do anything more than get themselves killed. Only a handful of men returned, empty-handed, except fer their tale of tha excursion."

"That doesn't sound like the nicest of places."

"T'isn't. From what was detailed in their reports, there are things in there that should not exist."

"And you even considered braving this?"

"Fer a short while before my cowardice got tha better o' me, I'll admit ta being curious. Maybe peeked around a few places I wish I hadn't." She paused briefly. "I have ta say that I am tha kind o' woman now who, upon hearing tha things that bump in the night, chooses not ta bump back. Not any more."

He nodded. "I understand that. No need to brave danger unless it's in your best interest."

Naze paused. Her mouth opened slightly and Gareth was certain she wanted to ask him something. When she shook her head, he took it as a sign that the urge had passed.

"Yew know that Dineothan's not so abandoned as she looks, right?" Naze commented without meeting Gareth's gaze. He was relieved that she'd not pried on matters he did not want to address.

"I've seen a few people already," he noted. "Not a lot, but—"

"More than that," she interjected. "More than those hidin' out in the Halls. Or whoever is still passin' fer livin' at tha College. I'd say there's a few hundred scattered here and there, 'bout the wards, still in hidin'. Some in their homes 'cause they think it's the safest. Others've taken up quarters in some of tha more public buildings."

Gareth's brow furrowed as questions came to mind. As he raised a finger into the air, Naze continued.

"Some're too scared ta leave the places they've always lived in. Others, well… they delude themselves in ta thinking everything's fine as long as they keep up tha façade of a happy home. I think you'd understand that many have lost their damned minds. Be it through grief, terror or merely a lack of understanding of how things got as they are."

That made a lot more sense to Gareth than he liked to admit. He, too, struggled against something that threatened to drag him under. His efforts to push on towards a goal that was always just out of reach kept the worst of it at bay.

Naze spoke up again.

"Did yew at least learn anything from Lyceed? I mean, I assume that's why yew willingly went in there. I've never had reason ta meet with him before and I don't think he was too happy ta see me."

With a sour look, Gareth shook his head.

"He mentioned something about…" Gareth scowled as he trailed off. "Well, he spoke about a lot of things that didn't make much sense. One might think he enjoys rambling. He spoke of someone known as the Ikkibu and a place called the Aurul Halls and the Black Basalt Fields. Any of that sound familiar to you?"

Naze nodded. "Ta some degree. I've read about tha Aurul Halls, erected long ago on tha edge of tha Black Basalt Fields. Tha kinda place no one goes out ta unless they must. Though, once Upelstbohr grew ta power, few people felt a need ta leave tha city. All that's out there now is a few structures from older eras."

"Well, it's as good a lead as any. And the Ikkibu?"

"Hints o' their existence, but no mention of who or what they were. Like no man wanted ta keep a record o' them. Not like tha natives: the Mericoinne. People wrote at length about them. While it was said that they were forced ta flee when tha settlers outnumbered them, I never got tha impression they were under attack. They retreated ta tha northern lands, and since Upelstbohr was established in the south, tha founders let them be. Or, that's how it was written in tha history books."

Gareth sighed. Lyceed had known far more than he was willing to divulge. He thought about the asylum's inhuman staff and a question came to mind.

"So, how did you escape the gaolers? You somehow reached Lyceed's lab unscathed."

Naze let out a small snort of laughter. "I managed ta not get seen."

CHAPTER TWELVE

The Aurul Halls

After a short while, they continued their trek. Gareth stomped out the dwindling fire and joined Naze as she climbed towards the nearby rise. When he inquired where they were headed, she replied with "North, fer now."

He shrugged in response. Though she had seemed reluctant to help him on his journey, Naze led all the same. If they got to higher ground and located a landmark or two, he might feel more confident. If he recalled correctly, Lyceed had mentioned the Aurul Halls were to the north. That helped to temper his uncertainty.

Soon, the pain in Gareth's head began to subside. Whether the walk helped, or time healed, he slowly got relief from the dull ache. Feeling better, Gareth became uncharacteristically chatty.

"So, do you have an idea of where we're going? I

mean, outside of *north*."

"Getting up and out of the shadow of Upelstbohr seems as good a plan as any," she noted without looking back. Her gaze remained focused on the hilltop in the distance.

As best as Gareth could gauge, they were roughly a half hour's walk from the apex.

"Once we get up there—" She pointed ahead of them. "—we should be able ta pick out where next ta head. Gonna be honest, I kinda don't have a solid idea where we are or where ta go."

Naze steadfastly kept facing forward, as if to conceal her expression.

"Shame that Lyceed didn't provide better directions," Gareth spoke drolly. "Probably figured tossing me into that pit was a death sentence. He would have been right if you hadn't come along." For a moment, he thought to thank her, but when he was overcome with embarrassment, he blushed. "I guess we're both running blind into this."

"I've ne'er been out this way afore," she admitted as her voice lowered. "Even in tha earlier days, when I was a bit more adventurous, I saw no reason ta come out beyond tha city limits. What I read about tha northern lands did nae... seem enticin'."

This struck Gareth as curious. Considering Upelstbohr's strange inhabitants, the fact that such a vacant space was deemed dangerous felt odd. "How so?"

"Too many stories of things out here, things that

dug inta tha blasted earth and called it their own. Too many… tales of old structures that pre-dated tha arrival of tha first settlers. Buildings far more complex than should be for tha time. Filled with *things* that even tha native Mericoinne thought ta give a wide berth ta. Too many foolish adventurers went a'lookin' and didn't come back. Tha Tower o' Gomar. And then there was Fort Haederon, this fifteenth-century fortress established on tha frontier, which was lost. They d'know how or why, but by tha time they sent a second squad ta investigate tha outpost, too many men failed ta come back and the commandant at the time, Lord Henry Aultodor, decided ta call it a total loss. I read an entire series dedicated ta that particular stretch of history and that was all it took ta make me want to stay put in Chorazin."

And yet, here you are, Gareth thought as he let out a sarcastic snort. While her suspicions of Alharrad rang true, Gareth began to wonder if there was some other reason she chose to assist him. "Well, you seem to have a fair handle on this situation as it now stands. I'll follow your lead, then."

She looked at him with a scowl. "I guess yu'r not one for makin' yur own decisions are yew?"

Though this irked Gareth, he couldn't exactly argue. While her unvarnished comment was blunt, she wasn't entirely wrong. "I was always paid to take orders. Never spent too much time thinking on my own. Never needed to. Never was a part of a chain of command, so it wasn't in me to think *tactically*. To plot and plan out my course. To figure out where I was going. Pay me enough and I'd do pretty much anything I was told."

"Anything?"

"Well, not anything. There are rules on the battlefield. Certain things that are and aren't acceptable, even to sellswords. A man has to live with himself when he eventually gets home." He nodded solemnly for a moment.

As they continued up the gradual incline, something occurred to Gareth. "And yourself? You have all the signs of someone experienced, though I'm not sure where it comes from. Can't exactly place where you learned. Definitely have some form of survival training from the looks of your equipment."

"Self-taught," she replied matter-of-factly. "Not everyone in tha Collette family took ta tha sword as their first choice of vocations. Those o' my ancestors who could'a taught me were already gone by the time I was old enough ta learn it."

To Gareth, this seemed unlikely, but he let the topic drop. The pair fell silent as they continued their hike.

As Naze neared the cliff's edge, she dropped into a crouch and snuck forward. A few feet from the earthen rim, she crawled on her hands and knees across the raw stone. Though he wasn't certain why, Gareth did the same. Except for the howl of the wind as it tore through the canyon below, he could hear nothing that would warrant such caution. Still, Naze's attentiveness had already served him well.

She stopped within inches of the overhang and peered downwards. Once Gareth came to rest beside

Naze, he did the same.

Spread out below them was a downward-sloping valley that extended for hundreds of yards. On either side was a series of rocky crags. The graded earth formed a natural set of steps in the ever-narrowing gorge until they eventually reached the open plains. There was very little foliage and the soil itself was almost colorless in its grayish hues. Gareth wondered if anything could survive out in such an unforgiving landscape.

In the distance, almost lost among the dusty flatlands, was a group of interconnected buildings, which were surrounded by a barrier wall. Gareth noticed the massive portcullis gate on the fortification's southern face.

"Is that…" he trailed off as he pointed.

"Tha Aurul Halls? Yur guess is as good as mine. If I was a bettin' person, though, I'd say that there is a pretty high chance. Considerin' I don't see nae other place out here and there's only so much land ta cover. It matches the descriptions, especially the recountin' by Earl Margol Petty. Sixteenth-century bloke who braved tha wilds in a so-called pilgrimage. In truth, he was rich and bored—a combo I don't think is so smart fer one wantin' ta live a long life—an' came out this way with tha notion that he'd write about all he saw. He only lived ta write about it because he'd paid some mercenaries ta act as bodyguards fer him."

Gareth rose and brushed the soil from the front of his pants. "Well, we should at least get closer. To get a better view before we climb down into the valley," he suggested.

Though she lingered for a long moment, Naze slowly got to her feet.

They made certain to hug the upper edge of the gorge as they headed to the east. During this leg of their trek, Gareth snuck frequent glances at the landscape below them. Had some natural disaster befallen the northern lands to leave it such a near-lifeless waste? Though he'd never seen such a spectacle before, it reminded him of stories passed on to him by other soldiers; some told of volcanos in the southern kingdoms that ruined large swaths of the countryside in the wake of their violent eruptions. If this area was anything like what they witnessed, he now understood the awe-tinged voices with which such descriptions were relayed.

After some time, Naze dropped to her knees against a craggy overhang. With a flick of her hand, she directed Gareth's attention to the north. Gareth settled in beside her.

He could now make out details of the aging estate. A drab exterior of limestone slabs covered the blocky, interconnected buildings, giving no clue as to its purpose. Certain elements, like the sharply-angled rooflines, suggested that it once served as a plush mansion for someone of eccentric tastes; other structures defied common conventions. A three-story wing, not unlike the one he'd witnessed at the Grand College, stood on the eastern side of the main hall. A bronze dome, now patinated dull green, was erected to the south. Atop this were statues, eerily reminiscent of those he saw on Golyat's Ascent. A chapel spire rose from the back of the property, near the northern boundary.

This alone did not enough to render Gareth speechless. However, the manor was constructed right at the edge where the gray valley met acres of basalt, as if a line had been drawn straight across the earth itself.

Stretching out beyond the complex of aged buildings was an expanse of darkened earth which extended for miles to the fog-obscured coastline. Gareth's eyes narrowed as his neck craned forward. All he could make out was the clear demarcation across the plain where the earth turned a near-black hue.

Without prodding, Naze spoke up.

"If this isn't yur Aurul Halls, I can't imagine what would be. Matches what I've perused ta a 'T.' "

Really? Gareth thought to himself. *Didn't Lyceed refer to it as some kind of temple? Doesn't look a bit like any house of the holy I've seen before.* It occurred to Gareth that, despite his dry nature, Lyceed may have spoken in a mocking fashion. Perhaps it wasn't a religious site in the literal sense.

As he peered intently, his vision failed him for a second. It was as if the buildings flickered out of existence, only to be replaced by an amorphous glimmer of light. Granite and marble were replaced with some blue metallic substance. These iridescent panes slowly pivoted back and forth, as if mounted on clockwork mechanisms.

Before Gareth could make sense of the sight, the

hallucination was gone. Everything returned to its original form and he was left questioning his sanity. He turned to Naze.

Sadly, she was already gone from his side. She'd continued along the cliff's edge. By now, it began to slope downwards into the gorge below. After gawking for a few seconds longer, as if that would provide additional information, he chased after her.

Naze eventually ended the next leg at a small rise in the bluff. She knelt on one knee and waited for Gareth to join her. They were no more than a few hundred yards from the campus.

As they waited and observed the scene from the ridge, Gareth's noticed human forms gathered around the entrance. Extending for hundreds of yards to the south of the portcullis were dozens of statues. These were unlike anything he'd seen before. While each was draped in a grayish-tan robe, they were posed differently, some on their hands and knees in supplication. On the head of each was a similarly-dyed hood, two feet in height and often bent over in one direction or another, adorned by a wreath of entwined twigs.

Before long, Gareth realized that these were not statues, but actual people who remained patiently in place. A stiff breeze barreled through the valley, ruffling the fabric of their clothing. One figure shifted just enough to move his headpiece back to its place.

He recoiled in shock as comprehension sunk in.

"Is that… are they…" he eventually sputtered.

Naze leaned in, as if that would allow her to see them

clearly. After a few seconds, she nodded as she let out a faint hum.

"Worshippers. Mericoinne faithful, if tha uniforms are any indication."

Gareth turned and gave her a look, but said nothing. She responded all the same.

"Lithographic plates from tha collection at tha Grand Ilu's Archives. Back when there were more of them ta be found, I gather." After a few seconds, she stood up and began to move to their right.

He cast another glance at the unmoving congregation before he eventually followed.

"You said they were 'worshippers?' Of what?" he called out to Naze, who failed to respond.

Gareth found the supplicants unnerving. Initially, he thought they were being punished for some offense, but there was no guard or goaler present. Perhaps this was a pilgrimage, where they were forced to linger in anticipation of a future event. Except for the rare moment when one or another gathered up their robe in the face of a particularly stiff breeze, none of them tried to move.

Once they traveled up a ridge to the east of the valley, Gareth was able to catch sight of a few faces. Unlike their bare hands, which were ruddy, their visages were covered in a white, plaster-like coating. Strange symbols, many simple, overlapping circles and arcs, were painted in black on this skin-tight mask.

Before he could repeat his earlier inquiry, Naze

spoke up.

"Are yew certain of this?" Naze cast a sideways glance. "That *this* is where yew want—need—ta go? I get the feeling that this is somewhere, once yew walk through that door, yew don't get ta come back from."

"I've come too far to look back. My family… my family is sick with the plague. This may be my only chance to get something. A cure? Who knows? Lyceed suggested I might find help here. I'm running out…" His jaw set tightly as his eyes narrowed. "If whoever's in there can't help me, well…" A twinge of desolation ached in his chest. The more he considered his situation and what he already knew—what he'd recently learned—the more likely it felt that he was losing precious time. That was if he wasn't already too late.

Time is so strange here. I was already running out when I left. It *was running out… time was,* He corrected himself. *I don't even know how long I've been here. They could already… No, don't think that way.*

He attempted to push his doubts back down.

"Are you certain?" There was concern in her voice.

He turned and met her gaze.

"Look, I'm not tryin' ta pry, any more than I already have. I tried not ta get inta yur business before, because I didn't think yu'd get this far, but now I gotta ask: is all this really worth it? Is there nae other way?" Her mouth hung open, as if she wanted to say something else. That she showed restraint kept Gareth from barking at her.

Gareth fought the impulse to lay it all out for Naze.

He wanted to unload about all his previous failures to find a remedy and the reasons why he couldn't just abandon his quest. There would be nothing left for him if he returned home empty-handed. Dying was a better option than admitting he'd failed to uncover a cure. Gareth might have to concede to the nagging thoughts that he'd left his family behind to die without him. He couldn't decide if he was a coward or a hero at any given moment.

Still, he balked out of a deep-seated fear. Naze was knowledgeable enough about Dineothan's history that she might know if his efforts were in vain—that there was no one in the Aurul Halls to help him. Unlike the others, she might not be happy to just send him along on the next leg of a futile quest. She might care enough to tell him the unpleasant truth. Even if it was to delay the inevitable, he avoided having his hopes dashed.

"Ya know what…" she eventually spoke up as their eyes locked. "Just… uh, just forget it. Yew have yur reasons." Her voice then lowered as she added, "We all have our own reasons fer tha things we do."

The relief was palpable but temporary. Naze was on her feet, moving towards the nearby rocky slope.

"Hey, what are you thinking of doing?" Gareth inquired as he looked over at Naze. He reached out with a flailing hand that just missed her arm.

"Well, if yu're so damned and determined ta get in there, then someone's got ta draw their attention away. I can'nae imagine they'll be so receptive to yew just walking in how you please."

"I… hmmm….." Gareth grunted as he bit at his lip.

"Yew got any *other* questions ta ask?" She hovered on an outcropping that looked poised to collapse. Though he had nothing to add, he paused. Before a full shake of his head was finished, she began her descent.

Gareth waited and watched as Naze crossed to the valley below. Once on the ground, she began to trot towards the nearest cluster of Mericoinne. With each stride, Gareth felt a sympathetic nervousness.

The Mericoinne remained fixed as she scurried towards the outer fringes. Gareth was certain that Naze's approach had not gone unnoticed. Just as she drew within a few yards of the nearest worshipper, Naze picked up her pace. She was upright and in a full sprint by the time she passed the first few.

As she drew in close to the Mericoinne, Gareth finally noticed the size of the natives. Standing at least seven feet in height, they towered over Naze.

None of them even shifted. There was no attempt to turn on the new arrival, even out of curiosity. Surprised, she slowed and cast appraising glances from side to side.

Undaunted, Naze shrugged her shoulders and rushed onward. She only decelerated long enough to yell a few taunts over her shoulder. Gareth struggled to make sense of her words. They garnered no response from the Mericoinne.

Just outside of the barrier wall, Naze came to a stop. She reached down and gathered up a handful of loose rocks. One by one, she began to pelt the nearby Mericoinne with the stones. When this failed to elicit a reaction, she ran over and pushed one of them to the ground. Before the man could return to his feet, she moved on to another and did the same. After toppling a third, she sprinted away to the west, as if they were hot on her heels. She soon became lost to sight beyond a craggy outcropping past the gorge's end.

At first, it seemed as though a few of the Mericoinne would give chase. Eventually, after dusting the soil from their robes, they returned to their places. Before long, it appeared as if nothing had changed.

Gareth steeled himself and began his own descent into the valley. Those posted outside the Aurul Halls seemed unlikely to interfere. Maybe they were forbidden to do so. At least, he thought, with his approach. Perhaps once he attempted to breach the property, they would become more aggressive.

Naze was yet to return; she must have realized that no one had followed her. If she was smart, she'd found somewhere to hole up and observe. He had no choice but to brave the same path himself.

While Naze had moved with cat-like grace, Gareth clumsily stumbled down the sloping rock-face. More than once, he lost his footing and slipped. He picked himself up, each time a little sorer than before, and dusted off his clothes. Once at the bottom, he paused long enough to check himself. He had only a bruise and scrapes, and all of his gear appeared to be in place.

Though he was wary, Gareth continued forward. Despite her best efforts—and she'd made herself particularly unpleasant to a few—the Mericoinne did not chase Naze. As he began to walk among them, he perceived no aura of malice. He felt nothing at all from the statuesque faithful. Still, he didn't feel entirely comfortable. Their unnatural height alone gave him pause. Instinctively, one hand dropped to his holstered gun.

As he strode past them, Gareth examined the Mericoinne with furtive glances. The bare skin of their hands and their necks, which was a dark, reddish hue, was weathered and raw from the bracing wind that tore through the valley. This caused him to wonder how long they'd maintained their vigil. The clay coverings obscured their faces, except for their eyes, most of which were a cold blue. When he looked at the markings on their plaster-coated visages, the icons themselves meant nothing to him, but he had seen something similar before.

The sanctuary... The glass flooring in the sanctuary. The markings are similar to those painted on the floor. These must have some meaning. Too bad I don't have a head for this... science? Math? Writing? Whatever...

He nodded to himself and continued. There was nothing to be gained in lingering among the Mericoinne. They were silent. While he could see twitches of eyelids flickering and the pulses in their taut muscles, they remained immobile.

When he reached the open portcullis, Gareth let out a sigh as though he'd held his breath for hours. The muscles along his back went slack as he slipped through the entryway. He paused under the latticed grill of iron which hung over him like a guillotine's blade. A quick glance over his shoulder confirmed that none of the Mericoinne had moved from their posts.

Once in the main yard, Gareth discovered the ground to be as gray and near-lifeless as the rest of the valley. What Gareth imagined had once been a lush series of topiaries was now row-upon-row of dried-out twigs. A lone paved walkway cut through the desiccated property and led to the porch-lined main hall.

While the exterior had signs of disrepair, the buildings themselves seemed to have weathered the years without too much permanent damage. Except for a few battered windows and some broken shutters, the façade had held up well. Though caked with years of dust, ornately-carved ornamentation cast sharp shadows in the afternoon sunlight.

Even as he nervously looked behind himself on more than one occasion, Gareth continued towards the oak double-doors. He still expected the Mericoinne to break their watch and come for him. Their ceremonial vigil must have some purpose behind it that they wouldn't welcome intruders.

And yet, he walked alone and unmolested.

He scaled a trio of short steps and reached for the brass handle on his right. After a tug, it slowly gave way, as if it had remained unopened for some time. A swath of soil on the terrace's flooring scraped aside in a noticeable arc as Gareth forced just enough of an opening to slip inside.

Once within, he discovered an interior marked by

excess. The architect had a baroque sensibility only made worse by décor that bordered on gauche. Furniture was laden with overly-ornate carvings and many of the glass-paneled doors were etched with overlapping circular patterns. Hallways were choked with furnishings. Almost every swath of the green damask wallpaper not covered by bookcases or curio cabinets was hidden with oil paintings; though many were portraits of men and women in their finest clothes, there were a few depicting landscapes. None of the locations were familiar to Gareth. One such artwork, which hung just inside the entrance hall, reminded him of the Lord's Chapel, though without the overbearing structures that now choked the surrounding ward of Chorazin.

He quickly realized that he didn't have the faintest clue as to where to begin. Once again, he'd arrived somewhere with only the barest hint as to what his next step might be. As usual, there was no one here to greet him, no one to provide ready answers. All he had to go by were Lyceed's ramblings, which included talk of someone—or something—known as the Ikkibu in residence.

Cautiously, Gareth strode from the foyer into the adjoining study. Once inside the room, he recoiled from the dense aroma of dust and mildewed paper. He placed a hand over his mouth and made a beeline for the door on the other side. The room itself had not seen use in some time.

Beyond stood a narrow hallway with no additional branches. This led him directly into a two-story atrium which looked much like a hotel lobby. Painted on the vaulted ceiling was a mural of geometric patterns, decorated with reflective metallic inks. A desk on the far end was bookended by staircases curling to the upper balcony. As he strolled slowly out onto the tiled floor, Gareth scanned his surroundings. The home's strange configuration unnerved him. It felt like an assemblage of random rooms tacked together to form some mutated puzzle.

Before long, he discovered another of the familiar obelisks; this one atop a dais on the second-story landing. Unlike the others he'd seen all over the island, though, there was no bas relief of a person. Instead, a series of overlapping arcs and circles covered the entire surface.

For some reason, he was drawn to the pillar. He climbed the stairs and went directly to it, only pausing once he was within an arm's length. With a moth-to-a-flame obsession, he reached out towards the etched surface. As his fingers were about to brush the exterior, he felt something, like a charge of static snapping at him. Even then, he kept his hand in place, welcoming whatever effect the obelisk had on him.

The longer he examined the image, the more nervous Gareth became, as if its meaning affected him on some subconscious level. His muscles grew uncomfortable under his skin. His stomach roiled and he could feel a sourness rise in his mouth. He forced himself to look away.

Just as he was about to retreat, Gareth was shocked

to hear his name. Though he'd come to the Aurul Halls to find help, the sound caused him to jump.

"Welcome, Wanderer Gareth Solomon," a voice, which buzzed like a swarm of insects, called out. The deepest tones rattled against the room's wooden interior. Gareth thought he saw one of the paintings shake against the wall.

Gareth shifted into a defensive posture, with his legs spread and his weight on his back boot, as he scanned the vaulted hall. Except for the haze of unsettled dust in the air, he saw nothing. He felt exposed.

"It would do well for you to join me," the speaker continued. "Your arrival is expected. We have much to discuss."

"Who are you? How do you know my name?" he bellowed in response. Though he was wary, Gareth eventually began to creep forward.

Ignoring Gareth's inquiries, the voice continued. "When you are through with your investigation of the premises, go through the western door and down the attached hall. You have plenty of time to indulge your curiosities."

Despite assurances to the contrary, Gareth rushed back down the steps and headed for the entryway on his right. At the far end of the corridor, he barged into the room and met the building's host.

CHAPTER THIRTEEN

Elgretamon

Gareth came to a skidding stop. His jaw dropped as his eyes bulged in their sockets. Shocked, he made no effort to retreat. His head began to spin as he struggled with the sudden confusion.

How had he returned here? It wasn't possible.

Gareth was back in Lyceed's laboratory. Though Gareth would admit he wasn't at his most observant during his time there, the similarity was undeniable.

The furnishings appeared exactly the same, even in their placement. Tables were choked with equipment and a seemingly endless collection of tomes lined the walls of the two-story chamber. The restraining board was suspended from the track railing on his right, empty, with leather straps that hung limply.

Gareth stumbled backwards into the now-closed door. The barrier was sealed tightly and refused to budge against his weight. He fully expected Lyceed to step out, to welcome his return to the asylum. A part of Gareth— the same one that begged for him to flee—waited for the gaolers to come out of the shadows for him.

Though gripped with panic, it wasn't long before he realized that this place was slightly different. Even in the increasingly-confused state in which he found himself, he recognized the truth. There was no gaping, brick-lined hole leading to the catacombs beneath. In its place was bare flooring and another workspace, loaded down with a variety of scientific equipment. Some of the more visible book spines were made of carved stone and dyed reds, browns, and greens.

Though he wanted to explore the room, Gareth held his place. The muscles of his shoulders tightened as his back knotted up. Something roiled in the pit of his stomach and he fought against sickness. The taste of vomit in his mouth held peppery hints of the dried beef from before.

Gareth's fear heightened as a form appeared out of thin air on the other side of the chamber. Taller than him by almost a full yard, the lanky humanoid was draped in layers of cloth similar to priest's robes. Though the colors were faded and dull, there was a reflective quality about the thin fibers from which they were woven. Each of the figure's limbs had extra hinge joints and each hand featured seven independently-moving digits. Rising from its torso was a serpentine neck, atop which sat a featureless face. A carapace-like shell formed from a tough hide concealed its features. Gareth saw no eye sockets, ear holes, or tufts of hair on its bald scalp.

"Wanderer Gareth, your arrival is as predicted." The voice issued from behind the chitinous faceplate. A subtle vibration along the hide-like skin accompanied each syllable.

Rendered mute, Gareth stood in place. When he failed to respond, the entity continued.

"I am sired Elgretamon, of the Ikkibu, former servitors of those Begeondan who crossed the void to explore this physical plane. It was their desire, insomuch as they exhibit motivations, to observe worlds unlike their own, but in doing so, the Begeondan have induced an unexpected influence on those they wished to oversee. Now long-separated from my designers, I serve as curator of Dineothan's complex history."

It took a Gareth a few seconds to grasp the Ikkibu's comments. Elgretamon made no effort to draw near. In fact, when Gareth stepped forward, it retreated in kind.

Gareth then spoke up. "I, uh, what? You'll forgive me but this is an awful lot to take in."

"Surely, you've seen hints of my creators on your journey. The Begeondan came to your world with my kind, the Ikkibu, to act as intermediaries on your mortal plane. In our time with man, we became deeply entwined with those of Dineothan's greater scientific minds. Some of my fellow Ikkibu influenced the direction of their work."

This did little to improve Gareth's understanding. Instead of belaboring the matter, his thoughts turned to the Mericoinne. "And your friends? The ones waiting outside? Are they *influenced*?"

"The Mericoinne? They are but the last of their kind, driven from their own territory by foreign settlers with an inclination for conquest. That their forefathers were not erased from this plot of land was providence, or perhaps a lack of foresight by foreign conquerors looking for new territory to claim. In some foolish degree of benevolence, the founders of Upelstbohr have left the remnants of a tribe to wait for a time where a settling of old debts will be theirs. They long for the day when all will be returned to them. It is in the minds of the Mericoinne that the Ikkibu can turn the world back to its original state, but to do so one must entreat with our former masters, the Begeondan, for theirs is the source of all that now binds Dineothan."

Gareth reached up and rubbed at his temples. It seemed as though his brain had been rattled. Beyond his strange host and the eerie surroundings, there was something else. Gareth felt as if his own will was slowly being eroded. He was growing more agitated by the second.

Eventually, he was able to focus long enough to address something that caught his attention.

"Wait, wait a minute… you said earlier that I was expected," Gareth spoke up. "H-how is that possible? I didn't even know I would be coming here—or where here was—until I was on my way."

Elgretamon motioned to the rows of tomes. It strode to the far side of the room and began to scan the shelves. "All that is ever known is writ within. All time—past, present, future—is known to us. Much like those of my kin still in Dineothan, I exist in all moments of time within Dineothan simultaneously."

Gareth shook his head violently. The longer he spoke with Elgretamon, the more confused he became. The Ikkibu's speech that wore on him, as if it corroded his mind from within. "And that means what?"

"That from the moment of your arrival as you were ushered across the Gape, your path, in its entirety, is known to me. Your course, to its end beneath the Coemeterium, is already established. Your role in Dineothan is set in stone." Due to its height, the Ikkibu was able to reach a shelf on the second floor. One of its lengthy digits stopped on a gray-colored tome.

As Gareth's mouth opened, Elgretamon continued.

"You would query how such a scenario is possible. They are expected, the words that would birth from your mouth in a fumbling attempt to pose queries which properly communicate your confusion. Your mind struggles valiantly against such concepts, not because you desire to understand but that, for the sake of your existence, you must." With book in hand, Elgretamon turned away. "So many of man's years before your arrival, one of my kin thought to shift Dineothan with the aid of those at the College. Through calculations and formulae, it desired to create a bridge which would cover the distance between realms. So that our Begeondan makers would converse with it once more. Rather than allow them to address more viable pathways, it convinced those at the College that the scientific theorems, taken from the Begeondan, would provide them with greater leaps than even they expected. Even with the aid of those of your kind considered most knowledgeable, its efforts proved to not only be futile, but harmful." There was a pause, as if Elgretamon felt something like regret.

"What you see about you are the fruits of this failure. A sun that never sets. A populace that never ages. Death is an inconvenience for those defeated without the immediate consumption of their flesh. In sanctuaries, they reawaken a little less than they were. And yet, mankind is prone to the corruptions inherent in the condition that has descended upon their city streets. A lust for akaluma'elusepsu that has turned man into Dalhakhu. The Begeondan influence has altered a populace that should have perished under its own hand long ago. All the greatest of empires of your history eventually fall, especially ones who've grown debauched. Upelstbohr's fancy for cannibalism should have been the beginning of their inevitable end."

Gareth groaned as he struggled to make sense of the Ikkibu's speech. Elgretamon crossed the room.

"Read the passage recorded of your time on Dineothan. You will find it enlightening."

It extended the open volume, laid out flat. Gingerly, Gareth received the hardback and held it in his own hands. He was immediately surprised by the heft of the object.

Where he expected to see two pages filled with writing was only a single, unfolded slab of granite on which was etched a series of lines. When he attempted to close it, the book refused. As he let out a thin sigh, Gareth focused on the passage.

> *Long and dark 'tis the way f'r man to follow*
> *Through hellish 'scape is he madeth hollow*
> *Even in twist'd prose th're is much to kent*
> *In deceit, sooth is hath found in the descent*
> *Wilt englut the slain ones to groweth stout'r*
> *To entreat with timeless one in the out'r*
> *Anon learns the futility of his eff'rts*
> *Is broken and strewn across blackened des'rt*
> *Within ag'd vaults, sought a hope declined*
> *At the edge of the black void, the eldest mind*

After reading it through to the end, Gareth's brow knit. His jaw clenched as he studied it a second time. He shook his head as the words permeated his brain. There was something there, but he couldn't quite grasp it. Even though the phrases themselves were obtuse, Gareth perceived some meaning, as if there were fragments of other lines hidden within the verse. Before he could mull over it too long, his frustration came to a head. He was tired and exasperated and this only aggravated his condition.

"And this means *what* now?" Gareth asked as he discarded the book with a hasty flick of his wrist. It dropped to the ground with a dull thud.

Elgretamon issued a series of annoyed clicks. "In the words lies the reality of your existence, accept it or not. In truth, your arrival in Dineothan and the subsequent trials were predetermined. In the newness of your spirit there is value in your toil, seen by the few that remain. An elderly madman wishing to steal unearned power from one who is his better. Shadows of men at the College who'd toyed with the fibers of your realm's existence and the lone survivor who sent you along. The educated man of the Sanitorium who sought not to aid but to make the most of how events transpired. These are the generators of looming transformation of Dineothan. If you, callow swordsman, were deemed an undesirable agitator, many anuphilim would have been dispatched to strip you bare. The walls surrounding every sanctuary in the city would be lined with those compelled to strike you down at every step. That you've made it this far is merely a series of events foretold which transpired in your favor."

During the diatribe, Gareth felt the tenuous grasp on his temper slipping by the second. The dismissive tone in which Elgretamon spoke only acted to goad him. Gareth had endured it long enough. "I'll have you know, damn it, that I fought my way here. I'm not some lucky half-wit who stumbled over myself to get here! Slayed foulkin and even that *thing* called Sindex in the Lord's Chapel, so don't think you can talk down to me like I'm some rank amateur! I didn't just fluke my way here!"

"Sindex?" Something that might have been laughter warbled from Elgretamon's head. "His sire long ago returned to the catacombs beneath the Coemeterium, beyond the Black Basalt Fields. He will not be missed. That you sundered him was only a kindness to a mongrel taken to hiding in an empty congregation hall. The blade you no longer carry was only effective in striking down naught but vermin—the bastard children of a maker's folly in sciences mankind has yet to understand."

This dismissiveness was the last straw.

"I'm tired of all this bullshit!" Gareth barked as he pulled out his revolver and aimed it at Elgretamon. The Ikkibu did not recoil. "All I ever wanted was a straight fucking answer from someone in this nuthouse. I've yet to find someone who knew shit or wasn't wanting to fuck with me. I have no more time to WASTE ON THIS!"

With his thumb, he cocked the hammer.

After a few seconds spent contemplating the weapon, Elgretamon ultimately responded. "Wanderer Gareth, you came in search of a cure for a scourge that besets your kind, did you not? Not for money, king, nor country. This quest is but a personal errand, one undertaken for the noblest of human reasons. For the love of kin."

Gareth could feel its verbal prodding, as if Elgretamon was jamming spikes into his head and chest with every barb. His limbs weakened and he struggled to keep the firearm level.

"Damn it, man! Do you *know* if there is a cure? I w-was sent here to ask f-for your aid. Every word you spit out i-i-is a second *lost*."

"The masters and creators of the Ikkibu, the Begeondan… only they have the capability to correct your malady, however not in the manner in which you expect."

A twinge of hope forced its way through Gareth's anger. He lowered his weapon. Elgretamon continued.

"You will not find them so readily available, though. All but one of their kind has departed, returned to their own domain as they pass through the space between spaces. The last is imprisoned by others of my breed. The Ikkibu grew tired of their role as servitors and rebelled against the authors of their existence. Perhaps it was anger or jealousy that turned us against our creators. With the birth of the anuphilim by Begeondan hands, some of my brethren questioned the necessity of their own purpose on this mortal plane. As such, the Ikkibu imprisoned our darkest, immortal mother, trapped her in the catacombs beneath the Coemeterium and siphoned her essence for the Ikkibu's own goals. Some, wishing to meddle with humankind, bequeathed scientific knowledge that would propel their learning beyond what they'd already earned. Even though my own name was cast as instigator, I saw the danger in such machinations. So alike were the Ikkibu in appearance that misunderstood words between the Ikkibu and mankind has left me branded as lord benefactor."

Elgretamon raised a hand to its face and scrawled its pointed fingertips along the chitinous surface.

"Once the Ikkibu felt in command of the collective existence of their kind, my kin turned to the humans and began to exert influences of our own. In our foolishness, we aided mankind in toying with the properties of the universe. Cut off from the outside world was Dineothan, trapped in a static prison of their own making. And as this folly was unfurled, I and my brethren retreated. The damage done, we chose to remove ourselves as we waited and watched. The Ikkibu had a hand in disaster and instead of offering aid, they hid."

Gareth's ire returned in full force. "Why are you telling me all of this? What purpose is there in going on and on if you yourself cannot help me? Just tell me where I can find this… Begeondan, and I'll be on my way."

Another series of clicks issued from behind the carapace. "Akaluma'elusepsu, mortal. It is forever about akaluma'elusepsu. Even in the transference of knowledge there is perceivable growth. It is in these stores that you will find resolution. I must satiate you if you are to succeed. Many times, you've tasted the rewards of physical victory. Little do you understand that you need not slaughter to grow in strength."

Gareth raised his gun again.

"Tell me *where* to find the Begeondan," he seethed, nearly growling. "I grow tired of your yapping."

"In your previous state, before you possessed enough akaluma'elusepsu, you would not have been able entreat with the Begeondan," was Elgretamon's response. "Through trial and education, you now grasp what you need."

Gareth wrapped his index finger around the trigger. He began to squeeze, fully aware that the bullet would end this conversation. The Ikkibu was merely delaying Gareth.

"This—" Elgretamon made a sweeping wave over their heads. "—is but illusion, a façade made for the benefit of humankind. Your frail minds become so entranced with the simplest of trappings, that one must present the stage in a fashion you can comprehend. Lest you lose yourself in a childish awe bordering on insanity. With these cast aside, your mind might collapse in on itself rather than comprehend a world beyond your own."

In that moment, the Ikkibu's fingers twisted into a series of overlapping arcs. Joints bent in unexpected angles as the bony digits formed into a mass of geometrical shapes. After a few spins of his wrists, the world around Gareth shifted.

Gone was any hint of the laboratory's original form. In its place were stacks of the same iridescent metal plates he'd spied earlier, all lined up in rows as they slowly spun about on posts mounted into the floor. Each pane was taller than him and stacked in columns of three. As they turned, he could see reflections of the other slabs as they rotated in kind. Beneath him was a transparent surface, covered by a pattern of arcs and circles which glimmered like quicksilver. Below this, a greenish mist roiled, as if under the constant influence of a faint breeze.

The illusion of the Ikkibu's form likewise disappeared. Its torso was a mass of green-gray flesh from which a dozen, multi-jointed limbs protruded at various angles. Instead of legs, a trio of these appendages served as a tripod. Its neck was twice as long, and the head weaved with a serpentine motion.

Gareth struggled against the mental undertow. There was far too much stimuli and he was overwhelmed. He was bombarded by glints of light which reflected off the blue-hued surfaces. Visions of angled edifices built according to non-Euclidean geometry shifted from hyperbolic to elliptic as each second passed.

Gareth's perception of the world flickered.

Before he knew it, Gareth dropped to his hands and knees. Somehow, his revolver had returned to its holster. It was as if time itself had skipped and he was missing an essential moment. His heart was thumping loudly and he struggled to get his breathing in check. Sweat broke out across his brow.

Everything went black for a second. In his weakened state, Gareth was overcome with sorrow. All delusions fell to the wayside and he was gripped with the horror of his situation. Bits of previous conversations barraged him. He could hear the words of Lyceed, Redbletter, and Geddish repeated over and over. Phrases that he'd once disregarded as peculiar now fell heavy on his brain.

"You smell of sadness. Loss."

"You've come at a bad time to find a cure. The streets are the way they are for a reason, my good man."

"You've seen the Dalhakhu which infest the streets, have you not? Any man *capable of curing a plague for you has either become one of them or fallen prey to them. The College is in no state to help and I assure you there is no one* here."

"Yours... yours is a fresh grief borne of something unexpected."

Elgretamon's words cut through the miasma as they rang inside his head. "The hour for all within Dineothan's borders is confined in this stasis. To go forward with your quest to cure the plague, as you would require, would need the scientific knowledge of certain Begeondan no longer available to this world. To shift backwards... reverse the course to a point more favorable... that is a thing that can be accomplished, but not without the highest of costs paid by someone such as yourself."

It paused as its hands moved in strange patterns in the air.

"One does not travel back alone. We are all tangled together, locked in place. It would require a shift of some consequence for us all to accomplish. A feat only the Begeondan would have the capacity to complete. Only they would understand the sciences in such an undertaking."

"I need..." Gareth muttered, holding himself up with palms pressed to the floor. Even through his gloves, the surface felt cold. Every time he looked up, his senses were flooded. Only through sheer force of will did he stay on his hands and knees. "...help me."

Gareth had never been one for praying before. Now, as he plead to the Ikkibu, he wondered if his supplication would result in anything. Any threads of hope were pulled taut to the point of snapping. This was not what he imagined when he thought of God. What benevolence would lie within the alien creature's heart?

Even as he kept his head down, Gareth could feel Elgretamon draw near. The Ikkibu slid across the smooth surface. Time passed before it leaned in over his head. Its words echoed in the back of his brain.

"These humans you cling to, their time is long gone. Only in the past will you find them."

Gareth shook his head back and forth. His skull pounded and he struggled to grasp Elgretamon's comment.

"The PLAGUE. How do I cure it?" He eventually forced the words out of his mouth. Spittle dripped from his lips and splattered on the glassy surface beneath him.

"For you, there is no cure."

"My wife and daughter are sick with it." It took everything he had to keep conscious. His face became flushed as tears ran down his cheeks and rained to the floor. Hope was all that kept him from collapsing.

"You misunderstand the situation, Wanderer Gareth. You are not here in Dineothan to find a cure."

"But... I was sent..." Gareth sputtered as his arms finally gave out. The muscles became like rubber as his hands slipped outwards. He dropped face-first to the ground.

Elgretamon's words grew faint as the world darkened around him. "The latest in a line of Lyceeds only directed you here because it was his fate to do so. In ensuring you acquired enough akaluma'elusepsu, you may continue onto the last stage of your journey."

"But… my… my…"

Just before his consciousness faded, Gareth heard Elgretamon whispering within his head.

"Beneath the Coemeterium. Seek the last of the Begeondan, bound beneath the centuries of graves. If you truly wish to turn time back upon itself, to a point where your kin are not afflicted, submit to the Goetia formula to entreat with—" For a moment, Elgretamon's words became a garbled mess. "—If you hold out hope for a day in which you would see your kin again, you must be willing to forfeit all that you've consumed."

Whether because of despair or out of exhaustion, Gareth finally blacked out.

CHAPTER FOURTEEN

The Coemeterium

Gareth did not wake up as a broken mass sprawled out across the transparent floor. Nor did his eyes flutter open to the simulacrum of Lyceed's laboratory. Instead, his senses slowly returned as he continued a trudging march across a blackened waste that was initially unfamiliar to him.

After a glance over his shoulder, Gareth saw that the Aurul Halls and its alien occupant were nowhere to be seen.

Standing upright and plodding forward without any direction, Gareth was stunned. It made no sense for him to push on in such an autonomous manner. Perhaps his memory was failing him. Had the trauma to his weary head been so great that he disassociated entirely? Did his body move without conscious decisions from his mind? These were all questions he thought he'd never ask of himself.

Though aware of his surroundings and actions, Gareth was nowhere near recovered from his ordeal. Where there had once been a sense of purpose was a hollowed-out, blackened pit. His heart was gone and all he felt was a weight that threatened to crush him from the inside. Why did he continue on? Why didn't he just lay down and surrender to whatever end awaited those who lived… who *persisted* on the island?

To say they lived was a lie. He knew that now. Those left alive were trapped and the survivors weren't bound by the natural order of living things. Entropy had long ago taken root on the island.

Gareth didn't know whether this was crippling depression, a lingering confusion, or a combination of both. Though he'd been physically injured in the line of duty, it was nothing like this. Blood and open flesh was the kind of injury he could understand. Time and care could mend broken bones. Before now, he'd never failed to properly dispatch his duties. He'd never know true defeat.

His current state, though, was something he'd never experienced before. Gareth was pulled apart at the seams, mentally and emotionally, only to be reformed into this hollowed-out shell of a man.

Haunting memories only deepened his dismay. The Ikkibu had poured a wealth of knowledge into his head; so much that he doubted even the sharpest of men could grasp it all. The complexity of the concepts far exceeded his limited education. Still, there were hints of things he should know. Truths that he did not want to admit.

Even now, Elgretamon's words buzzed in his head, like hornets had formed a nest where his brain once was. Gareth halted and placed his hands against his temples. He squeezed his palms tightly, hoping that they would keep his skull from splitting open. As he stood in place, the flood of information all seemed to rush forward.

"The hour for all within Dineothan's borders is confined in this stasis."

Perhaps if he was a smarter man, he could understand it. He reconsidered his conversation with Naze, about the sun being locked in place and time itself no longer progressing. Such things were always taken for granted: the day was bookended by dawn and dusk. This pact between nature and man was how one could keep track of the date. That such processes ceased to work only taxed his understanding. The concept itself was still foreign to him and at that moment he'd merely accepted it blindly without considering the vaster implications. The week, month, and year were all based on the rising and setting of the sun. Without it, how would humans measure time? The breakdown of such a fundamental truth of civilization meant that nothing could be the same.

With Dineothan stuck, temporally, Gareth wondered about the outside world. Was it moving on without them, or did it wait patiently for his return? Another of Elgretamon's comments surfaced above the mental chatter.

"These humans you cling to, their time is long gone."

After a fit of frantic head-shaking, his shoulders

slumped in defeat. Nattia and Shea had been in the later stages of the illness when he left to hunt for a cure. He knew that, logically, they would have succumbed, perhaps even before his crossing of the Gape. Even if they had survived that long, there was no telling how long he'd been trapped on Dineothan.

At some point, his body began to move. His feet shuffled clumsily as he lurched northwards. Slouched over, he trudged onwards with no idea where he was headed. There was no compulsion, no pull, no force, no alien will.

He just walked, resisting the urge to lie down and wait for a death that may or may not come.

By all rights, he should have just joined those huddled in the Chorazin sanctuary. He now knew why they hid. Or perhaps he should let himself be feed for the foulkin. Maybe he would stumble across one of the anuphilim and they would devour him whole.

Would the creature take only his 'energy' and leave him hollow and useless? He'd watched as Sindex's minions gnawed on it. Would he need to be devoured, like a meal, to be destroyed? He wasn't certain that suicide was a permanent situation here.

Gareth recalled Elgretamon's final words. That he remembered them at all was some kind of miracle. Even as the Ikkibu destroyed the last hopes of success, it urged Gareth to head for the Coemeterium. There he would find the imprisoned Begeondan.

Elgretamon had given him a reason to continue. Gareth was exhausted by the ulterior motives of those beings he'd met, who'd been in their current condition for God only knows how long. He doubted any of them could recall when they'd last seen a sunset. It was likely that everyone, even the charitable Naze, was eventually driven mad by unnaturally long existence. Had he already joined them? If not, would he eventually?

Gareth's body marched on. From time to time, his eyes shut. When he thought of his family, tears carved paths down his dust-coated cheeks.

Now that his head felt clearer, he noticed where he was.

Towering clusters of basalt columns, some as tall as twenty feet in height, formed the gorge's walls. Though the formations pointed to a volcanic origin, he saw no sign of their source. No dormant mount lingered on the horizon. All he could see was the island's misty barrier. In its expected place was the afternoon sun, which struggled to burn through the gray haze.

Beneath his boots, the earth was hard and unrelenting. A thin layer of soot collected between the surface's spider-web of fractures.

Without a landmark in sight, he marched on. If he was to spot this Coemeterium, he would need to reach higher ground.

Eventually, he reached a rise in the valley. As he did, he took in the panorama. For what looked like an endless expanse all around him was more of the same scorched, black soil. Hundreds of yards away, the wall of fog lined the island's distant shore. At the bottom of the slope was another gorge, though this one was much shallower than those he'd recently traversed. Though too far away to see clearly, there were silhouettes of aboveground structures at the far end. A ridge of angled rocks obscured most of his view beyond the crag-filled canyon.

Gareth nodded solemnly and began his descent.

It took maybe an hour to reach the far end of the chasm. During the trek, he tried to be more observant of his surroundings. While foliage had once existed there, the land appeared lifeless now. A few bleached roots and limbs stuck out of the ashy soil at strange angles, as if skeletal hands reached out for the wanderer.

When he exited the ravine, Gareth felt a sliver of something like hope. It was the notion that his aimless drifting was nearing its end. Though greatly aged, the shadows he saw proved to be man-made structures.

There was no formal border, no fence to outline the graveyard's borders. The surrounding basalt fields merely came to an end and the cemetery began. Gravestones poked out of the dirt. It looked as though the markers and aboveground tombs just sprang from the earth.

The further he progressed, the denser the necropolis became. In between clusters of limestone slabs were the remnants of topiaries. A few trees were reduced to bleached, barkless husks whose limbs flailed in the howling breeze. Beyond the crooked rows that ran for dozens of yards to the north, was a huddled mass of mausoleums.

None of these structures looked particularly out of place. Gareth's time in Dineothan had shown him so many architectural oddities, he found himself looking for them. Gareth spotted nothing that stood out.

There was an air of neglect, as if the site had gone unused for hundreds of years. The location of the graveyard, though, struck Gareth as odd. Why were Upelstbohr's dead interred so far away from the city? The catacombs that now housed the Governess' lair were a more convenient location. He'd not seen sign of anything that could pass for civilization since his reawakening. The isolation might be for a good reason, even if he didn't know what that was. Maybe there had once been another settlement in the region.

He attempted to read a few of the markers. Though time and weather had worn the etched words down, there were a handful of legible names and dates. There were a plethora of Branes, Willcotts, and Holtzes; interspersed among these were a handful of Lochtes. Years ranged from the early 1200s up to the first decade of the 1500s.

No more than a few yards into the graveyard proper, Gareth came across a fountain that had long ago dried out. At the center of the dulled marble structure was another of the familiar obelisks. The bas relief, a gravedigger in a suit and hat with a shovel in one hand standing over a grave, was similar to the one in the Chorazin sanctuary.

As Gareth approached the carven pillar, he felt something strange. This caused him to pause mid-stride. There was a static charge pulsing around the object that threatened to shock him if he dared too close. Still, Gareth took a few careful steps forward.

When the electric sensation began to increase, seemingly in response to his approach, Gareth retreated. Within seconds, the obelisk brightened, as if it was hollow and illuminated from within. As this light amplified, the surrounding atmosphere felt as though it was about to crack open. There was a sensation, much like the air just before a thunderstorm, which caused the hair on the back of his neck to bristle. A rush of noise, like a violent wind, buffeted Gareth and forced him to cover his ears.

With a deafening crash and a flash, both the light and sound phenomena were gone. As he batted his eyes, Gareth heard the rustling of movement.

He glanced up to find a person standing beside the obelisk. A familiar set of rags caused Gareth to groan to himself. When the man turned around, Alharrad offered Gareth a crooked smile.

"Took the long way, did you?" he said with a tired cackle.

"How... You know what, I don't even care," Gareth snarled as he took a step back from Alharrad, who appeared to be a bit off balance. After a few seconds, the hunched madman ran a hand through his beard. His head bobbed back and forth as he took a few deep breaths.

"Takes a bit, even now, afore all my bits get straightened out," he eventually noted with a grin. With a crooked finger, he pointed to his bowels.

Though Gareth was annoyed by Alharrad's arrival, he felt a twinge of relief. Another human face, no matter the owner, provided a small comfort. Loathe as he was to admit it, he was grateful to see the old man.

Before long, Gareth's gaze returned to the obelisk. Noticing this, Alharrad spoke up as he flicked a hand back over his shoulder.

"A bit of their science, it is. The Ikkibu, that is. Or maybe not even theirs. Maybe it was taken— appropriated for their own use—from their masters, the Begeondan, as they slept. I always wondered how much of their knowledge was their own. Too much of it unearned, I say. Too much passed along to mankind in false goodness."

"The Begeondan," Gareth muttered at Alharrad's comment. He was immediately reminded of his discussion with Elgretamon.

This caught Alharrad's attention. His head craned upwards as his eyes widened. "Yes, yes. The Begeondan. That is the name of their masters, not used by many, outside of the Ikkibu and some of those who benefited from their aid. Not used by any man in a polite conversation. A fearful word it has become. To know it, you must have spoken with one of those educated in such matters. One of those who have looked past the folklore to the realness of it. Perhaps even someone who stood in their grand presence and was not made mad by their... unearthliness."

As if to refocus Alharrad's thoughts, Gareth motioned to the pillar. "And how do you use it?"

Alharrad reached back and swiped his fingers downwards in the air, only a few inches from the obelisk's surface. "All it takes is a touch—an intent to be where it will take you—but do not make that choice hastily. For you, it would send you back to the Halls. Disorient you something fierce. Steal days of your life. Your struggle to get this far would be wasted. You *could* return, but would your window of opportunity be closed then?"

"And you understand how it works? Or well enough to use it?"

"Yes, yes. I've had time to learn," Alharrad said with a droll cackle. "Even more time to travel and find as many of these as I could. Like checkpoints on a map. Still, there are locations not yet reachable but by a few. Twisting pathways, hidden from the eyes of man that only the Ikkibu dare to tread. Perhaps the Mericoinne, though they seem otherwise possessed."

"So, I take it then that you've been here before?"

"A time long ago, I fear. Then, I was merely exploring what Dineothan had to offer. Beyond the graves, I saw nothing of merit. Actual dead in actual graves. Nothing worth soiling one's hands or soul. Now, with seeing you here, I wonder if something grander is hidden beneath the soil. At first glance, it appears that not much has changed since last I walked this land."

This evoked more questions that Gareth chose not

to ask. He doubted that Alharrad would answer them without obfuscation. Without encouragement, Alharrad continued.

"Now that you've arrived, I can only wonder what you intend to find here," Alharrad continued. "Certainly no men of science here to aid you. Or none that are not long-buried and no longer mourned." He cocked a brow and peered into Gareth's face. "Or... perhaps... perhaps you already have. Spoke with one of the Ikkibu and was dispatched this way like a loyal hound to find their masters. Hid one of the Begeondan beneath the Coemeterium, did they?" He chuckled to himself. "Deep these holes must be dug to bury them so well."

Alharrad stood up and slowly surveyed their surroundings. After a few seconds, he turned back to Gareth.

"They tell you exactly where, then?"

Gareth snorted in reply. Alharrad continued.

"Not so lucky, I see. The Ikkibu were never one to do more than nudge a man forward, I gather. Left to the role of grave robber to find your next clue, yes? Dirty, foul work it is. Well, this is not the first time such a vile task has been forced upon me for the gain of others. Let us see what we can find."

Before Gareth could say anything, Alharrad scrambled off. He almost called out to tell Alharrad not to bother. However, he realized there was nothing to be gained by that. Even though he disliked the idea of the man's involvement, Gareth knew that two sets of eyes were better than one. Even if his quest was a failure, he didn't want to haunt the cemetery any longer than necessary.

In that moment, he began to reconsider. If he accepted that he could no longer cure Nattia and Shea, that they had already perished, why was he letting the Ikkibu drive him further on? What did he have to gain from continuing?

The droning words of Elgretamon clawed up from the depths of his memory.

Seek the last of the Begeondan, bound beneath the centuries of graves. If you truly wish to turn time back upon itself…

What did that even mean? Was there something— some miracle of science—that not even the Ikkibu had the capacity to perform? Could one truly go back in time?

As Gareth mulled this over, he considered the strange things to which he'd already been witness. The idea of akaluma'elusepsu suggested that other, more implausible concepts might be feasible. Perhaps not in the world beyond the fog barrier, but within the prison that was Dineothan.

If you hold out hope for a day in which you would see your kin again…

Could the Begeondan send him home to a moment before they became sick? With what he knew now, he could take them away to the countryside and hide them from the plague. Maybe they would charter a boat and leave for foreign lands before any of them could become ill. He could—

"Gareth!" Alharrad hailed from a handful of yards away. Behind him was the open iron gate to one of the larger tombs. "Come here! Come, come. I've an inklin' that something of interest to you is right inside this tomb."

Without comment, Gareth moved to join him. As he did, he heard faint noises in the distance, like the movement of small creatures as they scrambled along the earth. He paused once to investigate, but when he did, the sounds disappeared, as if they were a hallucination.

Though his shoulders clenched up tightly, he continued on. If something was out there—and the sound wasn't in his worn mind—Gareth would have to deal with them in due time.

Right now, all he cared about was the mausoleum before him.

CHAPTER FIFTEEN

Ancestral

When Gareth looked at the nameplate mounted above the mausoleum's lintel, he wasn't certain what he expected to find. Etched into the aged bronze placard was a series of angled lines. There were overlapping curves and arcs, often intersected by a series of diagonal strokes. Despite the appearance of random marks, Gareth thought he spied something within them.

Somehow, he understood that it was a form of writing, fashioned from characters and symbols he didn't recognize. That he knew the assumption to be true was curious enough. He was aware that the icons were not only an alien language, but that it was a mixture of alphanumeric and mathematical symbols. The infusion of knowledge from Lyceed and Elgretamon had changed him. They'd laid down a rudimentary foundation, via akaluma'elusepsu, of understanding. Though he didn't entirely comprehend what he was witnessing, he at least knew what it represented.

"Gonna stare at it all day?" Alharrad's query snapped Gareth out of his moment of introspection. He turned to catch the old man as he beckoned for Gareth to join him.

"You don't care to understand what it says?"

"All I care is *what* it is," Alharrad commented as he disappeared inside. A second later, his voice could be heard from within. " 'Tis the writin' of the Begeondan. Too crudely done to be the Ikkibu, I think. Clearly the work of men. Probably scrawled by the human hand of the Mericoinne to mark this place for what it was."

Gareth wanted to inquire for clarification, but he doubted that Alharrad wouldn't ramble on. Though disguised among the untended graves, this was an entrance to somewhere far more important. He had a fair idea of where the way forward led. Elgretamon did not send him out here to unearth more dead humans, or to find a burial plot for the Mericoinne.

"Come, come," Alharrad implored.

After letting out a long sigh, Gareth straightened his belt and passed through the entrance. He came into a small, marble-lined chamber. Afternoon light fell through a few decorative windows at the back of the structure. Geometric patterns from the colored glass painted the bare walls in a kaleidoscope of hues. At the center, instead of a sarcophagus, stood a set of stairs that descended sharply. On the topmost step waited Alharrad.

"You act like a man who knows what he's looking

for," Gareth commented as he carefully strode to join him. "One might think you've been here before."

"Aw, you, uh, you think so poorly of Alharrad, do you?" he moaned. "Perhaps, one day you'll be in Dineothan long enough to know what to look for. Put your head on a swivel and they'll stand out, plain as day. Within the abandoned structures, you'll come to understand what clues point you in the right direction. And when something changes, one thing becomes something else, you'll take notice of it. It'll stand out like the sorest of thumbs."

Gareth chose not to argue. Though pretending to be defensive, Alharrad's reasoning was sound.

"What was different?"

"Eh?" Alharrad muttered as he continued down the lengthy descent. In the weakening light, Gareth struggled to spot the staircase's end.

"What led you here? Something had to catch your eye."

"Oh, oh! In my earlier days, I sought to while away my time by walking what I could of Dineothan. What stretches of land I could get to, that did not—in their own ways—attempt to bar my passing. In my time, I saw many a passage written in Begeondan. Each was placed with care, usually beside entryways sealed off from those deemed undesirable by their occupants. One needed to be a wanted guest, either by the Ikkibu, or with enough akaluma'elusepsu, I hear, to see where these placards led, you see. How such was determined is something I never quite understood, or at least not until I was stuck in Chorazin. Despite my curiosity, I came to accept I was never in a position to be allowed access. Too lacking in what they determined to be vital, I gather." He patted himself on the chest. "Never before, though, in my time spent amongst the city of the dead, through the rusty gate which barred this tomb, did I witness a sarcophagus so easily replaced with a set of stairs."

This caused Gareth to pause briefly. Alharrad called out.

"And finally, we reach the bottom." He motioned to the archway a few yards below them. Through the stone entryway, the limestone brick floor was lit by a blueish glow.

Instinctively, Gareth reached across his shoulder for his sword. When his fist clasped over empty air, he let out a disappointed sigh.

Damn it, he swore to himself. His hand then dropped to the handle of his revolver.

They reached the last step and strode through the doorless entrance into some form of underground crypt. The catacombs were not laden with the remains of the long dead. Instead, the network of tombs appeared to have served as a home for a group—perhaps either the Ikkibu or the Mericoinne. Small alcoves off of the main corridor looked as though they'd once been in use. Sizeable slabs of stone were fashioned into a primitive form of furniture. In more than one was a ceremonial dais. Gareth recognized the strange alignment of curves and angles carved across their exteriors, though he struggled to discern what their use had been.

In iron sconces along the main corridor were burning coals that gave off a cerulean hue. The flickering flames cast tiny shadows that wavered hauntingly.

Alharrad only lingered for a moment before he continued. Hunched over, he gamboled forward with purpose, as if he knew where he was heading. From time to time, he peered into a side room, hummed knowingly to himself and pressed on.

Gareth quickly wrote off the behavior. He was aware that Alharrad was peculiar. Perhaps the years trapped on the island had been too much for him. He was briefly reminded of his conversation with Naze.

"Craziness runs in tha blood, Gareth. I'll say nae more than that."

With this in mind, Gareth knew that if he interrogated him about it, it would only lead to an unnecessary squabble.

Certain he overheard something, Gareth paused for a moment. He cocked his head to the side and listened intently. Just as he did, the echoes of scratching from somewhere deeper in the subterranean site faded.

When he eventually continued forward, with slow, cautious strides, Gareth was certain there was a strange quality to his own footsteps. Their reverberations sounded too long, as if something stalked behind them. It wasn't Alharrad, whose soft leather footwear made only the slightest scuffle on the hard surface.

He glanced at their point of entry, but when nothing appeared in the darkened arch, he shook his head. Once again, it was as if his senses were playing tricks on him. Considering his recent condition, he knew the possibility was not remote.

After blowing out a long breath, Gareth pushed on. At this point, it was better for him to continue looking for the Begeondan.

As they continued further in, Gareth took the lead. Focused on his surroundings, he didn't notice that Alharrad had dropped back and now trailed him by a few paces. To Gareth, it seemed that the old man grew increasingly intrigued. More than once, he stopped to run gnarled fingers over the strangely-etched walls.

"Bet with all the power you've accumulated, you could ask for anything from the Begeondan," Alharrad muttered low. For a moment, Gareth thought he heard the sound of the old man's lips smacking.

Before long, Gareth began to have doubts. Though the catacombs did not feature many side paths—and those that they came across only led to dead-ends— he felt as though they'd become lost. Many of the architectural features looked familiar, as if they'd passed by them before. He began to weigh the possibility that they were walking in circles.

He reached into one of his belt pouches and produced a stick of chalk. He would mark the next intersection.

Around the following turn, Gareth stumbled upon a welcome new sight. He felt relief to see something indicating that he wasn't entirely off-track. Instead of more countless alcoves and dead-ended alleys, he now saw an archway. While there was no clue as to where this led, he felt drawn to it all the same. Moving forward, in any direction, now felt like progress to Gareth.

Once through the entrance, his pace tapered off. Beyond was a massive cavern, over a hundred yards in length. Across this spanned a bridge, lit by lanterns mounted at intervals along the railing. On the far end was another doorway, which was illuminated by flickering blue flame. Even with the illumination, Gareth struggled to pick out the hollow's exterior walls. When he looked over the side, he saw more of the greenish mist which prevented any view of the subterranean cavity's bottom.

Something struck him as off. Though there was bare earth and a lake of roiling mist below him, like at the Chorazin sanctuary, something was missing. No prominent earthy aroma filled the air. He noticed a distinct lack of humidity, as if the air was bone-dry. He'd been in enough subterranean caverns to realize this was not normal.

He shrugged his shoulders and continued his march. He glanced back to see Alharrad as the old man stopped to look over the chamber. When Gareth put some distance between them, Alharrad hurried after him.

Once across the bridge and through the distant archway, he arrived in another room. A good thirty yards in length and half as wide, the chamber felt cozy after the previous cavern. Still, it was the largest compartment he'd yet seen in the catacombs. This realization alone was not enough to give him pause. What was concerning, though, were the rows of statues along either side. While he'd grown used to Upelstbohr's love of sculpture, these were unlike anything he'd witnessed before.

There were no well-crafted representations of men in armor, no humanoid-like illusions of the Ikkibu; the effigies were of completely inhuman entities. Some were merely masses of what might have been flesh with multi-hinged limbs that sprang outwards in odd angles. Others had multiple pairs of wings draped across their twisted bodies like cloaks. A few displayed features that reminded him of insects, though these aspects were so altered that Gareth wondered if this was merely his mind stretching, to fit the form into a known taxonomy.

The longer he examined them, the more Gareth felt anxiety. What purpose did these serve? What was the room itself for that matter?

As he pondered the limestone artifacts, he moved in closer to one. He peered carefully at the craftsmanship as he reached out with a hand to touch the surface. Though the stone carvings were horrifying themselves, Gareth was impressed by their detail. He began to wonder what inspired them. Were they the product of an ill mind? Someone who'd decided to display the monstrosities which haunted his dreams? Or was it possible that these were fashioned after something that existed?

That notion alone caused a shiver to run down his spine. Even if only for a moment, he'd seen the Ikkibu's true form. Other such horrors were no longer out of the realm of possibility.

Gareth slowly backed away. He heard the scuffling

of soft shoes as someone rushed towards him. Thinking that Alharrad was merely catching up to him, Gareth quickly remained focused on the alien sculpture.

"Gareth!"

A female voice cried out to him. It took him a half-second to realize that it was Naze. Was she the one tracking them the whole time? In that moment, he stopped in his tracks and turned to face her. A smile curled the corners of his mouth.

As he spun about, he saw the knife.

Without warning, Alharrad rushed, a curved blade clutched in one hand above him. Though a part of him half-expected betrayal, Gareth was still shocked by the incoming strike. Stunned, he failed to feint and avoid Alharrad.

Instead, Naze came out of the shadows and leapt between the two men. Alharrad's weapon came down hard and fast; striking first at her throat, it cut diagonally across her torso. Flesh and fabric alike split open as the honed edge tore into her. Blood from a major vessel sprayed into the air and peppered the old man across the face. The blade eventually deflected off the molded armor plate that wrapped around her left breast.

Naze began to waver as she placed a hand over her chest. Sanguine fluids seeped out between her fingers.

"No! Grandma, no!" Alharrad screeched hysterically as he released his grip on the knife. His eyes were wide with horror.

Naze stumbled backwards with both palms

pressed tightly against the wound. Even though he was still focused on Alharrad, who now recoiled from his handiwork, Gareth could smell the blood. The blade had struck something important and Naze was hemorrhaging profusely.

Without a second thought, Gareth moved on Alharrad and whipped out his revolver. In a single fluid motion, he leveled the firearm and took aim. Gareth squeezed the trigger and a round punched through Alharrad's forehead. A spray of gore, including chunks of brain matter, rained to the floor behind him. As a tiny red stream trickled down the bridge of his nose, Alharrad's body went limp and dropped to the ground.

Gareth strode over and put another two bullets into his chest. Though he knew it was unnecessary, he felt better for it all the same.

For a moment, he sensed a tingling sensation that tickled at his skin. Unlike before, this faded immediately. If he was not staring into Alharrad's dead face, he might not have noticed it.

After nudging the side of Alharrad's body with the toe of his boot, Gareth holstered his sidearm and went to Naze.

As Gareth attempted to reach in and check her injury, Naze flinched. Gareth scowled. Alharrad was her… grandson? Was that correct? Though he struggled for a moment to figure out how that was possible, Gareth brushed it quickly aside. Alharrad was Naze's kin and Gareth had coldly put him down like some feral beast. It made sense that, even in her wounded state, she would pull away from him.

"Gareth?" she eventually spoke. Her voice was weak. The effort alone caused her to cough. Tiny red dots splattered on the pale skin of her chin.

"Yes?"

"Is he… is he dead?" She pointed to Alharrad's limp form with her chin.

"None deader," Gareth stated as he knelt. The anger in his eyes softened as he noticed the sadness in Naze. "I'm sorry," he added.

She offered a faint nod as their gazes met. In her countenance, he could see acceptance of what had transpired. She began to hack violently. Once the fit, which came with blood that dripped from her lips, was over, she turned back to Gareth.

"They'll be… here before too long. They can smell it coming. I'll be done soon and they'll want a bite." She glanced at Alharrad. Beneath him was a growing pool of blood. "Not him, so much. Barely a taste, he'll be. Maybe tha lesser ones'll be forced ta take him as a prize…"

She winced as her body shuddered.

"Foulkin?" Gareth inquired as he glanced back to the entrance. For a moment, he thought he heard movement from elsewhere in the catacombs. If they were crossing the bridge, it would only be a matter of time before the creatures reached them.

"Something… like that."

"Let me help you—"

"Yew have ta… Yew must…" she sputtered as her

grip on the wound began to grow slack.

Gareth leaned in close. As the seconds passed, he could hear her breathing growing fainter. A deepening wheeze was turning into a gurgle. Her face grew increasingly pale. While he was not experienced in field medicine, he could tell that the cut was deep. She was bleeding out and there was nothing he could do.

"Yew have ta make sure… they don't eat me," she requested as she locked eyes with Gareth. He could hear the movements of creatures from nearby. Shooting Alharrad had been a bad choice. Maybe she was right and they could smell her. The gunshots, though, served as a signal flare to those looking for a meal.

"My pack… use what yew can. My gun…"

He nodded. He reached across her waist and collected the sawed-off shotgun. He slid it into the loose opening between his belts.

Gareth shifted as he collected her rucksack. He opened it and rummaged around. He withdrew the last of her explosives. When the creatures eventually arrived, he had a present or two for the first few. As he continued to root about, he spoke up.

"I… *need* to thank you for all you've done for me," he noted without looking up. "I'm not certain why I trusted in you, believed in what you had to tell me. Perhaps it's because you're the only person who didn't shun me or wasn't just plain bat-shit crazy." Gareth let out a dry laugh.

When he eventually glanced up, he saw that Naze only responded with a crack of a smile. Her eyes were listless and almost all color had drained from her skin.

Just as he reached over to brush a strand of hair from her face, he heard the scrambling of claws on the tiled flooring from the adjacent chamber. They'd arrived sooner than he expected.

Gareth gathered up the two explosives, tucked one in his armpit and rose to his feet. He produced a match and held it to his side as he turned to the open entryway. From the rising volume, he could tell they were nearing with haste; a meal was laid out for them and they hurried to partake before it was gone. It sounded like there were many, but he couldn't tell their exact numbers.

Gareth watched pensively as the first of the horde scrambled greedily into the room. No bigger than three feet in length, the hunched-over beasts scurried forward on all fours. Mottled gray and brown pelts bristled as the initial wave came to a stop just inside the room. Hisses filled the air as they watched Gareth with brown eyes. Snarling snouts opened to reveal rows of sharp fangs.

"Gonna have to earn your meal today," he muttered as he struck the match. The oil-soaked cloth was alight as he pitched it forward.

The flaming bottle landed with a crash just as the creatures attempted to retreat back through the doorway. The first wave was aflame almost instantly. Pained howls filled the air as those not immediately downed by the fire flailed about in a panic. Behind them waited a legion of others, kept at bay by the conflagration and burning kin.

One by one, the charred beasts slumped to the

ground. While Gareth watched, he felt adrenaline wash over him. He struggled against a growing compulsion to throw himself into the fray. He'd experienced a similar transference of energies multiple times before, but this occasion seemed noticeably more powerful. The swell caused his blood to boil. His eyes bulged in their sockets and his breathing accelerated. Only by constantly reminding himself to hold his ground was he able to resist the call to charge forward.

As the standoff continued, Gareth withdrew his firearm and raised it. He waited as the flames slowly petered out. Left in their wake was a smattering of dead creatures, their hides burned black. Once the fire finally died, the beasts renewed their advance.

Gareth knew he'd have to be quick. He only had three rounds in the cylinder. He'd need to fire them off, light and toss the second bomb, and then hastily reload the weapon. If need be, he'd use the shotgun to thin the crowd some. There were only two rounds chambered, so he'd have to make them count.

Gun in one hand and bottle in the other, Gareth stood in front of Naze and watched the creatures creep forward. A few clambered to his left. He held back. They didn't want Naze, or not yet at least. Instead, the first trio latched onto Alharrad's crumpled form. Rather than devour him right then and there, they drug him from the room. It was unsettling to watch. The old man's corpse was pulled in a herky-jerky fashion that made his limbs flail about, as if wracked by seizures.

Once near the doorway, others scurried out to join

them in the retrieval. A mass of fur and claws swarmed the corpse as they worked to drag him back to the bridge.

Soon, Gareth could hear them tearing into his flesh. Rips of shredding fabric were accompanied by the snarls of beasts fighting over their share of the meal.

Gareth retreated to Naze's side. He knelt down and placed a hand on her forehead. A check of her pulse with two fingers under her jaw confirmed what he already knew. He set her pack in her lap and made sure that her eyes were shut.

"You didn't have to…" He trailed off. She was merely a vessel without a soul now. Still, he knew what to expect. Muscles that were once slack would lock up as rigor took over. Eventually, putrefaction would remove all that was familiar about her. Out of the sun and heat, this would take some time.

And yet, he noticed that there was something about her supine form that didn't seem quite right.

A warm glow, like that of a faint lamp shining from within Naze, began to permeate her exterior. This caused Gareth to lean in as his eyes narrowed.

He watched with some amazement as her body began to break down. It wasn't accelerated decay, a speeding up of the usual process, but a strange dissolution of her corporeal existence. Not only her skin but her clothes as well grew colorless and began to flake off. Instead of floating to the floor, flecks were lifted into the air as if caught by the wind. Before long, even the pool of fluids beneath her lost its color and began to dissipate.

Seeing this, he withdrew the shotgun and placed it beside her. As he did, the armament began to disappear.

She'll be needing that wherever she turns up, he thought to himself. Though he didn't know why, for some reason it made sense to him.

As the seconds passed, more and more of her vanished; the fragments evaporated like flecks of snow in the heat of the noonday sun.

Was this how it had been for him, when he was struck down outside the entrance to the Lord's Chapel? Every single bit of her, including her pack, hastily faded from existence. Soon she would be gone entirely.

Would she turn up somewhere else? Would she eventually waken at the sanctuary in Chorazin? What of Alharrad, now that he was being devoured by the creatures?

He glanced over the burnt husks at the empty doorway behind him. Beyond, the horde's orgy of consumption continued. A morbid part of him wanted to see what had become of the old man. He turned back to Naze.

Once the last of Naze dissipated into the air, Gareth stood and solemnly waited for something. From the next room, the noise of the creatures had tapered off. Sated with their banquet, he assumed that they had scurried back to their homes within the catacombs.

As the faintest sounds of movement died off, he realized he was finally entirely alone. Neither of his human companions remained. Both were… Were they even dead?

He decided to move to the doorway on the far side. There was nothing to be gained by waiting any longer. Neither Naze nor Alharrad would be returning. He was certain of that.

In that moment, the world felt cold. His loved ones were dead, his associates, such as they had been, were in some damned state he didn't quite understand, and he was on his own deep beneath the earth. Somehow his only hope was that he could plead his case with something he'd never seen before to turn back time, affecting the whole world for his family's needs.

Something—a voice unlike any he'd heard before— entered his head. It didn't so much speak as it formed passages for Gareth's consideration. In doing so, though, it overwhelmed him and caused his body to lock up tight.

Come, have you, to entreat with me and mine? Rich with appropriated vitality, you wish to spend your gains for something beyond the capability of mankind? Now, without your companions, those who have not yet earned their passage, may you be permitted access.

It was a foreign intruder that entered his mind and spoke phrases like they were his own thoughts. The syllables irritated his brain, like an itch he was incapable of scratching. Gareth shook his head violently as his eyes and jaw clenched tightly.

"Get out of my skull," he seethed.

Undaunted, the voice continued.

See you the Coemeterium, a prison for the ages, formed by traitorous servitors, for what it is. When you grasp the vista in its truest form, come to find me. You will know what it is that you seek when it is before you.

With a blink, the illusion of aging catacombs was gone.

CHAPTER SIXTEEN

The Begeondan

Despite his prior experiences, Gareth was still thrown as the world shifted its configuration. For a moment, his legs grew rubbery and his head spun. It was as if everything blinked for an instant, only to be replaced by a panorama of alien design. Carved stone walls were now semi-transparent slabs, lined by a non-linear arrangement of quicksilver-inked symbols. Multi-layered passages floated back and forth along the surfaces, never remaining in place for more than a second. Beyond these could be spied other formations of similar materials, arranged at unnatural angles.

Multiple lights wavered back and forth above him. As the beams reflected off of the façades, their illumination caused the panels to become opaque, if only momentarily.

Beneath him, as in the Aurul Halls, a dense fog of greenish-gray mist floated only a few yards under his feet. From time to time, he spied clear sparks of electricity, arcing through the formless void.

Once he eventually regained his balance, Gareth moved onward. As the pathway behind him no longer existed, all choice was gone. After a few paces, the room once again changed form, as if in response to his presence. It grew longer as a series of columns extended from the walls. Before long, these pillars morphed into craggy towers of sparkling minerals.

The cavern eventually became covered in violet-hued chunks of crystal. Many of the multi-faceted slabs were bigger than a man and attached to the partitions at seemingly-random points with a black, tar-like substance. Upon closer inspection, Gareth could see some evidence of energies roiling within the larger chunks. He considered reaching out to touch one, but refrained. There was no telling what might transpire if he did.

As he tentatively continued on, he saw phantom images flicker along the glassy surfaces. The first of these was Alharrad, whose reappearance set him on guard. He retreated back and reached for his revolver. After a second, he came to realize this was only another illusion. Gareth swore under his breath.

On his right appeared an apparition of Redbletter, who waved him along. Just beyond him waited Geddish Pwarma, who did likewise. Before long, Gareth was sure that the visions were ushering him to some destination further in.

Gareth pressed forward. He stopped once, as a

reflection of Naze caught his eye. He felt a pang of regret at this and wanted to reach out to her. He caught himself as his arm was half-extended to the illusion.

"No," he muttered as he curled his fist tightly.

At some point, he arrived at the chamber's end. In the alien surroundings, he struggled to gauge both time and distance. He could have walked a few yards in less than a minute, or he may have spent an hour traversing four miles. Through an opening in the back wall was a corridor that led down.

The voice was now silent. No directions were provided.

The serpentine path curled back and forth, sometimes even to the point of turning backwards in on itself. Rather than let himself become confused by this, Gareth proceeded. No matter how disorienting the pathway seemed to be, he knew that marching forward was the only way. The Begeondan, if that was what had called out to him, had pulled back the mirage and beckoned to him. He had no choice but to believe it wouldn't lose him in the twists of the labyrinth.

Gareth struggled to take in everything about his surroundings. As noticed before, there were no familiar odors in the air. There wasn't the kind of antiseptic aroma that wiped out all other scents; there was nothing at all. As his hand brushed the corridor's wall, he felt its surface. At least that much was real. Even if it was temporary and only another trick, he was convinced that something was there.

Eventually, he reached another vast cavern of

indeterminate depth. His body expected to continue its declining path; as such, he stumbled for a moment until he regained his balance.

Gareth wandered into the chamber. He was forced to weave through the maze of crystal constructs until he was unable to progress. No matter which way he went, his path was blocked. After examining the barricade and wondering if he could climb over it, Gareth noticed that something at the center of the blockade moved. Slowly but surely, it heaved in an undulating pattern that reminded him of an abdomen moving with labored respiration.

At least ten yards across at its widest point, the pulsing mass was pinned in place by over a dozen of the crystal shards. Many were multiple times larger than any man and seemed specifically arranged to hold the entity. A constant arc of electricity appeared to flicker from within each.

The organism displayed a bizarre arrangement of mismatched extremities, all of which were covered in blue hide. Limbs, many of which resembled those of humans, cattle and predatory felines, flailed without purpose. On occasion, they would fold back into the main bulk, only to appear again elsewhere. A myriad of viscous orbs, which Gareth assumed were eyes, moved along the upper layers of its flesh. Since they had no sockets, they migrated to a patch near Gareth to examine the new arrival.

In that moment, Gareth recoiled as he realized that this was a living thing. He moved a hand towards his revolver as he took a step back.

As he did, the creature's skin pulsed red before returning to its original hue. The booming voice once again entered his head. He flinched as the syllables pounded against his brain.

Repulsed, are you, by the current presentation of my physical being? No artifice is provided to make this experience more palatable to those unprepared such as yourself. This arrangement of flesh, organs, and bone of which your realm's physical laws forces upon me is a pale representation of my native form. Upon my return, I would rejoin my Begeondan brethren in a splendor that no man dared comprehend with your limited understanding.

"O-okay," Gareth grunted as he placed a hand on his forehead. "My apologies…"

No umbrage is suffered as such considerations are for those concerned with the opinions of lesser species. The waste of words on unnecessary platitudes is a failing of the human condition.

"Look, I went through hell to get here," Gareth hoped that he might cut to the chase. "You have no id—"

All that is—past, present, future—is known to us. To advise that one is uninformed is to reveal your own limitless ignorance. In the span of time located on your mortal plane, it has become evident that your kind revels in obliviousness.

Instead of lashing out, Gareth drew in a long breath and exhaled.

"Well, then, that saves me the effort of bringing you

up to speed," he eventually replied.

Strode you, willingly, into Dineothan, with your head filled with fables of a knowledge unrivaled. Not for plunder did you cross the Gape, but for a chemical reaction termed "hope" that you might encounter a learned man of science or medicine. That a cure for your malady might be delivered unto you. When it became clear that such an event would not transpire as swiftly as you imagined it, you allowed yourself to be cajoled by other humans into a lengthy course, wrought with peril. Little did you know that the instant you appeared in the Halls of Perpetual Arrival, your progression through Dineothan was firmly etched. "Long and dark 'tis the way f'r man to fo—

"I'm familiar with it," Gareth snapped. His voice dropped as he turned away. "You don't need to go over it. I didn't exactly get it the first time around, anyway." He placed his hands against his temples and shook his head. Eventually, the Begeondan ceased its recitation.

After a brief pause, during which he felt the pressure on his head ease, Gareth spoke up.

"Since you *know all*, then I don't need to ask you for help, do I? You already know if you're gonna do it or not, right? I mean, that's how it works... correct?"

As its words hammered at him, Gareth grew tired of the obtuse discourse.

Consider you the nature of your request. Through what means are your decisions made? A series of hardships leveraged upon you for what reason? An obsession with prolonging your time invested with those to whom you have developed a preferred biochemical attraction. Firing neurons perpetuate memories, executing a longing for more of the same, which goads you into the present scenario. Humans, to a man, continue to eschew logic in favor of decisions formed from the volatile mixture of chemicals such as serotonin, norepinephrine, dopamine, and endorphins. You cling to emotional attachments of others of your kind with whom you have formed extended associations. Because of an ability to recall each other by familiar designations, you pretend to continue relations whether or not such interactions produce negative impacts to your own progress as a collective species.

Gareth groaned as he rubbed his forehead. He wondered what would accelerate the exchange towards some end, even if that was a flat denial by the Begeondan. The pressure on his brain was growing unbearable; he hoped that, once done, it would stop.

"What... what will it take to get to the point? I was sent here, as you well know, by one of your own—"

Traitorous servitors, the Ikkibu, who not only sought to usurp their masters but imprison them for their own purposes.

By the force applied to Gareth's mind, he could tell the topic was a sensitive matter. It was as if the Begeondan was yelling in his ears.

Spent too much time amongst mankind and grew to enjoy the taste of the species' less savory elements: jealousy, guile, and opportunism. Believed, did they, that the anuphilim were more than a passing fancy, an experiment by my kind to toy with the structure of those in this realm.

Patchwork creations, formed of flesh and bone with sciences foreign to your world. AND FOR WHAT—

Gareth flinched. It felt like a hot iron rod in his left temple.

—so that they could become the benevolent hand which bequeathed to mankind advances far beyond their ken? Stolen from their creators was all manner of knowledge, slivers of which were doled out over the years. To curry the favor of lesser beings. Greedy for gain were your men of science that they did not think twice about the nature of their progress. Not until their own loved ones showed all the evidence of their meddling. Not until their greatest minds cut at the fabric of all that makes your world exist. To rend this island from the flow of time in an act of monumental folly. In their error, the Ikkibu retreated from those of which they aided in the severing of your world, as they refused to offer continued aid. They had no solutions, not without their masters. The same creators who fled, returning home rather than putting their servants to heel. All of them, save one.

The Begeondan went silent. The last of its words echoed in Gareth's skull. As they faded, so did the throbbing ache.

Once his brain began to clear up, Gareth thought it was unlikely that the Begeondan would assist him. The creature would have to feel charity for a lesser being. The Begeondan seemed far more interested in its diatribes. Just as he considered turning around and leaving, the voice returned. This time, it was softer, as if they were sharing a private conversation away from the curious ears of others.

There is a means by which to fold back the years. It is why, when your initial objective to uncover a cure was deemed impossible, you were directed to the Coemeterium by one of the Ikkibu. Even as Elgretamon has ulterior motives, this guidance is without fault. All the Ikkibu of Aurul Halls has left to its existence is the task of providing direction. Of relaying what it already knows will transpire.

"And you're capable of making this happen? Turning back time? How far? To when?"

As you would expect, not without sacrifice.

"Whatever it needs to be," he responded instantly. Even though trepidation dogged him, Gareth knew he had no other choice.

So readily you leap at the opportunity.

There was a chuckle behind the Begeondan's words.

Any price you would pay to turn back the world to a time you perceive as more preferable. Attach you a happiness to this chronological sliver. Perhaps you think to alter the subsequent events towards an outcome more favorable.

"It doesn't really matter what it takes," Gareth stated. "I can't cure my family. I can't even…" He fought against tears. He bit at his lip and continued. "If this allows me to see them again, happy and healthy, I will pay whatever price you want. I will… I want to see them again. Maybe take them away. Maybe… maybe just stay with them this time."

Your payment is without doubt. Take this not lightly.

Once begun, there is no turning back from this process.

"What of the..." It took Gareth a moment to recall the term. "The Goetia formula? The Ikkibu said that I must submit to something by that name. I wasn't certain what he meant at the time."

Fret you not, on the matters of Goetia. It is a sequence of interconnected formulae powered by akaluma'elusepsu, once initiated, that will affect the world in total. Upelstbohr, Dineothan, the lands beyond. One such as yourself needs not to understand the intricate mathematics involved. None of your kind has the capacity for such tasks. In truth, you are but a battery to power the Goetia to its eventual resolution.

"I, uh..." Gareth wasn't certain what to say. As he considered what had been communicated, he asked, "And what do *you* get out of this?"

It is logical to be suspicious of such an offer. Let it be known that you are not the only entity to wish to fold back the years. In the dilated state in which Dineothan exists, the Goetia will have a greater impact. Where you would shift the span of a year, Dineothan would speed back decades if not a full century. With the correct application of enabled energies, one might arrive at a point on the timeline in which the Ikkibu have not enacted their betrayal.

"Ah..." Gareth said with a nod. Even through the Begeondan's dense language, he understood it. "And the Ikkibu? There had to be a reason he—*it* sent me this way."

Elgretamon is unlike the rest of its kin. Tasked

with curating Dineothan's history, Elgretamon is more interested in safeguarding that the path is followed. This is the task set upon the master of the Aurul Halls. Your recorded timeline was determined to end here, beneath the Coemeterium. Elgretamon only ensured that you arrived where you were preordained.

The Begeondan continued as if it knew what Gareth would ask next.

Even in reversing Dineothan's temporal position, Elgretamon and its kin alike can benefit. Were one would seek to prevent their treachery, they would plot to entrap more of my kind before their flight from this realm. The true test is in arriving at the single point along the timeline that fails to benefit the Ikkibu.

"I, uh... okay." Gareth had no desire to become embroiled in the machinations of other-dimensional creators and their progeny. All he wanted was to see his family healthy. As if sensing this, the Begeondan ceased its explanation.

The hour is at hand. Come forward. Within this physical form, Begeondan turned flesh, you will open the gateway which will return you to your appointed time. Though bound to this mortal plane, the capacity to execute such an event is beneath this coarse tissue.

If he was to see this to its end, inevitable as it was, he had to take the proverbial plunge. After a few hesitant steps, he marched forward. His jaw set tightly as he held his breath.

Originally, he'd thought that the Begeondan's exterior was a tough, chitinous hide, but as he placed a hand against it, Gareth realized this was not entirely true. Under the pressure of his fingertips, the skin became a soft, gelatinous semi-solid. Before long, the surface ceased resisting and instead drew him in. Ravenous, the Begeondan greedily pulled Gareth off his feet.

Before he knew it, Gareth was completely inside. He didn't get the chance to take a breath before his head was dragged under. His last sight was of light flickering within the purple-hued crystals.

The further he sank, the more liquid his surroundings became. Within seconds, Gareth felt as though he was caught in an undertow.

For a moment, instincts took over and he thrashed to swim free. On some level, Gareth knew that he needed to remain, that to free himself would be counterintuitive. If his death within the Begeondan was needed to initiate the Goetia—whatever that was—then he must remain where he was.

It took some time before his body to realize that it was not drowning. As it did, he relaxed and allowed himself to float. It was a strange sensation, one that felt primal. Though he could barely feel his body, Gareth wanted to curl up into a ball.

Aware of every instant, Gareth noticed his physical form eroding as it drifted within the Begeondan. Tiny sparks, like electrical pinpricks, danced along his skin. The sensation caused a strange giddiness to come over him. Once the flares faded, each patch of flesh was no more. Bit by bit, layer by layer, he ceased to be. There was no pain in this disintegration, none that he could perceive.

He could feel the energies within him slowly being drained. How many creatures had he slain to get to this point? He'd lost count. Gareth thought that if he could observe himself, that he would be glowing like the sun in the sky.

At some point, Gareth knew that his physical body ceased to be. Only a manifestation of his consciousness floated within the Begeondan. Gareth wondered, only briefly, if he had a discernable form.

As he considered this notion, a vision came to Gareth. Blurry colors slowly rearranged into familiar shapes. The kaleidoscope of imagery formed inside the core of his being, a display of his existence.

Memories of previous events flashed before him. The days, weeks, months even, rolled backwards like pages, one at a time. He was now a disconnected observer. Somehow detached as he was, he could examine the subtle details of his interactions.

Within the catacombs of the Coemeterium, he saw Naze in the shadows, between two of the larger statues, waiting for Alharrad's eventual betrayal. She watched Gareth as he peered intently at the inhuman effigy. Minutes earlier, while Gareth and Alharrad were diverted by one of the many dead-ends, she'd slipped past them.

Gareth witnessed a broken man, hopeless and barely conscious, stumble across the Black Basalt Fields. Somehow, he'd walked through the back wall of the Aurul Halls and directly into the blackened landscape. Elgretamon's illusion merely parted as he lurched forward. The Ikkibu patiently stood by as it watched him depart. The creature never resumed its more humanoid form.

Minutes before, Naze scurried up onto the nearby cliffside. She'd failed to draw the attention of the Mericoinne. Their vigil proved far more important than her presence. Instead of going back to join him, she decided to observe from afar as Gareth marched through the gorge. She nodded to herself as he stepped inside the property.

Familiar scenes flickered before him as he continued backwards. A moment of peaceful reflection at the campfire morphed into the frantic flight from the Governess's tomb. He watched as Naze dashed past Lyceed, latched her grappling hook to the lip of the well and jumped after Gareth. A second later, he was back inside the Sanatorium.

As he saw himself dragged through the halls of the asylum, he could clearly see some of the prisoners. Now that he saw them without the glare of the gaoler's spotlight, he noticed that many were similar in form to those statues he'd only seen minutes ago, before the Coemeterium's illusion was discarded.

More sequences flashed. His trek up Golyat's Ascent soon became his time in Bethsaida. He was then leaving the Grand College of Amaru-ma-mudu. He could see the Umbral as they descended from the upper floors. Even as he spoke with Redbletter, they flocked from classrooms and laboratories and moved in waves through the darkened halls.

An image of the massive sigil gate gave way to a view of the rooftops and Naze. He watched as Sindex's body burned, only for the flames to turn into the candles that littered the Chorazin sanctuary. He threatened Alharrad before his departure. As the doors closed behind him, Alharrad produced a knife from the folds of his robes and swore under his breath.

Gareth could see his body, bloodied and broken, just outside the Lord's Chapel at Burngwent. Facedown and unmoving, he was on the ground. Time passed, then his fresh corpse began to break down. Exactly how Naze's body had paled and faded, his exterior lost all color and began to flake away. A few of Sindex's minions, who had caught his scent, watched his deteriorating form from the open doorway as the last of his remains were carried off in the wind.

Next was the massive form of the Gatekeeper, who looked at Gareth's crushed figure for a moment before it turned aside. It had no appetite for this victim. In one of the open archways above, observing, was an Ikkibu in a humanoid guise.

The final scene was that of Gareth as leaving his home with a scowl on his face. He'd made up his mind that he was going to find a cure. The sounds of Nattia coughing violently from her sickbed were cut off as the front door closed behind him. He went in spite of deep sorrow of leaving them in their time of need.

Everything became still as the world fell dark.

CHAPTER SEVENTEEN

A Return

Gareth awoke in the living room of his own home. He'd fallen asleep in one of the hide-coated, padded chairs, next to the fireplace. A small flame still flickered with life. If not tended, it would soon die out.

As he shifted in place, soreness made itself known. It felt as though he'd run for miles before crashing into the first seat he could find. Despite the pervasive discomfort, he reached up and rubbed the sleep from his eyes.

Once the blurriness went away, Gareth scanned the interior of his family's abode. Everything seemed in its place. A stack of clean, unfolded laundry was left on the dinner table. Nattia likely placed it there until she found the time to deal with it.

After a few seconds, Gareth realized that neither Nattia nor Shea were around. Visible through the west-facing windows, the sun was still out. Usually, during the day, the pair rattled on incessantly as they performed chores or worked on Shea's schoolwork. Though he wouldn't admit it aloud, Gareth enjoyed the constant babble generated by his family.

With creaking muscles and joints, Gareth got to his feet. His legs were a bit rubbery and he reached out to the fireplace mantle to steady himself. He looked at the clock on the far wall. It was an heirloom, given to Nattia by her grandmother, with an ivory face and brass numbers. He was relieved to see that it was still ticking away and that the time was now 4:02.

He felt a strange joy to see something so simple. He shook his head and stepped away. As he moved aimlessly through the house, he caught a whiff of Nattia's floral perfume. This caused a smile to curl his thin lips. If she wasn't around, she'd only just departed. Perhaps she and Shea left him to rest as they went on an errand.

For some reason, he examined his body, as if he'd uncover some answers there. He was dressed in casual clothes; a linen shirt, wool trousers, and a pair of well-worn leather boots. He was wearing none of his gear. He went to the wooden chest that sat beside the fireplace and flipped the lid open. Within was all of his equipment, cleaned and packed away for a future date. By the polished sheen of the boiled leather cuirass, he could tell his return was recent.

Why wouldn't I already know that? Gareth thought as a scowl creased his forehead. That he could forget such a thing was unlike him. Perhaps he was more tired than he first thought.

Before long, he heard rustling from elsewhere in the house. His head cocked to the side. The cottage wasn't big by any measure.

"Nattia?" he eventually called out. When his voice sounded strange to his own ears, he paused to clear his throat a few times. "Nattia, where are you?" he inquired. This time, the timbre felt right.

"In here." The muffled response came from the other side of the house.

Needing desperately to check in on his wife, Gareth strode to the bedroom door. It was slightly ajar and only took a nudge to open with a creak.

As he stuck his head in through the doorway, he quickly spotted Nattia, placing new linens on their bed. Her floral dress swayed playfully as she danced about. The quilt was clumped in a pile beside the foot of the bed.

"Nattia?" Gareth wanted to charge across the room and wrap his arms around her. He felt an overwhelming need to be close to her.

"Yes, dear?" she looked at him. Her cheeks were rosy, her eyes alert. Upon seeing this, he nodded to himself. If Nattia was in here, then Shea was certainly somewhere in the house. "Gareth? What is it?"

"Nothing. Just woke up and wanted to… to see you."

This caused Nattia to blush as she continued her chores. "Afternoon nap even after your long night's rest?" she asked with a coy grin.

With a sideways glance, Gareth located his sword in the stand at the back of the room. Despite the fact that it was where it should be, he felt reassurance upon seeing the blade again.

"Is Shea in her room?"

"Yes, dear."

"Good. Love you." Gareth said as he slipped to his daughter's quarters. Much like her mother, Shea was attempting, with much less success, to change her sheets. Gareth entered and watched her struggle with the fabric for a moment.

"Daddy!" Shea called out as she finally noticed his arrival. Gareth crossed to help her.

Once the bed was made, he pulled her close to him. For a moment, Gareth ran his fingertips through Shea's bangs. She giggled joyfully as he tousled her hair. He could feel warmth radiating from her forehead.

He was overcome by a powerful feeling, as if a burden was lifted from his shoulders. While he'd always been happy to see his family after every trip, this was something more. Disturbed by this sensation, he thought back to his recent travels as he rested a hand on Shea's shoulder.

Gareth struggled to fill in the hole that was his recent past. What memories were there felt stitched together over a void. The longer he contemplated this, the more his brain ached. Before long, he shook his head and knelt beside his daughter.

"What is it, Daddy?"

He kissed her on the forehead.

"Do you want to go on a trip?" he asked. His own

words came as a surprise. It was as if the suggestion came out of nowhere. For some reason he didn't understand, he needed to take his family to the countryside. Maybe they would stay for a while. Something nagged at him, from the recesses of his mind, just out of reach.

"Oh yes, Daddy! Can we?" Shea exclaimed as she wrapped her arms around his neck.

About the Author

Author of *Not Gods But Monsters*, Joshua Banker was born in Greece in 1973. He grew up in the San Francisco area before moving to Chattanooga where he attended the University of Tennessee at Chattanooga and received a BFA in Graphic Design. After moving to Charlotte, NC, he ran an independent entertainment review website from 1999-2006. Now living in Greenville, NC, Josh is a writer, painter and illustrator, loves all things H.P. Lovecraft, is married and has two cats and a dog.

Visit **joshuabankerbooks.com** for updates.

Follow the author on social media at
facebook.com/joshuabankerbooks
instagram.com/joshuabankerbooks